A Love Heist

Jamar Berry

DEDICATION

To the vibrant cultures of the Caribbean and Japan, as well as the rich heritages of China and beyond—this story is a celebration of your beauty, resilience, and the love that bridges the gaps between us. May we honor our diverse backgrounds while embracing the strength we find in unity.

Let this tale inspire us all to break down barriers, celebrate our differences, and foster connections that enrich our lives. In a world that often seeks division, let us stand together, hand in hand, forging a path of understanding, acceptance, and love. Together, we can build a future where every heart is free to love without boundaries.

CONTENTS

ACKNOWLEDGMENTS

My dearest fans; without you my passionate pencrafts would not flourish so.

Thank you!

Follow : @PrestigedFuture
All Social Medi

CHARACTER PROFILES

Main Characters

Kai Amara
Age: 17
Descent: Caribbean and Japanese
Personality: Passionate, creative, charming, warm, and comfortable in his own skin. Demonstrates strong artistic talents and values deep connections with others.
Interests: Art, music (plays guitar), capturing life's beauty through creativity, exploring diverse cultures.
Background: Values family and pursues meaningful relationships; deeply cares for Mei and is willing to face challenges for their connection.

Mei Suki
Age: 18
Descent: Chinese and Japanese
Personality: Spirited, fiercely loving, occasionally obsessive in her desire for closeness. Creative and sensitive, grapples with family expectations and societal pressures.
Interests: Photography, art, expressing feelings through creative outlets, exploring the interplay between different cultural backgrounds.
Background: Navigates family dynamics as she seeks acceptance within her relationship with Kai; her obsession at times complicates her emotional state.

Supporting Characters

Mei's Parents
Personality: Strongly rooted in traditional values, yet deeply care for Mei's well-being. They display concern about her relationship choices and desire to protect her from potential heartache.

Roles:
Mother: Nurturing but cautious, concerned about societal standards and what is best for her daughter. Wishes to ensure Mei's happiness while upholding cultural values.

Father: Supportive yet practical, concerned about the complexities of Mei's relationships, and engages in grounding conversations about love and expectations.

Akira

Age: Mei's peer 18 years old.

Personality: Supportive, energetic, and optimistic friend who offers comic relief and encouragement. Acts as Mei's confidant and stands by her during challenges.

Interests: Socializing with friends, engaging in lighthearted banter, loves food, and aims to support Mei in understanding her feelings about Kai and facing societal judgments.

Themes Associated with Characters

Cultural Identity: Kai and Mei navigate their mixed backgrounds and how that affects their relationship.

Love vs. Societal Expectations: Mei's emotional struggle with her parents' traditional values as she pursues a relationship with someone considered "different."

Growth and Understanding: Characters evolve through their experiences, learning to embrace authenticity and face outside pressures.

CHAPTER 1

A CHANCE ENCOUNTER IN HARAJUKU

The vibrant streets of Harajuku pulsed with energy, alive with the rhythm of laughter, music, and the tantalizing aromas of festival food. Mei Suki stood at the edge of the crowd, a kaleidoscope of colors swirling around her—neon hair, eclectic fashion, and joyful faces shaped the scene as she clutched her camera tightly in hand. Today was the annual Harajuku Matsuri, a celebration of youth, creativity, and cultural fusion, and she had every intention of capturing its essence through her lens.

As she maneuvered through the throngs of excited festival-goers, the tantalizing smell of yakitori wafted through the air, inviting her to join in the festivities. Mei's heart fluttered with anticipation as she snapped pictures of the splendid sights—the laughter of children, couples adorned in matching outfits, and friends sharing cotton candy as they danced to upbeat music. It was her favorite time of year, and she felt an electric energy tingling in her fingertips as she clicked away.

"Mei! Over here!" Her best friend, Akira, beckoned her from a nearby booth decorated with colorful lanterns and origami. Mei turned to see him waving enthusiastically, his excitement as infectious as always.

She rushed over, her eyes bright. "What did you find?" She quizzed, already guessing from the glorious spread of food in front of him. They had a sort of tradition, a routine where they tried to taste every delicious offering the festival had to offer.

"That," Akira pointed dramatically to a stall featuring towering stacks of fluffy cotton candy. "And this!" He gestured to a table piled high with different flavors of mochi. "We should try them all!"

With her camera in one hand and a skewer of yakitori in the other, Mei laughed at Akira's enthusiasm. The joy of the festival was contagious, filling her heart with warmth. Yet beneath the surface of her excitement lingered an ache—a longing for something more, something that had yet to fall into place in her life.

As they savored the sweet mochi and airy cotton candy, a live band began to set up nearby, and a small crowd gathered near the stage. The thumping bass filled the air, and curiosity piqued her interest. She lowered her camera and took a step forward, drawn to the music.

"Come on, let's check it out!" Akira urged, already pulling her toward the gathering crowd. They worked their way to the front, where the stage shimmered with bright lights and a lively atmosphere pulsed with youthful exuberance. The band started playing an upbeat number, and Mei felt herself beginning to sway, the rhythm enveloping her.

But as her eyes scanned over the crowd, her gaze suddenly landed on him.

Kai Amara stood at the edge of the stage, a boy with deep brown skin that glistened under the colorful lights. His hair was styled in loose curls, framing his face just the right amount. He wore a casual black sleeveless shirt and dapper shorts, a simple outfit that accentuated his physique and playful nature. Something about him caught Mei's attention, drawing her in like a moth to a flame.

As the music swelled, she observed him from afar, captivated by how effortlessly he danced to the beat, his body swaying rhythmically as if he were born for the stage. Kai's carefree spirit radiated from him, the way he smiled broadly and laughed with friends, unbothered by the world around him. Time seemed to slow as their eyes met for a brief moment, a spark igniting between them that sent a shiver down her spine.

"Mei?" Akira's voice broke through her reverie, pulling her back to reality. "Are you coming?"

She blinked, trying to shake off the daze that had overtaken her. "Yeah! Sorry, I was just… distracted."

"By what?" Akira grinned, nudging her playfully. "You saw someone cute?"

— She could hardly admit it, but a part of her wanted to tell him about the captivating boy under the stage lights. Instead, she laughed, feeling heat rise to her cheeks. "Maybe. Let's dance!"

The music surged, and as the crowd moved, Mei lost herself in the moment. She and Akira danced, twirling and laughing amid the swirling colors. Yet, her gaze frequently drifted back to Kai, who remained engaged with his friends, every laugh and gesture amplifying her fascination.

After what felt like hours of joyful dancing, the band took a break, and the energy of the crowd shifted. Mei felt a sudden urge to step away and catch her breath, her heart still thumping with excitement—both from dancing and the lingering sensation of Kai's gaze.

She excused herself, stepping away from the main gathering. The festival still buzzed around her, but she found a quiet corner near a vibrant mural depicting

she felt strangely drawn to. The mural was an explosion of colors—red and gold koi fish flowing through waves of blue, artistic brushstrokes blending harmoniously, creating a lively scene that sparkled under the sunlight. As she stood before it, she captured a few pictures with her camera, attempting to weave the colors and emotions into tangible memories.

Her heart still fluttering, she took a deep breath, trying to calm the frenzy of thoughts swirling in her mind. She tried to shake off the distraction of the boy who had caught her eye. Yet, every click of her camera felt empty without the spark of magic that had enveloped her moments before.

"Excuse me," a smooth voice interrupted her thoughts. Startled, Mei turned to see Kai standing a few feet away, his brown eyes twinkling with warmth and mischief. "I couldn't help but notice you were taking pictures of the mural. Are you an artist?"

She felt her heart race as he approached, and her voice caught in her throat for a moment. Gathering her thoughts, she managed to respond, "Um, I'm trying to capture the essence of the festival. I'm not an artist, but I love photography!"

Kai's smile widened, and she couldn't help but feel her cheeks warm under his gaze. "It seems like you have an eye for it. The way you were lost in thought… I thought you might be."

Taking a shaky breath, Mei felt her confidence build. "Thank you! I just think there's beauty everywhere, especially in moments like these." She gestured around, hoping to keep the conversation flowing.

"I completely agree!" Kai nodded; his enthusiasm infectious. "There's something magical about how vibrant everything is during the festival. It makes me feel alive!"

Mei laughed, her nerves easing as they conversed. In that moment, she felt a connection that she couldn't quite articulate, a sense that their souls were resonating on the same frequency. "Do you come here often?" she asked, tilting her head slightly as she studied him.

"Every year, actually. It's one of my favorite celebrations. I love the blend of cultures— the music, the fashion, the food!" His eyes sparkled with excitement. "I'm Kai, by the way."

"Mei," she replied, extending her hand shyly. When their hands connected, an electric jolt coursed through her, and she quickly withdrew, heart racing.

"Nice to meet you, Mei," Kai said, a playful grin on his lips. "Are you here alone?"

"Not completely. My friend Akira is around somewhere," she explained, scanning the crowd for him. "We always come together to try all the different foods."

Kai nodded knowingly, glancing at the festival's attractions in the distance. "You have to try the takoyaki; it's the best here! And there's an amazing floaty drink stand over there." He gestured to a stall filled with colorful drinks that sparkled under the sun, many topped with rainbow tropical fruits.

Mei's mouth watered at the thought. "I might just have to get one," she said with a grin.

"I'll join you! I know just what to order." Kai's enthusiasm was so infectious she found herself nodding eagerly.

As they made their way toward the drink stand, Mei felt her heart fluttering like the banners whipping in the breeze. It was as though her world had shrunk down to just the two of them, the noise of the festival fading into the background. Each moment he spoke filled her with warmth; she seemed to hang onto his every word.

"Do you do this just for fun or for a project?" Kai asked, breaking her reverie as they reached the stall, and she turned to face him.

"A little bit of both, actually. I want to capture moments that tell stories, emotions. This festival is perfect for that!" She glanced up at him with excitement. "What about you? Do you do anything creative?"

"I dabble in music!" he said proudly. "I play the guitar and sing a little. I love performing at places like this—it's invigorating to share that part of me."

"Wow, that's amazing! Do you play in a band?" Mei asked, genuinely interested.

"Not yet, just some friends and I jam together sometimes. But someday, I'll be on a big stage," he said with determination, a fiery spark igniting in his eyes. For a moment, she could envision him under bright lights, a voice that echoed into the night, captivating audiences.

The two of them ordered drinks, punctuated by genuine laughter and playful banter. Mei savored every moment; it felt as if she was dancing along with the pulse of the festival around them—light, carefree, and joyful.

Once they found a small corner away from the bustling crowd, they raised their drinks in a toast. The sun glinting off the vibrant colors of the floaty, sweet concoctions. "To new friends and unforgettable moments!" Kai declared, his smile making her heart race.

"To new friends!" Mei echoed, and they clinked their cups together before taking a sip. The drink was refreshingly sweet with a hint of tartness, and she couldn't help but smile at Kai's delighted expression as he tasted his.

"See? I told you they were good!" he said, grinning like a child. She couldn't help but giggle at his enthusiasm.

They found a nearby bench under a shady tree, a perfect spot to escape the bustling crowd for a moment. As they settled in, Mei stole a glance at Kai, his carefree demeanor igniting something deep within her—a desire for connection, a sense of belonging, and a spark of attraction that felt unexpected yet exhilarating.

"So, Mei," Kai said, leaning back with a relaxed posture. "What do you like to photograph the most? Moments? People?"

"Everything," she replied honestly. "I love capturing emotions—those fleeting instants when people are truly themselves, lost in joy or laughter. It feels like magic to hold those memories in a shot."

"That's beautiful," Kai said, genuinely impressed. "I can see why you love photography then. You capture feelings, like music does, right?"

A warm blush crept up her cheeks at his compliment. "Exactly! Each photograph has a story, just like a song. I think that's what art is all about— sharing stories, connecting with others."

"You seem to have a deep passion for it. I admire that." Kai's gaze held hers, and for a moment, everything around them faded into a blur. A sudden shyness enveloped her; it was a feeling she hadn't anticipated.

She shifted under his intense gaze, breaking the connection. "Thank you, but I'm still learning. There's so much I want to capture. I hope to get better each year."

"Don't sell yourself short. Art isn't just about perfection; it's about emotion." Kai's encouragement shone through, and her heart fluttered in appreciation. "Maybe you'll take some photos of me next time. I'd love to see how someone with your talent captures me!"

"Oh, um, I wouldn't want to intrude…" she laughed nervously, unable to hide her flustered reaction.

"Why not? That could be fun! I promise I won't be too awkward," he laughed, playfully tugging on his hair. The sound of his laughter mingled with the festival music, and despite the chaos around them, she felt as if they existed in their own little world.

"Okay," she relented, her heart racing at the thought. "If it helps you capture your own moments, I'll consider it."

They shared another moment of laughter, but all too soon, the festival seemed to beckon again. The music swelled, and the crowd began to move with renewed energy, rushing toward a performance zone where a traditional dance was about to begin.

"Let's go watch!" Kai exclaimed, his eyes sparkling with excitement. He grabbed her hand as he stood up, and Mei felt a jolt of electricity at the contact. She quickly stood too, following his lead with a racing heart.

As they wove through the crowd, Kai's hand had not let hers go, and she could feel the warmth radiating from him. Her mind raced with questions. What was happening? She was captivated by this boy who was a stranger just moments earlier.

They reached the front of the stage just as the performance began. The dancers, adorned in colorful kimonos, moved with grace and skill, their movements telling stories that resonated deep within Mei. She watched, enraptured, but couldn't deny how distracted she was by Kai's presence beside her.

"Isn't this incredible?" he said, leaning closer to speak over the music. "The blend of tradition with modern festival vibes—there's so much life here!"

"It really is!" Mei nodded, feeling an intoxicating mix of excitement and nerves. "I love how vibrant everything is, it's like a dream."

Before long, the dance concluded, and the crowd erupted into applause. Kai joined in, his joy evident, and Mei felt a swell of happiness within her. Watching him celebrate the moment made her heart flutter even more.

As the performance ended, they moved back a little, still caught up in the captivating atmosphere. "Want to check out more booths?" Kai suggested, his enthusiasm unyielding.

"Sure!" Mei answered quickly, grateful for the chance to spend more time in his warm company.

They wandered through the festival grounds, stopping at various stalls selling everything from handmade crafts to delicious street food. Kai encouraged her to take pictures of everything that caught her attention. Mei felt her camera come alive in her hands as she captured not just the vibrant sights, but the joy radiating between them. With each click of the shutter, she felt closer to Kai. As they strolled, he shared anecdotes about the festival, making her laugh with exaggerated impressions of the people around them.

At one stall, they stopped to sample some matcha-flavored ice cream, the cool sweetness melting on their tongues. Mei couldn't help but watch as Kai relished every bite, his eyes lighting up with genuine delight. "This is incredible!" he exclaimed, his enthusiasm infectious.

They continued their adventure, going from booth to booth, sampling exotic snacks and artwork while immersing themselves in the lively banter of festival-goers. In one corner, they even joined a game where festival attendees tried to knock over stacked cans with a ball. Kai's competitive spirit shone brightly as he enthusiastically shouted encouragement, urging her to take her turn.

"You've got this! Just aim straight!" he cheered, and Mei felt buoyed by his confidence in her. She took a deep breath, focused, and threw the ball; it knocked down a few cans, and her cheeks burned with pride as Kai erupted in applause.

"See? I told you! You're a natural!" He spun her around in excitement, and laughter spilled from them like sunlight. Mei felt the world around them fade away once again, as if they existed in their own little realm tucked away from reality.

As the sun began to set, casting a warm, golden glow over the festival, the atmosphere shifted to a more intimate tone. Suddenly, the music softened, transitioning to a gentle melody that encouraged couples to dance, while groups of friends gathered to enjoy the beauty of the evening.

"We should dance!" Kai suggested, raising his eyebrows in playful encouragement.

Mei felt her heart race at the thought. "I'm not great at dancing," she admitted, her nerves creeping back.

"Neither am I. But it would be fun to try!" he replied, his sincerity making her feel safe.

"Okay... I'll give it a shot, then!" she said, summoning her courage. Kai took her hand and led her to a small open space in the crowd.

They started swaying to the music, the rhythm guiding their movements as they laughed off concerns about their lack of coordination. Mei felt a rush of freedom envelop her; lost in the moment, she surrendered to the music and the electric connection growing between them.

As they danced, the world around them faded again, and all she could see was Kai—his laughter, his reassuring presence, and the way he effortlessly drew her into the moment. There was something liberating about this connection, something that felt destined and true.

The song continued to play, drawing them closer together. Time seemed to stand still as they shared smiles and playful spins, and Mei felt the magnetic pull of attraction grow stronger. Her heart raced, the feelings within her welling up more than she'd anticipated.

But then, amidst her joy, a pang of reality began to bite. The thought of her parents crept in, and the blend of fear and uncertainty clouded her mind. "What if they don't accept him?" she worried silently, envisioning her mother's stern disapproval and her father's protective nature—the expectations that clung to her like shadows.

As the final notes of the song faded into the air, the bustling festival resumed around them, breaking her enchanting moment. Kai gazed down at her, eyes sparkling with excitement. "That was so much fun! Thank you for dancing with me!"

"Thank you for making me dance! I had a blast," Mei replied, forcing a smile to mask the mix of emotions swirling inside her.

But before she could say more, a loud announcement crackled over the speakers, signaling the beginning of a lantern release—one of the festival's highlights. The joy and color of the evening suddenly shifted to a serene beauty, as people began to gather at the riverbank nearby, eager to participate.

"Let's go!" Kai exclaimed, grabbing her hand—her earlier hesitation melting away as they hurried toward the river.

As they reached the edge of the crowd, people began to release lanterns adorned with colorful wishes scrawled in ink. The sight was mesmerizing as the lanterns floated gently into the night sky, each one representing a hope, a dream, or a desire. Mei felt a tear prick the corner of her eye as she watched everyone's wishes ascend higher and higher.

"Wow..." she whispered, her heart swelling with emotion. In this moment, standing beside Kai, she realized how deeply she wanted to capture this feeling—not just in photographs, but in her memory. She raised her camera to her eye, framing the glowing lanterns against the darkening sky.

Kai leaned in closer, his voice slightly muffled by the sounds of the festival. "What's your wish, Mei?" His breath was warm against her ear, making her heart race as she turned to face him, their noses almost touching.

Mei hesitated, her heart quickening. For a fleeting moment, her truth danced on the edge of her tongue—I wish for this moment to last forever, for us to explore the depths of this connection. But instead, she offered a playful smile, lightening the mood. "If I tell you, it won't come true."

With a sly grin, Kai leaned in a little closer, his eyes sparkling. "Come on, just one little secret. I promise I won't tell anyone."

Feeling emboldened by his openness, she replied, "Okay, fine! I wish for adventure. I want to experience every beautiful moment life has to offer."

"That's a good one," he said thoughtfully. "Adventurous souls are the best kind. I wish for... to never stop learning about the world and meeting amazing people."

"Like me?" she teased, her heart fluttering again.

"Definitely like you," he said without missing a beat, and she felt her cheeks heat.

After sharing a brief laugh, they turned their gazes back to the river as a new batch of lanterns floated away, glowing softly against the starry night. Each lantern had a unique design, casting beautiful reflections on the water below—a hypnotizing dance of light that enveloped the atmosphere, enhancing the enchantment of the festival.

But amidst the magic, Mei felt a familiar shadow creeping back into her heart. What will my parents think? What if they won't understand? The thought lingered, threatening to overshadow the joy of the moment.

Noticing her silence, Kai turned to her, concern flashing across his face. "Hey, you okay?"

"Yeah, I'm fine! Just... thinking," she replied, but the concern in his eyes made her want to open up. Why was it so hard? Why couldn't she just let go of her worries, if only for tonight?

The moment hung between them, fragile and full of silent questions. She felt a wave of intensity building as she met his gaze again and realized how connected she felt to him. Perhaps he could understand if she shared her thoughts; after all, they had both expressed their dreams aloud.

But before she could formulate her words, the crowd erupted into cheers as the last lanterns were released, swirling upwards into the night sky. A brilliant display of fireworks lit up the horizon, sparkling bursts of color that filled the air with crackling joy.

"Look!" Kai exclaimed, pulling her gently toward the river's edge. "This is the best part!"

Mesmerized by the fireworks' brilliance, Mei allowed herself to be swept away in the moment, temporarily pushing aside her worries. She couldn't help but laugh at the wonder in Kai's eyes as he pointed out shapes in the sky. "That one looks like a dragon! And there's a heart!"

As they became absorbed in each other's company and the display overhead, Mei found herself leaning closer, feeling the warmth radiating from him. The connection she felt was undeniable, a tether pulling her ever closer to him.

"Thank you for this," she whispered, only half-aware of her words. "It's been amazing."

Kai turned to her, sincerity shining through in his eyes. "It's just the beginning, Mei. There's so much we can experience together."

Her heart swelled at the promise hidden in his words, and she found comfort in the thrill of possibility. "Together..." she echoed, feeling the weight of the word linger in the air between them.

As the fireworks faded, punctuated by the final bursts of color, the crowd around them began to disperse, but Mei felt reluctant to leave. The energy in the air buzzed and crackled like unresolved tension—alive and exhilarating. "So, what now?" she asked, hoping to prolong their time together.

"Well…" Kai said, rubbing the back of his neck with a shy grin. "I have a few ideas."

"Do tell!" she replied, her interest piqued.

"Let's find an open space and draw those lanterns! Or at least, I could try to sketch them while you take pictures," he proposed. "We could make a fun project out of it!"

"Now that sounds like an adventure!" Mei agreed, excitement blooming within her.

And just like that, their footsteps mingled with laughter as they maneuvered through the remnants of the festival, leading them toward a quieter park area adorned with lanterns still flickering in the gentle evening breeze. The world felt full of promise, possibilities, and moments waiting to be made.

As they settled on the grass, Kai pulled out a small sketchbook from his bag. The cover was slightly tattered, revealing its well-loved nature. "I always carry this with me to capture ideas and moments," he explained, flipping it open to reveal an array of sketches—some were rough still-lifes, others were lively designs inspired by the urban landscape of Tokyo.

"Wow, these are incredible!" Mei exclaimed, genuinely impressed. "You've got some talent!"

"Thanks! I just do what I can. It's more about expressing what I see rather than making it perfect," he said modestly, looking a little shy but pleased with her compliment. "Do you want to take some pictures while I sketch the lanterns? We can create a visual memory of tonight together."

"I'd love that!" she replied, her enthusiasm bubbling over. She pulled her camera from her shoulder, adjusting the settings as she prepared to capture the scene before her.

As she began taking shots of the softly glowing lanterns woven together in the night, she stole glances at Kai, who was carefully focusing on his sketch. He had a look of intense concentration, his brow furrowing slightly as he captured the shapes and shadows dancing under the lantern light. Mei felt a warm flutter in her chest—there was something incredibly beautiful about his determination and passion for his art.

A gentle breeze rustled the leaves above them, bringing with it the faint sound of festival music that still lingered in the air. It was peaceful, magical even, and Mei felt as if they were in their own world, isolated from the noise and chaos that surrounded them.

After a few moments, she caught Kai glancing at her. "How's it going over there?"

She smiled into her camera, a playful glint in her eyes. "Just capturing the magic of this festival—one moment at a time!" She snapped a photo of him concentrated on his work, and a contagious laughter erupted between them.

"Make sure you take plenty of me in action," he joked, striking an exaggerated pose with his pencil, trying to mimic a serious artist. Mei laughed and took another shot, feeling the joy of the moment seep into her very being.

They worked side by side in harmony, exchanging stories about their lives, dreams, and aspirations as the night unfolded—a beautiful mix of laughter and thoughtful discussions. Mei felt at ease, more so than she had in a long time, and she couldn't shake the feeling of connection growing deeper than mere friendship.

"Hey, do you want to draw together?" Kai suddenly asked, pulling out a spare pencil and offering it to her. "We can take turns sketching our view of the lanterns. It would be a fun challenge!"

Mei hesitated for a moment, her heart racing at the thought of sharing something so personal. "I've never really drawn before," she admitted, feeling a hint of nervousness creep in.

"Don't worry! It's all about having fun. Just let your hand flow; it doesn't have to be perfect," he encouraged, his gaze radiating warmth and sincerity. "We're in this together, right?"

With a deep breath, she took the pencil and smiled, finally deciding to dive into the moment. They sat side by side, sketching their interpretations of the glowing lanterns. Mei felt a rush of adrenaline as she let go of her own expectations, focusing on the gentle strokes on the paper and the connection blooming between them.

As they sketched, Mei threw glances at Kai, watching how he carefully translated what he saw onto the page. There was a certain passion in his movements, a natural grace that inspired her.

"I think you're really talented, you know?" Mei said, a compliment born from admiration.

"Thanks! But honestly, it's you who makes me feel inspired," Kai replied, his voice earnest and sincere. "Seeing how much you love capturing moments reminds me of why I create in the first place."

A warmth spread across her cheeks at his words, a blush that betrayed the impact he had on her heart. "That means a lot," she mumbled, unsure of what else to say, her heart racing with exhilaration and shyness.

As they continued to sketch, the conversation shifted to deeper topics— of dreams, of fears, and aspirations. Mei shared her ambitions to pursue photography seriously, while Kai spoke of his desire to bring music and art together, of wanting his creations to inspire others.

Time faded away, enveloped in their shared laughter and words. The festival began to wind down as the lanterns floated higher and disappeared into the night, replaced by the twinkling stars above.

At last, judgment settled in Mei's heart again, and the weight of reality began to intrude, reminding her of her parental expectations. Her blissful evening felt like it was teetering on the edge, waiting for a single word or action to ruin it all.

CHAPTER 2

HIDDEN FEELINGS

Dawn broke gently over Tokyo, painting the city in shades of pastel orange and soft lavender. Though the festival had ended hours ago, the magic of that night clung to Mei like a warm blanket, wrapping her thoughts in a hazy glow. Her heart felt lighter, yet a fluttering unease lingered at the edge of her excitement. She relished the memory of Kai, their shared laughter, and those fleeting glances that seemed to hold more than mere friendship.

Back at home, Mei sat on the edge of her bed, gazing out her window at the early morning bustle. The sounds of the city provided a familiar symphony of life, but her mind was elsewhere. Her fingers absentmindedly traced the edges of her camera as she thought back to the sketches and lanterns, to the way Kai's eyes sparkled when he smiled.

She shook her head, trying to dispel the weight of her thoughts. You need to focus, she reminded herself as she looked over her photos from the festival. Each image captured the joy of that night—the laughter, the movements, the blend of colors—yet alongside that vibrancy lay the undeniable truth: a burgeoning connection with someone she barely knew.

With a sigh, Mei picked up her phone and scrolled through her messages. There were notifications from her friends about brunch plans and updates buzzing through her social media, but all she wanted to see was a text from Kai. When none arrived, her heart sank slightly, and she tried to shake off the feeling of disappointment. It's too soon, she reasoned. You can't expect him to text every moment.

Determined to clear her head, Mei decided to tackle the day. After her morning routine, she stepped into the vibrant streets of Tokyo, the lively surroundings pulling her focus back to the present. Colors danced before her, shops beckoned with their inviting displays, and the sun was already warming the air, promising a beautiful day.

As she strolled through the streets, taking in the sights, her mind couldn't help but drift back to Kai. Their time together had ignited a burgeoning affection within her—a feeling that felt simultaneously thrilling and overwhelming. She couldn't shake the awareness that something deeper was developing, enveloping her in a blend of excitement and apprehension. What if he feels the same? What if it's just me?

Hours passed as she visited various art shops and bookstores, but unsurprisingly, she lingered in the photography section. Eventually picking up a new photography magazine, she happened upon an article featuring a local festival—the very one she had attended last night. As she flipped through the pages, she marvelled at the photographs and felt a familiar pulse of inspiration rise within her.

But amidst her excitement over the photos, her phone buzzed in her pocket, startling her. Heart racing, she hurried to check and found a message from Kai.

Kai: Hey, Mei! I just wanted to see how you're doing after last night. I had a great time!

A flutter of joy erupted in her chest as she read the message. She immediately began typing back, her fingers flying across the screen.

Mei: Hi, Kai! I had an amazing time too! I loved our impromptu sketching session. Your drawings were impressive!

After hitting send, she felt a swell of anticipation mixed with nervousness. A few moments passed, each second stretching into eternity. Would he reply? What if he didn't?

As if reading her mind, her phone chimed again.

Kai: Thanks! It was fun drawing together. We should do it again soon! How about next weekend?

A smile broke across Mei's face. Her heart raced at the thought of seeing him again, of continuing their growing friendship.

Mei: I'd love that! Let's make more memories.

Kai: Perfect! I'll bring my guitar. We can jam and sketch!

Mei felt her heart skip a beat, the idea of being near him again causing excitement to bubble within her. "Sounds great," she typed back, barely able to contain her smile.

She put her phone away, walking through the streets with renewed energy, her mind dancing with possibilities. What do you have planned for us, Mei? a little voice chimed in her head, prompting a series of optimistic daydreams. They could explore new hidden gems around the city, share more stories, and perhaps… maybe… deepen their connection even further.

As the week passed, Mei found herself diving into her photography with newfound passion, yet Kai lingered in her mind more often than not. Each encounter with him felt electric—every laugh, every fleeting touch, and those magical moments they had together at the festival awakened something she hadn't fully experienced before, a blossoming affection that brought both warmth and uncertainty.

When the day of their planned meet-up finally arrived, Mei busied herself picking out the perfect outfit. She rummaged through her closet, pulling out pieces of clothing and tossing them aside—a bright sundress, a casual blouse, a favorite vintage shirt—seeking a look that matched the excitement fluttering in her chest.

Suddenly, she stopped to look at herself in the mirror, a wave of uncertainty washing over her. What if he sees me differently than how I see him? The thought made her apprehensive. Each piece she tried on felt inadequate, unable to encapsulate the whirlwind of emotions she was feeling.

With a determined sigh, she settled on a comfortable yet stylish outfit: a light denim jacket over a simple white tank top paired with her favorite high-waisted jeans. She felt confident in this—casual yet effortlessly chic. After a quick application of her favorite lip gloss, she glanced at the clock, realizing she was running a little late.

"Focus, Mei," she muttered to herself as she grabbed her camera, tucking it under her arm. With one last look at her reflection, she stepped out of her room and into the world outside.

The sun hung high in the sky as she made her way to their meeting spot, a small park she loved. Blossoms from nearby cherry trees danced in the gentle breeze, and the bright colors of flowers surrounded her, creating a picturesque scene that felt almost magical. She couldn't shake the anticipation building in her chest, the thrill of spending time with Kai unfurling like petals opening to the sun.

Breathing deeply, she arrived at the park and saw him waiting by a quaint gazebo, strumming his guitar. He looked effortlessly cool, dressed in a soft gray t-shirt and jeans, with his hair tousled in the perfect way that made her heart skip.

"Hey!" he called, his face lighting up as he spotted her. The moment their eyes met, her nervousness melted away.

"Hi, Kai!" she replied, her voice bubbling with excitement. "I hope I'm not too late."

"Not at all," he smiled, putting down his guitar. "I just got here myself! I thought I'd warm up a bit before you arrived."

"I'm glad I didn't miss you playing," she said, stepping closer. "You sound great!"

"Thanks! I can't wait to play a few songs for you later," he grinned, a hint of mischief dancing in his eyes. "But first, let's find the perfect spot to sketch!"

The park was alive with activity, children playing and families enjoying picnics, and they walked together, a natural ease growing with every step. As they found a quiet patch near a blossoming tree, a sense of comfort settled around her—yet beneath it, a current of unspoken feelings twitched like a living thing.

They spread out their things and settled on the grass. Mei took a deep breath, preparing herself to unravel her camera and start capturing the beauty around them. But when she looked to Kai, he already had his sketchbook out, pencil poised to draw.

"Okay, let's see what inspires us today!" he said, glancing around for ideas.

As she snapped pictures of the scenery—the vibrant blooms, the children playing, and the vibrant tapestry of life—she noticed how Kai drew with fervor, his pencil gliding smoothly over the page. His concentration was mesmerizing, and she couldn't deny the fluttering in her heart as she watched his focus turn into a joyfully creative expression.

"Do you ever think about what it would be like to be truly free," Kai broke the silence, his eyes still on the page. "To just chase after adventures?"

His words hung in the air, and Mei contemplated their meaning. She sensed a deeper longing beneath the surface—a desire they both shared. "Often," she replied softly, sweeping her gaze across the park. "I think about it a lot, especially at times like this."

Kai looked up, curiosity shining in his eyes. "Then what's stopping you?"

The question caught her off guard. She bit her lip, contemplating how to answer without revealing the confusion in her heart. "I guess… sometimes I feel like there are expectations, you know?" She tried to articulate her thoughts. "Especially from my family. They have this vision of what they want me to be."

Kai paused for a moment, nodding in understanding. "You have to follow your passion, Mei. Those expectations can be crushing."

His sincere tone resonated deeply within her, his words striking a chord. "Yeah, they can be. It's hard to chase dreams when you feel tied down."

Silence wove between them, a shared understanding passing like an unspoken promise. It felt so liberating to share this with him. "But what if we can be free," Kai said, his words laced with optimism. "We can define our own paths, create our own stories. What if we took the plunge and chased those moments that make us feel alive?" His enthusiasm ignited something within Mei, a flicker of hope that began to warm her heart.

"Like how we did at the festival?" she mused, a smile creeping onto her face. "It was such a spontaneous adventure."

"Exactly! That's the spirit," he affirmed, leaning closer with a spark in his eye that made her pulse race. "Think about it—we could explore places together, capture moments that matter. Just us, no boundaries."

His gaze was intense, and as he spoke, Mei could feel an exhilarating sense of possibility filling the space between them. For a fleeting moment, she let herself imagine a world where they could indeed embark on a journey—a world where rules didn't bind them, where passion led their paths.

"Where would we go?" she asked, her imagination ignited.

"Anywhere! Let's find hidden gems in our city, get lost in the streets of Kyoto, or even take a road trip to the countryside! There are so many adventures waiting for us," Kai replied, his excitement infectious.

The very thought of it sent a rush through her. A smile widened on her face. "That actually sounds incredible!" she admitted, her heart fluttering at the idea of exploring with someone as spirited as Kai. "Maybe even take photos and sketch along the way?"

"Definitely!" Kai exclaimed, his voice brimming with enthusiasm. "But remember, photography is about capturing feelings—if we let ourselves feel everything, we'll have all the inspiration we need."

Their eyes met, the unfiltered connection electrifying the air around them. Mei could feel her cheeks flushing as she was struck by the intensity of the moment. Was this more than just friendship? Did he feel it too?

They sat in comfortable silence for a moment, both engaging in their creative pursuits—Mei snapping photos of blooming flowers and Kai sketching the scenes around them. With every click of her camera and each stroke of his pencil, she felt the weight of words left unspoken brewing beneath the surface, the bond between them growing deeper.

But anxiety nibbled at the edges of her heart. As the day wore on, fleeting glances turned into lingering stares, and the tension between them began to build quietly. Every word, every gesture felt like a dance on a precipice of something wonderful yet terrifying.

"Hey, can I ask you something?" Kai broke the hush, his voice lower now, carrying an undertone she couldn't quite place.

"Sure! What is it?" she replied, her heart pounding with curiosity.

"Do you ever think about… what you want in a relationship?" The question hung in the air, charged with anticipation.

Mei's breath caught in her throat as she measured her response. Suddenly, she felt exposed, as if the vulnerability of the question dared her to confront her own feelings. "I… I think about it sometimes. But it's complicated."

"Complicated how?" Kai's eyes searched hers, determined to uncover the truths hidden beneath her hesitation.

"Because there are so many expectations from family and society… and then there's the fear of losing myself in someone else," she confessed, her heart racing. "It's hard to navigate what I truly want."

"I get that. But look at us," he said, a soft smile playing on his lips. "We've already started something real. We're here, sharing and exploring—and I think that's important. You don't have to sacrifice who you are to let someone in."

Mei was struck by his words, their simplicity stark yet profound. She felt a rush of admiration for him, the way he seemed to understand her so deeply despite their short time together.

But as a wave of warmth surged through her, another thought crept in, whispering doubts that clouded her joy. What if it all came crashing down?

Out loud, she said, "What if we ruin this friendship by moving too fast? I don't want to lose you."

"Mei," Kai said softly, his voice reassuring. "I don't think we're moving too fast. I think we're just acknowledging what's already here."

His sincerity washed over her like a balm, and she felt her heart ache with longing and fear. "I'd like to see where this goes," she breathed, her voice trembling with honesty. "But I'm scared. I really like you, Kai. More than I expected."

He met her gaze, and for a moment, the world around them fell away. Under the warm sunlight filtering through the cherry blossoms, they shared a moment charged with possibility—two souls connected, teetering on the edge of something beautiful.

"What if we take it one day at a time?" Kai proposed, his voice calm and steady. "Let's just enjoy what we have right now and see where it leads.

We don't have to rush anything. We can keep exploring and creating together, and if something more comes of it, great. If not, we still have each other as friends."

The weight of his words settled over her, a soothing balm to her anxieties. Mei let out a soft breath she hadn't realized she was holding. "That sounds good," she replied, a smile tugging at her lips. "I like that idea."

Kai grinned, the warmth of his expression making her heart leap a little. "So we're in agreement then?"

"Definitely!" she confirmed, feeling lighter. They shared a lingering gaze, and for a brief moment, everything felt perfect. The noise of the park, the laughter of children in the distance, and the rustling of the cherry blossoms faded away, leaving just the two of them suspended in their own world.

Gradually, the sun began to dip lower in the sky, casting a golden hue over everything. As the afternoon wore on, Mei and Kai continued capturing their surroundings—she clicked away with her camera while he sketched furiously, both attempting to immortalize the beauty of the moments they had shared.

While they worked side by side, an invisible thread seemed to grow between them, tightening around their unspoken feelings. Subtle glances lingered a little longer, brushes of their hands felt a little more electric, and when their laughter merged, it resonated like a shared secret.

Mei caught herself glancing at the sketches Kai created, admiring how he captured the essence of the park—the way the sunlight danced on the flowers, how the cherry blossoms fluttered like confetti in the wind, and how his lines seemed to pulse with life. "You have a real talent for capturing not just the visuals, but the feelings, too," she remarked.

"Thanks! I try to express what I see and feel as much as I can," he replied, his voice full of passion. "But you inspire me to dig deeper. I want to capture everything that makes this moment special."

As the sun began to set and the sky painted itself in brilliant hues of purple and pink, they padded their things, having spent the day immersed in their shared creativity. A sense of contentment enveloped them, but beneath that contentment lay an undercurrent of anticipation and curiosity for what would come next.

"Shall we get some food?" Kai suggested, glancing at her with that hopeful glint in his eye.

"Absolutely! I could use some energy after all that capturing," Mei replied, her excitement bubbling over. "I know a great little place nearby that has delicious ramen!"

"Lead the way!" Kai replied, and they set off through the park, their laughter ringing in the fading light. The walk felt natural, the distance between them shrinking as they shared thoughts on everything from their favorite foods to their future aspirations.

As they approached the little ramen shop tucked away along a narrow sidestreet, Mei felt an exhilarating mix of eagerness and nervousness bubble in her belly. Would tonight bring any significant changes to their newfound connection? Would the evening deepen what was lingering unspoken between them?

Once inside the cozy ramen joint, they settled into a small booth in a corner, the warm ambiance wrapped around them like a comforting embrace. The small menu options made the decision easier, and as they placed their orders, the intoxicating aroma of broth filled the air, enhancing her anticipation.

While waiting for their meals, they continued to converse effortlessly, exploring each other's thoughts and experiences. Kai shared a hilarious tale about a cooking disaster, and Mei, in turn, recounted an awkward moment from her childhood involving a school presentation gone wrong. The stories flowed, punctuated by laughter and the occasional shared intimate gaze that made Mei's heart flutter.

Even as they delved deeper into their shared experiences, a sense of worry crept over Mei. What if this moment solidified everything she felt but was unable to voice? As the appetizers arrived and they began to eat, the air hummed with unspoken emotions.

Kai paused mid-bite and looked at her, his expression shifting to one of earnestness. "So, now that we're here... I just want to say that I meant what I said earlier. Whatever happens next, I hope we can keep this momentum going."

Mei's heart raced, emotions crashing over her like waves. "I feel the same way," she said, her voice steady despite the whirlwind inside her. "This is all so new for me, but it feels like… something special."

"It is special," he affirmed, his gaze unwavering, etching the moment into her heart. "I'm glad we're taking the time to explore what this is. I really enjoy being with you, Mei." "In a world that often feels overwhelming, you make everything seem lighter," Mei confessed, her heart pounding as she met his gaze. She could feel the depth of her feelings bubbling to the surface—an urge to say everything that had been building inside her since their first meeting.

Kai's eyes softened, and for a moment, it felt as if they were caught in a bubble, shielded from everything else around them. "I'm really glad I met you," he said, his voice steady and sincere. "There's something about this connection between us that feels different."

"Different how?" she asked, curiosity dancing in her voice. She leaned forward on the table, pulling out the courage that had been simmering beneath the surface since their festival encounter.

"Like, I don't always feel this way with friends," Kai explained, a touch of vulnerability creeping into his tone. "It's like there's this… unspoken understanding. I feel freer to be myself with you, and it inspires me to explore what that means."

Her heart soared at his words, the thrill of mutual understanding dancing on the edges of her thoughts. "I feel the same. It's comforting, like we're in sync with each other," she admitted.

They shared a moment of silence, a world brimming with unvoiced possibilities expanding between them. Mei felt the urge to take a leap, to uncover the full range of emotions she felt for him, but the fear of those feelings terrified her as well.

Just then, their steaming bowls of ramen arrived, the fragrant scent captivating both of them. They exchanged delighted grins at the feast before them, momentarily distracted from the heavy conversation. They dived into their meals, the warmth of the broth sparking feelings of comfort and contentment.

As they enjoyed their ramen, laughter punctuated their conversation, the air filled with warmth and the sound of chopsticks clashing against bowls. Despite how effortless it felt, Mei couldn't shake off the tenderness in the air, the understanding that lingered beneath the surface.

After finishing their meal, Mei wiped her mouth with a napkin, feeling a mixture of satisfaction and the thrill of anticipation settling in her chest. "So, what's next for us?" she asked, her voice playful but tinged with seriousness.

Kai raised an eyebrow, a hint of a smile playing on his lips. "I don't know… maybe planning our next adventure? I'm really looking forward to spending more time together, but let's keep it light and fun for now. A clear path seems to bring clarity and excitement."

"Agreed! I could get used to this kind of adventure," Mei joked, but internally, she felt as though she had scored a little victory. The blend of excitement and fear she felt at the idea of moving forward became a thrilling prospect rather than an overwhelming uncertainty.

They made their way out of the ramen shop, but the night was still young, and the vibrant streets of Tokyo awaited them. The city glittered under twinkling lights, a canvas of possibility stretching as far as they could see.

"Let's walk a bit more," Kai suggested, gesturing for her to follow. They ambled down the illuminated streets, the ambiance of the city settling into a comfortable rhythm around them.

As they strolled, Mei found herself stealing glances at him, the way he lit up as he took in their surroundings, the spark of creativity in his eyes as he observed everything around them. It made her heart race—part admiration, part longing.

Eventually, they found a quiet spot on a bridge overlooking the water, where reflections of the city lights shimmered like stars in the river below. Kai leaned against the railing, glancing out over the water, the moon casting a silvery sheen over the scene.

"This place is beautiful," Mei remarked, leaning beside him and taking in the breathtaking view.

"Just like the festival," he replied softly. "It's moments like this that capture the essence of life, don't you think?"

She responded with a quiet smile, feeling the weight of the evening settle around them. The beauty of the moment felt fragile yet significant, holding potential for something more than friendship.

As they stood in companionable silence, an unspoken promise hung in the air, binding them closer together. The world around them dimmed, creating a cocoon of peaceful intimacy. And in that moment, Mei felt her heart open, recognizing the pull of something profound.

"Whatever happens, I want you to be a part of my journey," Kai whispered, breaking the tranquility.

Her heart swelled, feeling the truth of his words resonate within her. "And I want you to be a part of mine," she said, her voice barely above a whisper but filled with sincerity.

In that breathtaking moment, the possibilities of the future stretched out before them like the water below—endless and shimmering, waiting for them to explore.

With a shared smile that encapsulated everything unspoken between them, Mei felt as if they stood on the threshold of something more significant than friendship. The laughter and adventures from that day felt like mere beginnings, each moment a stepping stone toward a deeper connection.

As they gazed out over the water, the city lights twinkling like stars reflected in their eyes, the weight of unspoken feelings settled comfortably between them.

"Here's to new adventures," Mei said softly, raising an imaginary glass to the night.

Kai turned to her, that infectious grin spreading across his face. "And to discovering where this journey takes us."

In that instant, the world felt full of promise, the air vibrating with potential as they both leaned into the warmth of that understanding. Hand in hand, they stepped away from the edge of the bridge, ready to embrace whatever lay ahead—together.

As they walked back through the streets toward home, each footstep felt lighter, as if they were not just moving through the physical space of the city but also into the realm of possibility. Hidden feelings lingered in the air like the lingering glow of lanterns, just waiting to illuminate the path they would forge, side by side.

And in that moment of hope and connection, they couldn't know that this was just the beginning of a beautiful journey that would challenge everything they thought they knew about love, friendship, and what it truly meant to embrace life.

CHAPTER 3

THE SECRET GARDEN IN SHINJUKU GYOEN

Spring had fully embraced Tokyo, transforming the city into a palette of blooming colors and fragrant blossoms. With each passing day, the cherry blossoms unfolded in delicate shades of pink, greening the parks and bringing life to even the most hidden corners of the city. Mei felt a renewed sense of hope and excitement as she walked toward Shinjuku Gyoen, a place she had loved since childhood, yet it held the promise of something new.

After their meaningful evening together, she and Kai had agreed to meet here—a beautiful garden filled with serene paths, vibrant flora, and tranquil ponds—an ideal spot for them to explore their thoughts and feelings further away from the prying eyes of the city.

As she entered through the grand gates, the sights and sounds of Tokyo faded, replaced by a soothing chorus of rustling leaves and chirping birds. The air was crisp, infused with the scent of fresh blooms, and Mei felt a sense of peace wash over her—the kind of peace that invited introspection.

Spotting Kai near a cherry blossom tree, she smiled at the sight of him basking in the sunlight. He had already set down his backpack and was fiddling with his sketchbook, the soft breeze causing his hair to flutter. She approached him quietly, feeling a rush of affection.

"Hey there, artist," she greeted playfully, leaning against a nearby tree to observe him. "What masterpiece are you planning to create today?"

Kai looked up and grinned, his eyes lighting up upon seeing her. "Just waiting for the perfect moment to capture these blossoms before they start to fall. They're blooming beautifully!"

"Let me take a photo while you sketch! It'll be like creating a visual memory together," Mei offered, pulling out her camera and framing the scene in her mind.

"Sounds perfect!" he replied, positioning himself under the tree and striking a quick pose as if he were part of an art piece himself. Mei chuckled at his antics as she snapped a few pictures, feeling the warmth of laughter between them.

After photographing Kai, she walked around the garden, taking in the vibrant surroundings. Each blossom seemed to whisper stories of fleeting beauty and new beginnings, reflecting her own heart's blossoming connections. The tranquil atmosphere inspired her to open up—to express her thoughts and emotions with Kai, who stood at the brink of becoming something more than just a friend.

"Let's find a place to sit and relax," she suggested, wandering deeper into the garden. As they walked through the winding paths, she felt the weight of unspoken feelings loom over them, though she was determined to explore it further.

Finally, they reached a secluded spot by a serene pond, where willow trees gently dipped their branches into the water. The sunlight filtered through the leaves, casting playful shadows on the ground. Mei felt as though they had stepped into a secret world away from the hustle and bustle of Tokyo—a private haven just for them.

"This is perfect," she said, sinking onto a patch of soft grass. Kai settled beside her, and for a moment, they both took in the beauty around them, the atmosphere thick with possibilities.

With the sounds of nature swirling around them, Mei took a deep breath, trying to gather her thoughts. "So…" she started, her heart racing as she finally gathered the courage to express what had been swirling in her mind since their last encounter. "About what we talked about the other day… I've been thinking a lot."

"Yeah?" Kai prompted, his gaze steady and encouraging. "About our adventure?"

"About us, actually," Mei clarified, feeling a rush of vulnerability wash over her. "After everything we've shared, I think… I think I really like spending time with you."

Kai's expression shifted, deepening as he listened intently. "I feel the same way," he said quietly but firmly. "It's been hard not to notice how special our connection is, and I want to explore it more with you."

A warm blush crept up her cheeks at his admission. "I'm glad you feel that way. But I guess I worry about the weight of expectations—about where this could lead and how it might change our friendship."

Kai nodded, understanding evident in his gaze. "That makes sense. But maybe it's those expectations that can sometimes hold us back. We can't predict what the future holds. All we can do is embrace the present."

His perspective struck a chord within her. She had always tried to control the narrative of her life, afraid to let go and see where the current would take her. "You're right," she admitted, glancing down at her hands. "It's just... new for me. It's easier to hide."

"You don't have to hide with me," Kai reassured her, shifting closer until their shoulders touched. "You can be yourself. I want to know you—the real you, the good, the bad, everything."

His words washed over Mei like a gentle tide, soothing her worries and igniting a flicker of courage within her. She turned to face him, her heart racing at the sincerity etched into his features. "That's so encouraging, Kai. I've been afraid that if I let myself feel too much, I might lose everything I've gained, lose you in the process."

"Then we tackle that fear together," he said softly, his eyes meeting hers with unwavering confidence. "We won't let fear dictate our relationship. We'll make our own memories, no matter where that leads."

In that moment, everything felt possible. The blossoms bloomed around them, vibrant and alive, mirroring the connection that was blossoming between them.

Taking a deep breath, Mei let go of her worry, letting the beauty of their surroundings ground her. "I want to take that leap, to embrace this connection between us," she said, her voice steady. "I really do like you, Kai, more than I realized."

"I like you too, Mei," he admitted, a smile breaking across his face that lit up his entire being. "I've been hoping you felt this way."

Their shoulders brushed against each other again as an electric thrill coursed through her. For a moment, it felt as if the entire world melted away, leaving just the two of them in their own secret garden blooming with potential.

Suddenly, a soft breeze rustled the cherry blossoms above them, and delicate petals fluttered down like confetti. They landed around them, blanketing the ground in shades of pink and white, infusing the moment with an air of enchantment.

"Look!" Mei exclaimed, laughing as she raised her hands to catch the falling blossoms. "It's like nature is celebrating us!"

Kai joined in, attempting to catch a few of the delicate petals. "I can definitely take that as a sign!" he grinned, his excitement infectious. The atmosphere felt charged with happiness and a sense of shared adventure, a promise of new beginnings.

After the petals settled around them, they sat back, eyes twinkling. In that ethereal moment, Mei felt an awakening inside her—an understanding that it was okay to embrace the uncertainty of life, to be brave enough to taste the adventure of falling in love.

"What if we make an annual tradition out of this?" she suggested, glancing at the vibrant blossoms surrounding them. "A place for us to always return, no matter where life takes us."

Kai's eyes lit up. "I love that idea! We can document each year's adventures, see how we grow, and change together," he said, his enthusiasm making her heart swell.

"Yes, and we can take pictures and draw in the hopes of capturing our journey," she added, already imagining all of the future memories they would create.

"Deal," he said, extending his hand to seal their pact, and Mei eagerly took it, feeling a rush of warmth flow between them. The connection deepened, solidifying a bond that felt both exhilarating and comforting.

"I have so many ideas for our first official adventure," she exclaimed, her eyes shining with excitement. "We could explore the hidden spots in Tokyo I've always wanted to visit—quaint cafes, secret gardens—each location holds a story."

"I can't wait to hear all about them!" Kai said, squeezing her hand gently.

"And I promise to bring my sketchbook, so we can capture everything we find."

Their palms lingered together for a moment longer, and Mei could feel the fluttering in her heart intensifying. Beneath the blossoming cherry trees, in their secret garden, the world around them felt imbued with magic, possibilities, and something she whispered to herself: Hope.

As the sun began its descent, casting the garden in golden light, Mei leaned back against the tree, feeling at peace and paradoxically thrilled. She took a deep breath, allowing the fragrance of blossoms and the warmth of their shared moment to envelop her.

"So," Kai began, settling beside her, "what do you see for the future?"

She pondered his question, glancing at the colors painting the sky. "I see adventures, laughter, and infinite moments that help us grow. I want to discover more about the world and, hopefully, more about us."

Kai nodded, his gaze steady as he took in her words. "I'm excited to explore this world with you."

In that quiet moment of reflection, as the shadows lengthened and the stars began to appear, she finally let herself dream about the possibilities with Kai—the adventures, the laughter, and the connection evolving in ways she hadn't yet dared to imagine.

With a heart full of hope and a smile that illuminated the fading day, Mei knew this was merely the beginning—a beginning steeped in the promise of a deeper attachment that thrived amid the beauty of their secret garden, ready to blossom into something extraordinary.

As the soft glow of twilight enveloped the park, Mei felt a comforting warmth knowing they had crossed into uncharted territory together. Their relationship had shifted from playful friendship to something more profound, and she couldn't help but wonder what the future held for them in this growing connection.

"Do you ever think about what it will be like when we look back on moments like today?" she asked softly, glancing sideways at Kai, whose attention was fixed upon the distant horizon where the sun was setting.

His eyes sparkled with something akin to excitement. "Definitely. I think these are the markings of real memories—the kind that last a lifetime. One day, we'll reflect on these experiences and feel grateful we didn't hold back."

The sincerity in his voice resonated deeply within her as they sat side by side, allowing the tranquil atmosphere to sink in. But even amid this comforting moment, Mei couldn't shake the tingle of apprehension settled low in her stomach. The more she opened her heart to Kai, the more she feared the potential heartache that could lie ahead.

"I want to enjoy our journey, but I can't help but feel scared sometimes," she admitted, vulnerability threading through her words. "What if we drift apart in the end?"

Kai turned to her, his expression earnest yet gentle. "Life is unpredictable, Mei. But if we promise to communicate openly, we can navigate through whatever challenges arise. We can't let fear dictate our journey together."

His words were both reassuring and inspiring, and she felt the remaining heaviness in her heart begin to lift. "You're right, Kai. I want to be brave and take this chance with you," she said, her voice resolute.

"Then let's make a pact," he suggested, leaning in slightly, the bright colors of the sunset reflecting in his eyes. "No matter what happens, we promise to always be honest with each other about our feelings. This is a journey we take together, no expectations—just authenticity."

Mei nodded, feeling warmth blossom within her, dreaming of an honest and open relationship. With a grin, she said, "I promise. Here's to honesty and all our future adventures."

"Here's to us," Kai said with a wide smile, their hands still entwined, sealing their pact with an unbreakable bond.

As twilight deepened, they lingered in their shared space, the world around them gradually dimming into night. The stars began to twinkle brilliantly against the darkening sky, as if echoing their promises.

Eventually, as the air turned cooler, Mei shivered slightly. Kai noticed and nudged her playfully. "Looks like it's time to grab some warm drinks and continue our adventure. What do you say?"

"I say yes!" she laughed, feeling buoyed by the warmth of their connection. She rose to her feet, and together they wandered the paths of Shinjuku Gyoen, transformed by the glow of the night.

As they made their way to the park exit, the enchanting atmosphere lingered between them—a beautiful, fragile tapestry of unspoken emotions, hopes, and dreams. Each step away from their secret garden brought a bittersweet mix of comfort and anticipation for what lay ahead.

With their hands intertwined, they ventured back into the bustling city, excitement for their next adventure blooming in the spaces between them. The possibilities felt exhilarating, a new chapter unfolding as they navigated their way toward exploring the depths of their attachment.

And as they stepped out of the park, ready to engage in the world that awaited outside their little oasis, Mei couldn't shake the feeling that this journey had just begun—an adventure of discovery, vulnerability, and the enchantment of first love.

CHAPTER 4

SWEET CONFESSIONS UNDER CHERRY BLOSSOMS

The sun set behind the skyline of Tokyo, casting a golden glow that bathed the bustling city in warmth. After leaving the sanctuary of Shinjuku Gyoen, Mei and Kai made their way to a quaint café nearby, the echoes of laughter and distant chatter filling the night air. Their hearts were light, buoyed by a shared promise of openness and adventure, yet there lingered an unmistakable tension between them—a sweet anticipation that seemed to pulse with every beat.

The small café, with its charming atmosphere and aromatic coffee, offered a perfect backdrop for their heart-to-heart conversation. They settled into a cozy corner, a window framing the blossoms outside that danced in the gentle breeze. Below the cherry trees, the last remnants of light melted away, revealing a tapestry of silver stars twinkling overhead.

As they sipped their drinks—Mei with a creamy matcha latte and Kai with a rich espresso—the conversation flowed effortlessly. They shared stories, dreams, and laughter, but beneath the playful banter lay an undercurrent of feelings that both excited and terrified Mei.

"Remember when we first met at the festival?" she began, recalling the moment that had altered everything. "I was so nervous, but you were so easy to talk to."

Kai chuckled, his eyes sparkling. "Yeah, I remember thinking how captivating you were. I was mesmerized by your passion for photography and art."

A warmth spread through Mei at his compliment, and she could feel a shy smile blooming on her lips. "I think I captured you in a way that day. You just lit up when you danced and played music with your friends. It was… refreshing."

"Well, it was all because of you. I felt like I could be myself, and it made everything feel more vibrant," he said, leaning in slightly, his tone low and sincere.

As those words hung in the air, they both knew that the conversation was shifting—a transition into something more intimate. The atmosphere crackled with unspoken confessions, and Mei's heart raced, an anxious thrill pulsating within her.

The café's ambiance fell away, and she found herself lost in Kai's eyes, feeling the urge to share the deeper feelings that had been building inside her since that moment beneath the cherry blossoms.

"Kai," she began, swallowing hard, "there's something I've been wanting to tell you."

His expression shifted, his focus sharpening as he took her hand in his, the warmth of his touch sending shivers down her spine. "You can tell me anything."

This was it—a moment of vulnerability she had craved. "I've enjoyed every moment we've spent together, but being honest, it's been more than fun for me. I've come to realize that I like you a lot... more than just a friend. And it scares me because I feel this connection that I've never felt before."

She took a deep breath, her heart pounding as she compressed her emotions into words. "I feel so drawn to you, and it's exhilarating, but also terrifying. I want to embrace it, but I don't know what that could mean... for us or for me."

The words poured out like a long-held secret liberated into the night air. The vulnerability felt liberating yet terrifying, and she watched Kai carefully—his expression remained steady, his eyes never leaving hers.

"I'm glad you told me," he said softly, his thumb brushing over hers soothingly. "I've been feeling the same way. It's been hard to ignore this powerful connection between us, and I've been afraid to say it. I've never met someone who makes me feel so alive and inspired."

Mei's breath caught in her throat as she processed his words. Relief washed over her; she felt lighter, brighter. "Really? You feel that too?"

"Absolutely," he affirmed, a smile breaking across his face. "Being with you has brought out a side of me that I didn't even know existed. You've opened my eyes to so much, made me want to explore more than just what's in front of me."

His sincerity wrapped around her, filling her with warmth. "So, what does this mean for us?" Mei hesitated, still unsure but hopeful. "I don't want to rush things, but I want to explore this…whatever 'this' is."

Kai paused for what felt like an eternity, but then he nodded thoughtfully. "Let's take our time. We can navigate this together, openly and honestly, no pressure. I want us to be able to share everything—our fears, our dreams, and our hopes."

A smile bloomed on her face, gratitude swelling in her chest. "I'd like that. I really want to see where this journey takes us, to discover who we are together."

Just then, the café's door swung open, letting in a gust of cool night air, and the sweet smell of cherry blossoms drifted in. Just then, the café's door swung open, letting in a gust of cool night air, and the sweet smell of cherry blossoms drifted in. Mei inhaled deeply, feeling invigorated by the soft fragrance that reminded her of their cherished moments in the park. The atmosphere felt charged, and she could sense that the world outside was unaware of the transformation taking place within them.

As they continued to talk and sip their drinks, the conversation turned lighthearted once more. They recalled funny memories from the festival, exchanged ideas for their next adventure, and even playfully debated the best ramen spots in the city. Yet, woven into the laughter was the undeniable thread of feelings that had deepened in that small café corner.

"You know," Kai said, his tone shifting slightly, "I didn't expect to feel this way about someone so quickly. But then again, everything about being around you feels easy and right."

Mei's heart soared at his words, and she felt the flutter of excitement re-ignite in her chest. "It's so refreshing to have this connection with you, especially in a world that feels so chaotic sometimes."

"Exactly," he said, a knowing smile lighting up his face. "It's like we've created our little oasis among all the noise."

As they lingered over their drinks, the hours passed, and they both eventually knew it was time to leave. With a shared reluctance, they exited the café, stepping out into the night where the soft glow of the streetlights illuminated their path.

"Where to next?" Mei asked, her heart beating with anticipation as they began walking again.

"How about we take a stroll along the river?" Kai suggested, glancing at her with that charming spark in his eyes. "I've heard the cherry blossoms are still in full bloom down by the water. It would be a beautiful view at night."

"That sounds perfect," Mei agreed eagerly, feeling a sense of giddiness at both the blossoming night and the closeness they shared.

As they strolled towards the river, their fingers brushed against each other, and the contact sent tingling sensations up her arm. Slowly, as if drawn by an invisible force, they intertwined their fingers, and she felt an electrifying warmth flood through her. The touch felt natural, as if they had been holding hands for a long time.

As they reached the riverbank, the scene before them was enchanting. The moonlight cast a silver sheen over the water, and the reflection of the cherry blossoms danced like flickering stars on the surface. The sweet scent of the blossoms filled the air, and Mei felt a rush of serenity wash over her.

"Wow," she breathed, taking in the beauty of the moment. "It's breathtaking."

Kai stood beside her, basking in the atmosphere. "It truly is. It's like something out of a dream."

In that moment, Mei felt a surge of emotion bubbling to the surface, fueled by the tender connection they had forged. This place felt sacred—a canvas where she could express herself openly, far from the world's judgments.

"Do you mind if I share something?" she began softly, her heart racing again as she turned to face him.

"Of course! Whatever's on your mind," Kai encouraged, his gaze locking onto hers with an intensity that made her feel seen.

"I've often kept my feelings hidden—afraid of what might happen if I let them out," she confessed, a tremor in her voice. "It's just so easy to get lost in expectations and fears. But being with you has shown me that it's okay to be vulnerable. I want you to know what you truly mean to me. This connection feels so special, and I don't want to hide from it anymore."

She felt the weight of her words settle in the space between them, an act of bravery that filled her with both fear and relief. The very act of voicing her feelings felt liberating, like a breath she had been holding in for far too long.

"I'm so glad you said that," Kai replied, his voice soft yet filled with warmth. "I feel the same way, Mei. You've opened something in me that I didn't know needed to be explored. I want to be there for you, to support you… and to discover everything that lies ahead for us."

Realizing the depth of their shared feelings, Mei took a step closer to him, her heart thundering in her chest. "So, then… let's make a promise to each other," she said, feeling the exhilaration building. "A promise that we will always communicate openly, no matter how difficult or scary it may be."

With a gentle smile, Kai's expression turned serious. "I promise, Mei. We'll build something honest between us."

As the blossoms swayed gently above them, they sealed their promise with a shared gaze under the moonlight, both feeling the weight and significance of their commitment to open communication and honesty in the journey ahead.

Mei felt her heart soar as an exhilarating wave of warmth coursed through her. This shared understanding, this moment of vulnerability, brought them closer in ways she hadn't anticipated. The world felt as though it had shrunk to just the two of them, the soft rustle of leaves and the distant laughter of passersby fading into the background.

"Thank you for being so open with me, Kai," she said, her voice filled with sincerity. "I didn't realize how much I needed someone like you until now."

Kai smiled, a hint of pride shimmering in his eyes. "And I didn't realize how much I needed someone who could see me for me. You've brought out everything I've wanted to explore."

With a lightened heart, Mei took a moment to appreciate how far they had come since their first encounter at the festival. The blossoming connection felt surreal, as if they had scripted their own fairy tale among the cherry trees.

"Shall we take a picture to commemorate this moment?" she suggested, a playful grin crossing her lips. "A moment of us under the cherry blossoms to remember our promise."

"Absolutely! Let's capture this—our promise under the stars!" Kai agreed enthusiastically, pulling out his phone as they positioned themselves beneath the delicate branches.

As they posed together, Mei leaned into him, feeling the warmth of his presence envelop her. Kai raised the phone, and just before clicking the shutter, he whispered, "Say 'hope'!"

"Hope!" they exclaimed in unison, and the soft flash captured their radiant smiles, a testament to the bond they had formed.

After reviewing the picture and laughing together, their eyes sparkled with delight. "This will be the first of many adventures, right?" Mei said, her heart full of anticipation.

"Definitely! Just think of all the memories we'll create," Kai replied, the excitement evident on his face. "We'll fill this gallery of ours with laughter and love, one moment at a time."

Mei nodded, a sense of purpose pushing her forward. "And we'll always remember this night, this promise," she said, glancing up at the blossoms overhead that had become witness to their burgeoning relationship.

As the night deepened and a cool breeze swept through the park, they knew it was time to head back. The enchantment of the moment lingered like the sweet scent of the cherry blossoms, warm in their chests as they walked hand in hand alongside the shimmering water of the river.

But unbeknownst to them, every fairy tale has challenges to face, and as they stepped back into the reality of their lives, they would soon find themselves confronted with the very expectations and fears they had vowed to navigate together.

With their hearts light and full of hope, Mei and Kai left the enchanting embrace of the cherry blossoms behind, ready to embrace the journey ahead.

CHAPTER 5

CHAPTER NAME

The following week passed in a blissful haze for Mei. Each day brought new moments with Kai that filled her with joy—they visited hidden cafés, explored tucked-away galleries, and spent countless afternoons sketching and laughing in their secret garden. But despite the exhilaration of their budding relationship, a subtle weight began to press upon her heart.

As Mei settled into her routine, the thrill of newfound affection began to intertwine with the gnawing anxiety she had tried to push aside. She adored their connection, but lingering worries about her parents' opinions crept back into her thoughts. They had always held firm expectations regarding her relationships, adhering to traditional values that sometimes felt stifling, especially in the face of her feelings for Kai.

One evening, Mei returned home to find her parents in the living room, their voices low but clear from the hallway. She hesitated, sensing she was about to walk into a conversation that might deepen the anxieties swirling inside her.

"I just want what's best for her," her mother's voice touched her ears, laced with a tremor of concern. "I mean, she's been spending a lot of time with that boy. He's nice enough, but there's so much more to consider."

"Are you worried about the fact that he's mixed race?" her father's response was gentle but firm. "You know it's a different world today, and love can cross all kind of boundaries."

For a fleeting moment, Mei felt a sting of embarrassment, her heart racing as she fought the impulse to turn back and leave. Instead, she inched closer, subconsciously wanting to hear more.

"It's not just that," her mother continued, her tone rising slightly. "What if he doesn't understand our culture? What if he doesn't value the things we do? Relationships like this can complicate things for her. I don't want to see her hurt."

The words sent a chill through Mei, and she pressed her back against the wall, a wave of fear washing over her. What if they were right? What if their worries were justified? She had felt free with Kai, but the idea that her parents wouldn't accept him because of his background weighed heavily on her heart.

"Mei is still figuring things out. We need to let her make her own choices, even if they differ from what we envision," her father replied, but there was a hint of uncertainty in his voice.

Mei felt her heart race, caught in a battle between her desire to face her parents about her feelings and the fear that their doubts about her relationship were valid. How can I make them see Kai for who he is?

With her mind racing, she stepped back just as the front door creaked open. Her father turned around, eyes meeting hers, and she froze for a moment. "Mei! You're home!" he said, and the warmth of his tone was genuine, but she felt the weight of what had just been said hanging in the air.

"Uh, yeah," she stammered, forcing a smile as she walking closer into the living room. "I was just out with some friends."

Her mother's gaze shifted, scrutinizing Mei in a way that made her stomach twist. "How was your time out?"

"It was good," she replied, suppressing her feelings. "We enjoyed some time at the park." She glanced quickly at her father. "I should finish up on my homework. I'll see you both later."

"Alright, honey," her father said gently, but Mei felt her mother's eyes follow her as she retreated to her room. Once the door was closed, she released the breath she hadn't realized she was holding.

Sinking onto her bed, she felt a tidal wave of emotions crash over her. The doubts her parents voiced echoed in her mind, intertwining with the joy she felt about Kai. Torn between her feelings for him and her parents' concerns, she struggled to make sense of it all.

With trembling hands, she picked up her camera, instinctively looking to find solace in capturing the beauty around her. But no matter how hard she tried to focus, her thoughts swung back to the revelations she had overheard.

What if my parents don't accept this? What if I hurt them by pursuing something my heart wants? The conflict enveloped her, leading her to spiral deeper into anxieties she had hoped to avoid.

Mei spent the evening restless and lost in thought, her heart wrestling with hidden fears. She couldn't shake the feeling of obsession that had begun to consume her—an obsession with ensuring she did right by her family while navigating the intricate emotions growing for Kai.

The following day, she met Kai at their favorite café, but she felt a barrier between them that wasn't there before. As he chatted excitedly about a local art exhibit they could visit, Mei caught herself nodding along but remained distant, her thoughts swirling with uncertainty and the shadows of her parents' doubts.

"Mei! Are you even listening?" Kai laughed, teasing, his playful expression sliding into concern.

"Yeah, of course!" she replied, forcing a smile that felt more like a mask than her usual bright demeanor. "The exhibit sounds amazing. I was just thinking about the different art styles we might see."

"Okay, good. I was worried for a second," he said, his eyes scanning her face as if searching for the spark they usually shared.

But Mei realized she had slipped into a state of anxiety, overwhelmed by the weight of everything she felt—for Kai and for the expectations she knew her parents had. "I'm sorry; I guess just… I'm kind of all over the place today," she admitted, biting her lip.

"Is it something in particular? You know you can talk to me about anything," Kai said, his tone shifting to genuine concern.

A surge of temptation stirred within her to share the weight she carried, to divulge her parents' concerns and the fear it instilled in her. She wanted to be honest with him, but she hesitated, unsure if discussing it would push him away rather than draw them closer.

"It's just been a hectic week, that's all. School has been more demanding. I guess I'm just trying to keep things together," Mei said, her voice faltering slightly despite her best efforts to sound nonchalant.

"Mei, you know I'm here for you," he reassured her, placing his hand gently over hers. The warmth of his touch sent her heart racing and a wave of longing washed over her. "You don't have to pretend with me."

His words hung heavily in the air, and she could feel her barriers crumbling. She glanced down at their intertwined fingers, grounding herself in the comfort his presence provided.

"I appreciate that, I really do," she whispered, her heart heavy with the fear of sharing her uncertainty.

Just then, the weight of her longing felt unbearable, and she found herself glancing around to see if anyone was watching them. Despite the world bustling around them, this moment felt intensely private. A flicker of vulnerability seized her—a desire to unleash her thoughts but afraid of the potential fallout.

"What if… what if my parents don't accept us? What if they think that who I'm seeing isn't good for me?" she finally blurted, the words tumbling out before she could stop them.

Kai's expression softened as he listened, genuine concern etched across his face. "What do you mean by that?"

"My parents have always had specific expectations for me—what they want my life to look like, who they believe I should be with," she explained, her voice trembling with emotion. "I overheard my mom worrying about us, and it made me think… what if they're right? What if this doesn't work?"

"Mei…" Kai said gently, his brow furrowing as he absorbed her words. "I can't tell you how your parents will feel, but I want you to know that our connection is real. It's something we both feel. We can't let their doubts define us."

"But what if they don't understand?" Mei's voice cracked, a mix of fear and insecurity infiltrating her thoughts. "What if they make me choose between my family and you?"

Kai's grip on her hand tightened, and he leaned in closer. "That path isn't easy for anyone, but we can confront this together. You deserve to be authentic in your life and relationship. If they see how happy you are with me, maybe they'll come around."

Mei looked into his eyes, searching for reassurance, feeling the turmoil within her reeling from his words. "You really think so?"

"I do," he said, his conviction unwavering. "It might take time, but being honest with your parents is important. I want to support you, no matter what. Just because some people may not understand doesn't mean it isn't valid."

A part of her felt comforted by his words, but beneath that sense of security was the familiar heaviness—the fear of their judgments. How could she convince them to see the beauty of what Kai brought into her life? It felt like a daunting barrier that stood against their blossoming connection.

As the chatter of the café faded into the background, they shared a moment of silence, each lost in their thoughts. Mei's heart ached with uncertainty.

After a while, she took a deep breath and let it out slowly. "I'll try to talk to them soon. I'll try to find a way to bring it up. But I'm still scared."

"Scared is okay, Mei," Kai reassured her gently, his voice steady and calm. "You're allowed to feel that way. Just know that I'm here with you every step of the way."

Mei let his words sink in, a tentative smile breaking through the storm of her emotions. "Thank you for that, Kai. It means a lot to me to have you by my side."

"Always," he said with sincerity, his eyes softening.

Feeling a surge of gratitude, she squeezed his hand, comforted by the strength of their connection. "I want us to be able to talk about anything, even the hard stuff. It feels good to get it out."

"Exactly. Just don't forget that you don't have to take this on all on your own," he replied, a reassuring smile creeping back onto his face. "Besides, if we tackle this together, we'll be stronger for it. I'm rooting for you."

With a flicker of hope ignited within her, Mei nodded, knowing that confronting her fears would prove challenging, but she was ready to take that leap. "You're right. We can do this together."

Feeling a new sense of determination, she took a calming breath, letting the caffeine and warmth of their conversation recharge her spirit. There was so much that lay ahead, both the excitement of their relationship and the hurdles that life posed. But for now, the promise of their connection felt solid, a haven to which she could always return.

"Alright," she declared with newfound resolve, "let's plan our next adventure! We can't let anything get in the way of all the amazing experiences we have yet to capture."

"Yes! I love that idea!" Kai responded with enthusiasm, his eyes gleaming with excitement. "How about exploring some of the hidden murals around the city? I've heard there are some incredible street art spots."

Mei's heart raced at the thought of future moments they could share—beautiful sights, laughter, and artistic creation unfolding before them. "That sounds perfect," she said, her spirit lifting once again. "I can't wait to capture every moment with you!"

As they left the café together, hands entwined and spirits high, the sun began to set, painting the sky with brilliant hues of orange and pink. The comforting warmth of their shared connection blossomed within her, easing her anxieties and surrounding her with hope.

"Let's keep moving forward, one adventure at a time," she said, glancing over at Kai who matched her bright expression.

"Absolutely! Adventure awaits, and I'm ready to capture all of it with you," he replied, excitement ringing in his voice.

And as they walked side by side into the vibrant evening, Mei couldn't help but feel optimistic about the journey ahead. The worries about her parents lingered at the back of her mind, but she now understood the importance of courage—of embracing the present and the hope that thrived within their connection.

With the cherry blossoms still fresh in her memory and their promises echoing in her heart, Mei was ready to find a path that led to both her love for Kai and the acceptance of those she held dear.

CHAPTER 6

BONDING OVER CURRY AND KARAOKE

The following weekend arrived, carrying with it a sense of excitement that fluttered in Mei's chest. After her heartfelt conversation with Kai at the café, she felt rejuvenated, ready to embrace life with open arms and an adventurous spirit. Tonight would mark the continuation of their promise to embark on new experiences together—a night filled with good food, music, and shared laughter.

Plans were set for a cozy evening filled with curry, one of Mei's favorite dishes. She could already picture the symphony of flavors; the warmth of spices mingling with the rich aroma of coconut milk, all swirling together to create a mouthwatering experience.

As they gathered at a small, authentic curry restaurant tucked away in a lively street marked by animated chatter and colorful lanterns, Mei felt an anticipatory thrill envelop her.

"Kai, you're going to love this place," she proclaimed as they stepped inside, the fragrant air enveloping them in a warm embrace. The restaurant was quaint and inviting, filled with wooden tables and vibrant décor that celebrated Indian culture.

"I can already tell!" he replied, his eyes lighting up as they settled into a corner booth. "It smells amazing in here!"

As they perused the menu, Mei felt a familiar ease settle between them. Their laughter and playful banter filled the space, echoing with the warm intimacy that had grown between them since they first met.

"Let's do a curry challenge!" Mei suggested, her excitement bubbling over. "We should order different dishes and try each other's!"

"Great idea! We can rank them, but I'm warning you, I might be a tough critic," Kai teased, flashing his competitive grin.

A playful spark ignited between them as they placed their orders—a variety of curries, naan, and fragrant basmati rice—eager to indulge in a culinary adventure together.

When the food arrived, the vibrant colors and rich aromas set their mouths watering. Mei glanced at Kai, who practically glowed with anticipation. "Okay, ready? Let's dig in!"

They dove into their meals, the flavors bursting in their mouths as they tasted each dish. Mei watched as Kai savored every bite, the expressions on his face shifting from delight to exaggerated joy with each new flavor.

"This is so good!" he exclaimed, wiping a bead of sauce from his chin. "What is this one called?"

"That's tikka masala! It's one of my favorites," she said, her eyes twinkling at his enthusiasm. "You have to try the garlic naan with it—it elevates the experience even more!"

Kai nodded, grabbing a piece of naan and scooping up the spicy sauce, a look of sheer bliss spreading across his face. "Wow! This is incredible!" he declared, prompting Mei to laugh.

They continued tasting, dunking and savoring, exchanging opinions on each dish and relishing the moment. Amidst the delicious food, their conversation effortlessly shifted from light-hearted jokes about their mutual love for food to more intimate thoughts about dreams for the future.

"Have you ever thought about what it would be like to travel the world? Just meandering from place to place?" Mei asked between bites, her heart warming at the thought.

"Every day," Kai replied with enthusiasm. "I want to experience the different cultures, try all the foods, and see how art varies around the world. There's so much to explore out there." His passion radiated from him, invigorating Mei.

"Exactly! I want to capture all those moments," she said, her mind swirling with images of various landscapes and cultures. "I can already imagine the photos I could take—the sights, the people—every frame telling a story."

"Oh, man, I'd love to see how you bring your perspectives together through photography," he encouraged, his eyes shining as he leaned in. "There's something about the stories we tell through food and culture—like it's a universal language."

"Yes!" she agreed eagerly. "Food does connect us; it tells stories about heritage and identity that go beyond words."

As the dishes dwindled, their shared enthusiasm grew, the sweetness of the curry mingling with the warmth of their conversation. The bond they had formed over their mutual love for exploration and creativity felt all the more profound after sharing such a delightful meal.

Once they finished dinner, they strolled over to a nearby karaoke bar, laughter spilling between them as they entered the vibrant establishment. The atmosphere was alive with energy—musical notes and cheerful voices dancing in the air.

"This is going to be so much fun!" Mei exclaimed, her excitement palpable.

"Let's see just how brave we are tonight!" Kai grinned. "I'll let you choose the first song!"

As they perused the song list, Mei felt a surge of adrenaline mixed with nerves wash over her. She had always loved singing, but performing in front of others was another matter entirely. Yet, spurred by the camaraderie they had built, she felt emboldened. This was the perfect opportunity to share another piece of herself with Kai.

"Let's do 'I Want It That Way' by the Backstreet Boys!" she declared, giddiness bubbling to the surface as she pointed at the song in the list. It was a classic, one of her favorites, and she knew it would be fun to sing together.

Kai's eyes widened in mock horror and utter delight. "Oh, yes! This is going to be epic! Let's go full nostalgia!"

They took the stage, and as the spotlight illuminated them, Mei's nerves tingled throughout her body. The crowd outside their booth dulled instantly—she could only focus on Kai standing beside her, a look of excitement dancing across his face.

As the music began, Mei found a rhythm that eased her tension. They started singing in unison, pouring their voices into the mic, and she felt the rush of adrenaline mingle with joy as the lyrics flew by. The moment transformed into an exhilarating release, lifting her spirit as laughter and smiles flowed freely.

With each chorus, Mei's confidence grew, and as Kai added goofy dance moves, her laughter rang through the room, shaking off the nervousness that had previously held her back. "We're such dorks!" she shouted mid-song, unable to contain her mirth.

"Absolutely! But dorky is fun!" Kai replied, half-singing, half-laughing, and the energy between them sparkled like fireflies on a summer night.

When they hit the final notes, they stood triumphant, laughing and high-fiving each other as the audience cheered. Mei's heart swelled with happiness—this shared moment was electric, a combination of melodies and warmth that she wanted to last forever.

"See? You were amazing!" Kai exclaimed, ruffling her hair playfully. "Now you're officially a karaoke superstar!"

"I can't believe we just sang that!" Mei giggled, still buzzing with joy. "I feel so alive!"

"Ready for round two?" he teased, his eyes gleaming with extravagance. "Let's take it up a notch—how about something a bit more challenging this time?"

"Alright, but you're picking this one!" she laughed, feeling emboldened by their earlier success.

Kai picked another song, and they took turns singing solo verses, supporting each other through laughter and cheers. The dim lights and ringing laughter transformed the atmosphere into a joyful celebration—one that felt like only the two of them existed within its confines, oblivious to the external world.

By the end of their karaoke session, both of them were flushed with excitement and a lively sense of achievement, volunteering to sing even more songs. When they finally emerged from the stage, they were greeted with applause from a small crowd that had gathered.

"Wow, who knew you were hiding that talent?" a voice called out.

"Right? I'm telling you; she's there getting ready for her big break!" Kai teased, nudging Mei playfully, basking in the contagious atmosphere.

"Maybe this is the start of our duo superstardom!" Mei fired back, laughter spilling out as their camaraderie blossomed further.

After a few more songs, they stepped outside, the night air feeling brisk but refreshing after the heat of the karaoke room. With their hearts still racing from the fun, they found themselves walking through the vibrant streets lit by neon lights.

"I had such a blast tonight!" Kai said, a radiant smile plastered across his face as they meandered along the sidewalk. "We should definitely do more karaoke nights!"

Mei nodded, the thrill of the evening still buzzing within her. "Definitely! It's amazing how much joy music can bring."

Suddenly, she felt a twinge of vulnerability rise within her. As they walked past the bustling eateries and storefronts, the worries that had crept in days ago weighed back on her heart. She stole a glance at Kai, taking in how effortlessly he seemed to glide through life. There was something so magnetic about his spirit—it surrounded her, igniting both passion and uncertainty.

What would her parents think if they knew that their daughter, who had always followed expectations, was exploring feelings for someone who defied their ideals? The fear she had held back pressed against her, and she felt the urge to share her thoughts now more than ever.

"Hey, Kai…" she started, her voice softening, unsure but determined to broach the subject.

"Yeah? What's on your mind?" he asked, his expression shifting to one of gentle concern.

"I wanted to talk about something that's been weighing on my heart," Mei said, her voice trembling slightly. She licked her lips, searching for the courage to express the turmoil swirling within her.

Kai's brow furrowed with concern as he slowed his steps, giving her his full attention. "What is it? You can tell me anything, Mei."

She took a deep breath, steeling herself. "It's about my parents and… us."

A cloud of uncertainty hung in the air; she could see Kai processing her words, his expression remaining calm yet attentive. "What do you think they'll say?" he asked gently.

Mei paused, choosing her words carefully. "I overheard them talking about you the other day. My mom is worried because of her expectations—about your background and how that might affect us. They want what they believe is best for me."

Kai's brows knit together, a flicker of understanding reflected in his eyes. "You think they wouldn't accept me because of my background?"

She nodded slowly, feeling the weight of apprehension settle in her stomach. "It's always been pretty evident that they have ideas about who I should be with. It makes me feel torn between wanting to follow my heart and keeping them happy."

"Mei," he said softly, tilting his head as he regarded her, "you can't let their opinions dictate how you feel or who you choose to love. This journey is yours, and it's about what makes you truly happy."

"I know that," she replied, biting her lip. "But the fear of disappointing them is big. I care about what my parents think, and the struggle between being myself and adhering to their expectations is overwhelming. I don't want to hurt them."

Kai took a moment to reflect before responding, resting a hand on her shoulder reassuringly. "Have you thought about talking to them about it? Shining a light on how you feel about me might help ease their concerns. If they see how much joy I bring you, it might shift their perspective."

Her heart raced at the thought, but doubts infiltrated her mind once again. "What if they can't see it? What if they refuse to understand? I don't want to walk into a battle over something that feels so pure."

"Sometimes love requires us to face challenges boldly, and this might be one of those times," he offered gently. "It's okay to be scared, but you don't have to face it alone. I'm going to be right here with you."

His unwavering support washed over her, granting her a fleeting sense of courage amidst the turbulence. "I wish I had your confidence, Kai."

"You've got more strength inside you than you know, Mei. You've already stepped out of your comfort zone in so many ways, and I know you're capable of this too," he encouraged, his voice steady and warm.

As they continued walking, Mei felt a spark of determination breaking through the haze of fear that had clouded her mind. "You're right. I want to have that conversation. I need to be honest with them, for both of our sakes. It's time to embrace the love I feel, no matter how difficult it might be."

A smile returned to Kai's face, and she felt a rush of warmth spread through her. "That's the spirit! And remember, no matter what happens, I've got your back. It's a journey we'll navigate together."

Mei nodded, feeling a sense of purpose bubbling inside her. They walked a little longer in silence, letting her thoughts settle. The lively street filled with laughter and chatter felt more inviting than ever, echoing the promise of new beginnings and the strength that came from confronting fears head-on.

As they reached a beautiful lookout point over the city, the twinkling lights mirrored the stars above, and Mei felt a renewed connection to Kai. "Thank you for always being there for me," she said sincerely, her heart swelling with gratitude.

"Always," he affirmed, turning to her with a playful glint in his eyes. "And who knows? Maybe next karaoke night, I'll have you sing a love song to me."

With a laugh, Mei shoved him playfully. "Only if you agree to sing one back!"

As they shared laughter, the worries she had been carrying felt lighter, and the road ahead seemed clearer. That night, beneath the stars, they had created memories filled with hope and laughter—a foundation for a deeper understanding of their bond.

As they walked home hand in hand, Mei felt the strength of their connection fortify her resolve. She was ready to face the upcoming conversation with her parents, knowing she wouldn't be alone.

CHAPTER 7

THE FIRST KISS AT TOKYO TOWER

The day had arrived, a radiant Saturday that illuminated Tokyo in all its glory. Mei felt a delightful mix of excitement and nervousness as she prepared for the evening ahead. After mustering the courage to speak to her parents about her feelings for Kai, she was ready to change the trajectory of her heart's journey. Yet, there was still one magical element yet to unfold—the anticipated visit to Tokyo Tower, where the skyline would frame their connection in a perfect view.

She arrived at the base of the iconic structure, her heart fluttering with anticipation. The tower loomed high, a beacon of the city, glowing softly in the fading sunlight. Kai was already there, leaning casually against a railing, looking effortlessly handsome as he took in the sights around him.

"Hey, you made it!" he smiled, his eyes lighting up upon seeing her. "I was starting to think you'd walk right past me!"

"Not a chance! I wouldn't miss this for the world," she replied, feeling the tension in her chest ease at his infectious energy.

As they approached the ticket counter, they bantered back and forth, Kai joking about the various activities they could attempt at the top—like a photo op portraying them as adventurous explorers. Mei laughed, envisioning their playful antics and thrilled in the prospect of the evening.

Once they had their tickets, they ascended in the elevator, the anticipation building with each passing floor. As they rose, the city began to unveil itself beyond the glass panels. Mei's heart raced as Tokyo revealed its breathtaking landscape; millions of lights dotted the city, creating a dazzling urban sprawl below.

When they finally stepped out onto the observation deck, a cool breeze swept over them, and they were greeted with an astonishing view of the sprawling metropolis. The sun had set, painting the sky with deep purples, oranges, and hints of indigo, while glittering stars began to peek through the twilight.

"Wow…" Mei breathed, her voice barely above a whisper as she took in the breathtaking panorama stretched out before her. "This is more beautiful than I imagined."

"It truly is," Kai agreed, stepping beside her and casting his eyes over the cityscape. "There's something magical about experiencing it with someone special."

Feeling a thrill at his words, Mei turned to him, noticing the way the lights reflected in his deep brown eyes. This was the perfect setting for a magical moment, but anticipation skipped like a heartbeat—the kind that made her pulse quicken with a mixture of excitement and trepidation.

They wandered along the observation deck, taking in the illuminated landmarks—Shibuya Crossing, the glittering skyscrapers, and the river reflecting the city lights. The buzz of the city below felt like a heartbeat, alive and invigorating.

"Do you remember our first date at the café?" Kai asked, leaning on the railing casually, and the playful comfort in his voice made her smile.

"Of course! You were so enthusiastic about the curry challenge. I thought you were going to eat everything on the menu!" she replied, laughing at the memory.

Kai turned to face her, a laugh sparkling in his eyes. "I could have if you had challenged me!"

In this moment, Mei felt the camaraderie between them shift to something deeper. As they shared laughter and fond memories, she sensed the air around them thickening with unspoken feelings. The night felt charged, as if it held its breath in anticipation of what was to come.

Kai looked at her with an intensity that made her heart skip. "Mei, I…I really appreciate what you said about facing your fears with your family. It's brave."

"Thank you," she replied softly, feeling the warmth on her cheeks. The vulnerability they both shared brought them closer, forging a connection that felt like a binding promise—the willingness to be honest and face whatever challenges awaited them.

"Honestly, I didn't know how I'd handle the pressure from my parents. But thinking of you and what we share… it inspires me," Mei said, her words flowing easily as she gazed into his eyes. "I feel like I can be who I am around you."

"I feel the same way," Kai responded, his gaze unwavering as he stepped closer to her. "It's like I can truly be me with you. It's liberating."

As they stood facing each other, the world around them faded into a blur—a backdrop to the moment charged with the weight of unvoiced feelings. Mei felt the pull of something deeper, a burgeoning desire, as their hearts danced in unison under the stars.

With the city twinkling beneath them and the sound of distant laughter in the background, time seemed to slow. It was as if this moment was just for them—a delicate capsule of magic swirling in the air between them.

"Maybe it's the energy of this place, but I've been wanting to say something…" Kai began, his voice dipping to a soft whisper.

"What is it?" Mei asked, her heart pounding as she held her breath, eager yet anxious to hear his words.

Kai took a step closer, the gentle night breeze ruffling his hair. "I just… I need you to know how much I care about you. Everything feels different when I'm with you, and it terrifies me and exhilarates me all at once." His tone was earnest, filled with a vulnerable honesty that made Mei's heart flutter.

"I feel the same way," she whispered, her voice steady yet infused with emotion. "Being with you makes everything seem brighter, and I can't imagine not having you in my life."

The air between them crackled, charged with unspoken promise and anticipation. Kai's gaze never wavered as he leaned in just a fraction closer, and Mei could feel the magnetic pull between them. It felt as if the entire world had narrowed down to this moment, everything else falling away—the skyline, the city below, and the bustling life that existed beyond this observation deck.

In that magical silence, Mei's heart guided her. She took a breath, and before she could think, she moved toward him, drawn by an irresistible force. "Kai…" she began, searching his eyes for reassurance.

And then, in a heartbeat, he closed the distance. Their lips met first in a tentative brush, a gentle exploration that sent shockwaves through her. As the kiss deepened, all of Mei's nerves melted away, replaced by warmth and softness. Kai's hand found its way to the small of her back, drawing her closer, pulling her softly into the warmth of his embrace.

The kiss felt electrifying, alive with all the emotions they had been building since the moment they first met. Mei felt the sweet rush of joy and tender affection ripple through her, blooming like the cherry blossoms around them—their own blossoming love.

When they finally broke apart, they stood breathless, foreheads resting against each other, their hearts racing in rhythmic unison. The soft sound of the city drifted into the background, leaving only the two of them suspended in this unforgettable moment.

Mei's pulse still raced, and she couldn't help but smile as she gazed into Kai's eyes, which sparkled with delight. "That was… incredible."

Kai chuckled softly, his cheeks tinged with a rosy hue. "I was hoping it wouldn't be a disaster."

"It was anything but!" she laughed, her voice ringing with joy. "I didn't realize how much I needed that until now."

"I'm so glad," he replied, his expression turning serious for a moment. "I wanted it to be special. You're special to me, Mei."

Her heart swelled at his words, a warmth rushing through her, affirming the connection they shared. "You're special to me too, Kai. I've never felt this way about anyone before," she admitted, unable to hold back the sincerity of her feelings.

They stood in comfortable silence, the sky above them now sprinkled with stars. The height of Tokyo Tower created a dreamy vantage, the bustling life below a reminder of the adventures that awaited them.

"Why don't we take a picture to remember this?" Kai suggested, breaking the tranquil reverie. "Our first kiss at Tokyo Tower!"

"Great idea!" Mei beamed, excitement bubbling up again. They both fished their phones out and positioned themselves under the soft glow of the tower lights, her heart fluttering as they struck a playful pose.

"Ready? On three!" Kai counted down, and as Mei smiled at the camera, capturing both their joy and the magic of the moment, she couldn't help but feel that this was just the beginning of something beautiful—a new chapter unfolding before them.

As the click of the camera went off, the sound echoed in their hearts, sealing this moment of promise and affection.

Stepping away from the camera, Mei felt the warmth of emotion surge through her. The kiss had not only solidified their feelings but had also ignited a bold new chapter in their relationship.

"Here's to more adventures and memories," she said, her voice light but filled with intention.

"Definitely," Kai replied, his jovial tone returning. "And to more beautiful sunsets!"

With laughter spilling between them, they began to stroll hand in hand along the observation deck, ready to soak in the breathtaking view of Tokyo sprawling beneath them while feeling the warmth of their connection deepening.

The city lights, the cherry blossoms, and the promise of blooming love filled Mei's heart as they walked together, ready to face whatever challenges lay ahead—with the knowledge that they had each other to lean on every step of the way

CHAPTER 8

RUMORS AT SCHOOL

The early morning light streamed into Mei's bedroom, casting a warm glow around her as she prepared for school. Despite the excitement of her recent experiences with Kai and the blossoming feelings they shared, a knot of apprehension twisted in her stomach. The weight of uncertainty loomed heavily, a contrast to the joy she had felt since their first kiss against the backdrop of Tokyo Tower.

As she donned her school uniform, lingering memories of their magical moments replayed in her mind—the laughter, the tenderness, the promises of shared adventures. Yet the joy of that intimacy faded beneath the surface as thoughts of school and potential judgment crept in. What would her classmates think? Would they support her and Kai?

Once she arrived at school, the familiar rush of students flowing through the hallways did little to alleviate her unease. She found Akira waiting for her at their usual spot, his energy bright as always, but Mei could sense a subtle change in the air.

"Hey, Mei! Did you hear?" he said, voice brimming with excitement. "There's some big buzz circulating around school about you and Kai!"

Her heart dropped at his words, and uncertainty flooded her senses. "What about us?" she asked, trying to keep her voice steady, but the tremor of fear seeped through.

"Apparently, some people saw you two at Tokyo Tower and are saying you're dating!" Akira grinned, oblivious to her growing tension.

"Oh…" Mei felt a chill run down her spine. "I didn't think it would matter to anyone." She attempted to maintain an air of nonchalance, but the fluttering in her stomach intensified, warning her of the storm brewing ahead.

"What do you mean? It's exciting!" Akira stated, clearly enjoying the gossip. "You and Kai make a great couple—it would be a shame if people didn't notice!"

"Yeah, but…" Mei faltered, her mind racing. What if they misinterpret our connection? "What are they saying? I mean, are they supportive of it?"

Akira paused, his expression shifting to one of concern. "Mostly positive. I've heard comments about how cute you two are and how you're finally dating someone. But you know how people are—there's always speculation."

The thought of speculation made her heart drop. Her parents' doubts echoed in her mind, merging into a symphony of insecurity. Suddenly, she felt as if she were being placed under a magnifying glass, the excitement of her feelings clouded by vulnerability.

"Have you heard any specifics?" she asked, trying to push down the fear clawing within her.

"A few people were saying stuff about you not being able to balance your family's expectations with who you want to be with. Some think it's complicated because of your differences," he replied lightly, trying to mask the seriousness of the matter.

Mei's heart sank further. Of course, they'd think that. The idea of her classmates witnessing what she and Kai had built, only to twist it into gossip and doubt, settled heavily on her shoulders.

"That's ridiculous…" she murmured, feeling her face heat with both embarrassment and frustration.

"Hey, don't let it get to you. Just ride out the wave. They'll get tired of talking soon enough; school gossip tends to die down." Akira patted her shoulder in reassurance.

But as the bell rang, signaling the start of school day, the knot in Mei's stomach deepened. Class felt long and tedious, her mind elsewhere as whispers floated through the hallways; each giggle felt like a piercing reminder of the scrutiny she was under. Despite Akira's encouragement, uncertainty gnawed at her confidence, leaving her feeling exposed.

As the lunch bell rang, Mei shuffled through the cafeteria, eyes darting around for Kai. She longed for the comfort of his presence, hoping to find solace in their shared connection. When she finally spotted him at a table with a group of friends, excitement surged within her—only to be met with a wash of insecurity.

She approached with cautious steps, but as she got closer, she overheard snippets of conversation that made her heart race with tension.

"Did you hear about Mei and Kai? They're dating now?" one girl whispered, her voice laced with mockery.

"Yeah, I don't know how that's gonna work out. Her parents are so traditional," another voice piped in, snickering. "They'll freak out when they find out!"

Feeling as if she'd been slapped, Mei froze at the edge of the table, the whispers swirling around her like a storm. Thoughts raced in her mind: What if my parents really can't accept this? What if I can't face the fallout?

Kai caught sight of her, his gaze brightening as he waved her over. "Hey, Mei! Come join us!" he called, oblivious to her inner turmoil.

She hesitated for a moment, her heart racing as she stood there at the periphery, surrounded by the echoes of unsupportive whispers. But the warmth in Kai's voice drew her in, a beacon of comfort amidst the swirling tide of uncertainty.

"Hey," she murmured as she approached the table, forcing a smile that felt heavier than usual. She settled next to Kai, feeling his presence ignite a spark of reassurance, but the weight of the curious eyes around her made her feel exposed.

"Did you have a good morning?" he asked, nudging her playfully. His easy disposition gave her a little comfort, even as her insecurities lay heavy in her chest.

"Yeah," she replied, trying to focus on him instead of the whispers. "Just the usual stuff."

"Great! We were just talking about what we should do this weekend—any fun ideas?" Kai's upbeat energy was contagious, and she felt a flutter of hope at the thought of planning their next adventure.

"Oh! I was thinking we could check out that new art exhibit downtown. I've heard amazing things about it!" she suggested, her voice lightening a bit.

"Oh, I love that!" Kai replied with enthusiasm. "I'll bring my sketchbook! We could make a day of it."

"Yes! That sounds perfect." Mei felt a flicker of excitement return as they discussed their plans. For a moment, it felt like they were in their own little world, insulated from the outside noise, but the reality soon crashed back in.

"Speaking of art, did you hear about Mei and Kai?" one of the girls at the table piped up, her tone laced with faux sweetness. "They're officially a thing now! Isn't that cute?"

Mei's stomach twisted as the remarks brought the previous whispers flooding back to her mind. Kai glanced over at her, a frown crossing his face. "That's one way to put it," he said, voice steady, but she could sense the tension beneath his facade.

The girl continued, "I wonder how long it'll last? I mean, you know her family doesn't approve of people who are different."

"Seriously." Another classmate chimed in, rolling her eyes. "Can she really make that work? Isn't it harder for them to be together?"

Mei felt her heart sink, a rush of embarrassment spilling into her cheeks. Their comments hung in the air, heavy and suffocating, ripping apart the carefree atmosphere she had hoped to maintain.

"Can we not talk about this right now?" Kai cut in, glancing at Mei with concern. "We're just hanging out like anyone else."

"Relax, it was just a joke," the girl shrugged, but her laughter was sharp, cutting through the small moment of respite that had begun to blossom.

Mei turned to Kai, feeling the weight of his gaze as he silently sought to reassure her. "Hey, it's okay," she said softly, though inside, her mind raced with doubt. What if they were right? What if her parents wouldn't accept their relationship?

"It's not okay," Kai said, frustration simmering beneath the surface. "You don't deserve to be the subject of gossip. We're better than that."

"What do you mean?" one of the girls retorted, feigning innocence. "We're just wondering if this will actually go anywhere."

Mei swallowed hard, feeling a lump in her throat. "Can we just change the subject?" she asked, her voice barely above a whisper as she tried to hold back the emotions threatening to spill over.

Kai reached for her hand beneath the table, providing an anchor she desperately needed. "That sounds good to me," he said firmly, not letting the atmosphere waver in his gaze. His touch emboldened her, but the impact of the gossip still hung heavy in her mind.

The conversations shifted, but Mei struggled to shake off the weight of the comments and her parents' concerns. The discussions around her felt like a storm brewing, threatening to wash away the budding connection she had formed with Kai.

As the lunch period came to a close, they exchanged polite goodbyes with their classmates, and Kai walked Mei to her next class. "I'm sorry about those comments. Don't let it get to you; you know what we have is real," he said, squeezing her hand once more.

"I know, but it still hurts," she confessed, her chest feeling tight. "Their words remind me of the doubts I've been struggling with myself."

"Mei, you have every right to be who you are, and there's nothing wrong with how you feel," Kai reassured her, sincerity lighting up his eyes. "If you want to confront your parents about us, I'll be right by your side."

She felt that warmth once more dissolve the tension in her chest. "Thank you. It means so much to have your support," Mei replied, her voice softening as she met Kai's gaze. "I want to talk to them. I just have to find the right moment."

"Just remember, no matter what, your feelings are valid," Kai said, intertwining their fingers as they walked down the hall. "And no one should dictate who you should be with. Your happiness matters most."

With every step beside him, Mei felt a renewed sense of determination washing over her. Despite the clouds of uncertainty and judgment surrounding her, she felt grounded by Kai's unwavering support. "You're right," she said, feeling a flicker of courage igniting within her. "I'll talk to them soon."

They reached her classroom door, and Kai stopped, pulling her gently to a halt. "I'll be waiting for you after school. We can brainstorm together about how to approach your parents. You've got this."

"Thanks, Kai. I really appreciate it." The sincerity of her words hung in the air for a moment before she leaned in, planting a quick peck on his cheek, her heart racing at the spontaneity. "See you later!" she said before stepping inside the classroom, feeling the flutter of emotions from their kiss linger in her chest.

As class began, Mei felt herself drifting in and out of focus, her thoughts preoccupied with what lay ahead. The rumors continued to swirl in her mind, mixing with her doubts. Each glance from classmates reminded her of the pressures and uncertainties, threatening to overshadow the warmth she had felt moments before.

When the bell rang at the end of the day, she eagerly made her way outside, scanning the sea of students until she spotted Kai waiting for her near the entrance. As he caught her eye, a huge grin spread across his face, and the warmth of his presence melted away her insecurities, if only for a moment.

"How did class go?" he asked, falling into step beside her as they walked toward the exit.

"It was okay, just trying to ignore the rumors," she admitted, fidgeting with the strap of her backpack. "But I've made up my mind. Tonight is the night I'll talk to my parents."

Kai's expression turned serious and encouraging. "I know you can do this. You're strong, Mei, and you deserve to live authentically."

His words gave her the strength she needed. "Thank you for believing in me. I want them to see how wonderful you are—and what we share," she said as they headed toward a small park nearby, where they could talk more privately.

As they settled onto a park bench, surrounded by the gentle rustling of leaves, the air filled with the sweet scent of blooming flowers. Mei felt the tension in her shoulders begin to melt away in the peaceful environment, but her heart still thudded in her chest, echoing her nervousness.

"Just think about how much joy you have in your life now," Kai said gently, sensing her anxiousness. "Focus on that."

"Right," Mei said, nodding in agreement. "I just have to remind myself that this is about my happiness, too. I want them to understand that."

Kai smiled, clearly pleased by her resolve. "Exactly! And you're a fantastic person. If they can see how happy you are with me, they'll come around."

Mei took a moment to absorb his words, feeling the connection spark between them even more. "I'll do it, Kai. I'll speak to them tonight."

"Good! I'll be here waiting for you," he said, leaning in and placing a gentle kiss on her cheek, causing warmth to spread through her entire being.

As they talked, the sun began to dip below the horizon, painting the sky in shades of pink and gold. The beauty of the moment felt inspiring, and Mei allowed herself to linger on the dream of a more harmonious life—a life where she could freely love Kai without fear of judgment.

When they finished their time at the park, the sky was almost fully dark, and Mei felt ready to face her parents, though a spark of anxiety still flickered in her heart.

"Let's head home," she said, taking a deep breath. "Tonight's the night."

With Kai by her side, they walked toward her house through the softly lit streets, the closeness of their hands still intertwined. As they approached her home, a mix of emotions emanated from her—fear, hope, and determination—all clashing together, creating a whirlwind in her heart.

"Remember to just speak from your heart," Kai said as they paused outside her front door, a reassuring smile on his face. "I'll be right here waiting for you when you're done."

Mei nodded, appreciating that he had come with her as support. "Thank you for being my strength," she said, her voice filled with gratitude. "I honestly don't know what I'd do without you right now."

Kai grinned but the seriousness in his eyes reflected his understanding of the weight of what lay ahead. "You don't have to think about that right now. Just focus on what you want to say. You've got this."

Taking a deep breath, Mei squared her shoulders, feeling a surge of determination mixed with nervous anticipation. "Okay, here goes nothing," she said. As she reached for the doorknob, her heart raced again, nerves threatening to overwhelm her resolve.

"Just remember—be honest, be you," Kai encouraged, squeezing her hand one more time before stepping back. "I'll be here waiting, no matter what."

With one last reassuring smile, Mei pushed the door open and stepped inside. The familiar scents of home enveloped her—sage and incense wafting through the air. Her parents were in the living room, sharing tea and discussing their day, and for a split second, she felt overwhelmed by a sense of comfort.

"Mei, you're home!" her mother exclaimed, glancing up from her tea with a smile. "How was your day?"

"It was good, Mom," she replied, trying to inject enthusiasm into her voice. "I was with friends."

"Always good to see you making time for your friends," her father added, his voice warm but laced with the typical parental scrutiny.

"Can I talk to you guys for a minute?" Mei asked, her heart pounding as she watched their expressions shift from casual banter to curious concern.

"Of course, sweetheart. What's on your mind?" her mother responded, setting her tea down.

Mei took a deep breath, feeling the gravity of the conversation weigh heavily on her. "It's about my friends… and, um, well… it's about Kai."

Both of her parents exchanged glances, their smiles faltering slightly, and worry crept into her mother's features. "You mean that boy we heard about? The one you've been spending time with?"

"Yes," she said, her voice steadying as she continued, "and I really like him. He makes me happy, and I wanted to talk to you about it."

There was a brief silence before her mother cleared her throat. "Mei, sweetheart, we just want what's best for you. We worry about you."

"I know," Mei interjected, feeling the adrenaline surge as she fought against the knot in her throat. "But what I feel for Kai is real. I want you to try to understand him. He's not just a boy… he's kind, supportive, and caring. He makes me feel seen in a way I've never felt before."

"Mei, it's important to consider things beyond what's right in front of you," her father said, his tone earnest but concerned. "You need to think about your future. Relationships can be complicated, especially when there are differences in backgrounds."

"I understand your concerns," she replied, her heart racing with a mix of fear and determination. "But it shouldn't matter where he comes from or anything like that. What matters is how I feel when I'm with him."

Her parents exchanged another glance, and Mei felt the tension in the air grow thicker with each passing second.

"Mei, honey," her mother said carefully, "we just want you to be cautious. We don't want you to get hurt."

"I appreciate that," Mei replied, determination giving her voice strength. "But I want to make my own choices, even if they differ from what you expect. I want to experience love on my own terms. I want you to see Kai for who he is, not just who you think he should be to me."

Another charged silence followed, and Mei could feel her heart pounding in her chest. Her parents were deep in thought, likely mulling over how to reply.

"Sweetheart, we love you," her father finally said, his voice steady. "And we want to support you, but it's just hard when we're not used to these kinds of situations. People's differences can lead to misunderstandings."

"Then let me help you understand," Mei urged, her voice rising slightly in passion. "I want to show you just how great Kai is. Can we meet him? Get to know him as a person? I really believe you'll like him."

Her father's expression softened, and for a moment, the tension began to ebb. "If this is truly what you want, we can give it a chance," he said, his voice careful but open.

"I want you to know him," she affirmed, her heart swelling with determination. "I want you to see how much joy he brings into my life."

"Okay, but we want you to promise to be honest with us about how you feel, regardless of what happens," her father said, his expression shifting to one of cautious acceptance.

"Of course! I promise." A wave of relief surged through Mei, and hope blossomed in her chest. This was the first step toward bridging the gap between her world and the expectations imposed upon her.

"Let's set up a time to meet him," her mother suggested, her tone softening. "We can have dinner together. It's only fair."

Mei's heart felt like it could burst from the happiness swelling within her. "Thank you! I'll coordinate with Kai, and I promise to make it fun," she replied, a huge smile spreading across her face.

"But remember, Mei, our main goal is to ensure you're making the right choice for yourself," her mother said, a hint of concern threading her words. "Love is beautiful but can also be complicated. We just want you to take things one step at a time."

"I know, and I'll keep that in mind," Mei promised, feeling lighter now. "This is just the beginning, and I appreciate your willingness to meet him."

As the conversation wound down, Mei felt a sense of accomplishment simmering beneath her skin. She had faced her parents' doubts head-on, but she couldn't shake the nagging feeling that the path forward would still be filled with challenges.

After expressing their love one last time, Mei slipped out of the living room and into the sanctuary of her room, her mind buzzing with hope and anxiety. She couldn't wait to tell Kai the news—a tangible sign of progress, a bridge toward reconciliation between her heart and her family.

Later that night, she texted him with excitement, recounting the outcome of her conversation with her parents and the invitation for him to join them for dinner.

Mei: Hey, I just talked to my parents and... they're willing to meet you! Can we set up a dinner?

The response came almost immediately.

Kai: Really? That's amazing! I'd love to! When?

Mei: How about this weekend?

Kai: Perfect! I'm looking forward to it!

As the warmth of his enthusiasm washed over her, Mei sank back onto her bed, smiling brightly at the ceiling. Maybe everything would be alright after all.

But as the night light dimmed in her room and she prepared for sleep, the earlier insecurities began to creep back in. What if they don't like him? What if they notice our differences and let it overshadow everything? Every fear felt amplified in the stillness of the night, and the excitement of the day began to swirl with apprehension.

Over the next few days, the buzz of Kai's impending visit loomed over Mei. She couldn't shake the feeling of reservation despite Kai's infectious enthusiasm. Would dining with her parents undermine what had already felt so comforting?

On the day of the dinner, Mei felt her stomach twist with nerves, butterflies fluttering wildly. She wore her favorite blouse, hoping to feel a sense of confidence, but apprehension loomed over her like a shadow.

As the clock ticked closer to the dinner hour, thoughts raced in her mind about how the evening would unfold. She paced back and forth, rehearsing what she would say and how she would introduce Kai, hoping to ease her parents' concerns while expressing her own excitement.

When the doorbell finally rang, her heart raced. "He's here," she said to herself, feeling giddy yet terrified.

Her mother greeted Kai warmly as he stepped inside, a first impression she hoped would ease any tension. But as Mei watched from the hallway, she felt a rising wave of uncertainty. How would they interact? Would they vibe?

Mei stepped forward, a friendly smile plastered on her face. "Kai! I'm so glad you made it!"

"Thanks for having me!" he replied, his charm shining bright as he stepped into the home.

With her parents joining them, the applause of conversation began, but Mei could feel her heart racing as if the stakes had been raised higher.

After introductions, they all settled at the dining table, and as the meal began, she held her breath, eagerly anticipating everyone's reactions, her pulse quickening with apprehension.

The evening felt like a whirlwind of emotions—the warmth of Kai's humor against the backdrop of her parents' cautious facade. As the conversation flowed, she searched for moments where everyone might connect, to merge their worlds, but insecurities quickly clawed at her.

In the thick of the evening, Mei caught a glimpse of her father's discerning look toward Kai, and she sensed his watchful scrutiny. It was a reminder of the unspoken expectations that hung heavy in the air, putting pressure on the evening's atmosphere.

Yet, as the dinner went on, the initial tension began to ease slightly. Mei watched as her parents engaged with Kai, their cautious approach transforming into tentative curiosity. They asked questions about his interests, and to her relief, Kai answered with the same charm and confidence that had drawn her to him in the first place.

"Your artwork is impressive, Kai," her mother remarked, her tone softening as they discussed art. "Mei has told me so much about your sketches. We'd love to see more of it sometime."

"Thank you!" Kai replied, his enthusiasm shining through. "I actually have a portfolio of my work. I'd be happy to share it. I love capturing the beauty of daily life, especially here in Tokyo."

Mei felt her heart swell with pride, resonating with the connection building before her eyes. It was surreal watching Kai navigate the conversation, and for a moment, the room felt light. Her father even chimed in, sharing stories about their neighborhood and the local art scene, and Kai responded with friendly banter—laughter breaking down barriers that seemed to separate their worlds.

But even amid the growing warmth, an unsettling twist lingered in Mei's mind. She could sense her mother's lingering apprehension; her gaze occasionally flickered toward Mei when she thought no one was watching, gauging the dynamic between her daughter and the boy seated across the table.

As dinner progressed, they transitioned into dessert—delightful mochi and a warm matcha cake that Mei had suggested. The atmosphere felt festive, filled with laughter and shared stories.

"Mei is quite the photographer. She has an eye for capturing the essence of a moment," Kai complemented, looking directly at her with a smile that made her heart leap.

Mei blinked, surprised that he had chosen to highlight her passions. "It's nothing special," she replied, trying to downplay it, not wanting to steal the spotlight.

"Are you kidding? Your photos are amazing," Kai insisted, his tone earnest. "You capture emotions that really resonate with people. I think you have a real talent."

A blush crept onto Mei's cheeks, and she was taken aback by the sincerity in his voice. "Thank you, Kai," she said, feeling a blend of happiness and embarrassment.

Her father chimed in, "You know, Mei has been taking photos of the cherry blossoms. Maybe you can both collaborate on a project. It would be nice to see how your artistic styles come together."

The idea caught her off guard; a project involving both her passions and Kai's felt exciting yet daunting. "That could be fun," she said, unsure of how it would really work but eager to explore such opportunities together.

As dessert came to an end and the conversation began to wind down, Mei noticed the flickers of uncertainty return to her mother's expression. She could feel the tension silently growing once again, wrapped tight around the edges of the conversation.

With a deep breath, Mei seized the moment, wanting to ease her mother's worries. "Mom, I wanted to thank you for being open to meeting Kai. I know this is different from what we've discussed before, but I really believe we have something meaningful."

Her mother's gaze flickered toward her before settling on Kai. "It's important to us that you pick someone who supports you and understands your values," she replied carefully.

"I understand that, and I appreciate your concern," Kai said, his voice steady and respectful. "I genuinely care about Mei, and I promise to always respect her and the values she holds dear."

There was a moment of silence, the atmosphere thick with unspoken thoughts, and Mei felt her heart race as she waited for her mother's response.

"Well, it's still early for us to make any judgments," her father finally said, breaking the tension. "But I can see that you're both passionate about what you do."

Mei seized the opportunity. "I'd love for you to get to know him better. You'll see how amazing he is," she remarked, glancing from her father to her mother, hoping to bridge the gap.

"Perhaps we can spend more time together, as friends," her mother said, her voice softening slightly. "But it's important that love is built on mutual respect and cultural understanding."

Mei nodded, knowing her mother was speaking from a place of care. "I want to be honest about how I feel. This is about my happiness and what I want, too."

The weight of the conversation felt significant, as if the future of her relationship with Kai balanced precariously on these moments. As dessert plates were cleared, Mei's resolve solidified, feeling the driving force of her feelings push her forward.

When the evening came to a close, and Kai said his goodbyes, promising to contact her soon, Mei felt a rush of relief. The night had gone better than she had anticipated—her parents had surprised her with their willingness to engage, and there was a hint of acceptance that stirred hope within her.

As she watched him walk away, his silhouette gradually disappearing into the night, she turned back toward her house, her heart fluttering in her chest. A blend of excitement and anxiety bubbled inside her. She had taken a monumental step, daring to bring her relationship with Kai into the light, and for now, it felt like a significant victory.

"Did you have a nice time?" her mother asked, her voice breaking Mei's thoughts as she leaned against the doorframe, arms crossed.

"Yes!" Mei replied, the brightness of her smile spilling over. "It was really nice getting to know Kai better with you both around. He handled everything well."

Her mother regarded her thoughtfully, a flicker of pride crossing her features. "I'm glad. It's important that you feel comfortable sharing parts of your life with us. Sometimes it just takes time to get used to new experiences."

"Thank you for being open to it," Mei said, feeling genuine gratitude for her parents' willingness to see Kai for who he truly was.

"That being said," her mother continued, her tone shifting to a more serious note, "you must remember that feelings can be complicated. It's vital to stay true to your values while navigating relationships."

Mei nodded, processing her mother's words. She understood the caution behind them but felt deep within that she was ready to embrace whatever unfolded with Kai. "I know, Mom. I assure you that I'm being careful. But I also want to experience this—what it feels like to let love in."

Her mother smiled softly. "Just hold onto that courage, sweetheart. That way, you'll always find your way through."

With their conversation winding down, Mei felt a renewed sense of hope settling around her. The darkness outside began to envelop the neighborhood, but inside, there was a comfort that warmed her heart.

After a little while, she retreated to her room, reviewing the moments of the day. She picked up her camera, scrolling through the photos they had taken on their recent adventures—each snapshot filled with laughter and joy immediately reminded her of the connection forged between them.

As she sat on her bed, the glow of her desk lamp illuminating her thoughts, her phone buzzed. A message from Kai lit up the screen, and her heart raced.

Kai: Hey! I just wanted to say thank you for tonight. It meant a lot to me. Let's plan our next adventure soon!

A smile spread across her face as her fingers danced over the screen.

Mei: I had a great time too! I'm really glad you came over and got to meet my parents. They warmed up to you!

Kai: I'm relieved! 😄 I was a little nervous, but I'm glad they seem supportive!

Mei: They still have some reservations, but I think they'll come around. I can't wait for our next adventure!

Kai: Me neither! How about next week? We can do that art exhibit we talked about!

Mei: Perfect! I'm excited!

After sending the message, Mei's heart felt light, filled with the hopeful promise of their upcoming adventure together. She allowed herself to linger on thoughts of Kai, of their chemistry, of how easy it felt to be with him, pushing aside the whispers of doubt that surfaced earlier.

But as the night wore on, layers of anxiety resurfaced, unwelcome but persistent. The reality remained that the rumors about their relationship were still out there–whispers from their classmates fueling insecurities about whether her family would truly accept Kai or if they would stand in the way of her happiness.

Mei resolved to stay strong and keep communicating openly with Kai.

She knew she would face challenges, both at home and at school, but inside, she felt a fire igniting. Her relationship with Kai was worth every bit of uncertainty that came with it.

The next day at school was marked by tension as whispers about her relationship with Kai circulated among her classmates. As Mei walked through the hallways, she felt the weight of gazes following her, the murmurs floating around her like shadows. There go Mei and Kai, the odd couple.

Whenever she passed by groups of skeptical friends whispering and giggling, her heart dropped slightly, the anxiety creeping back in as insecurities bubbled to the surface.

"Mei!" Akira called, rushing to catch up with her. "Have you heard the latest? People are saying things about you and Kai... again."

"Yeah, I'm aware," she said, attempting to maintain a brave face. "It seems like every time we make progress, the gossip just gets louder."

Akira tilted his head, concern etched on his face. "Do you want to talk about it? I mean, I see how this is affecting you."

Mei glanced around the crowded hallway, feeling a twinge of vulnerability. She lowered her voice. "Honestly, it's hard not to think about what they're saying. I just want to enjoy my feelings for Kai without worrying about everyone else's opinions."

Akira nodded, his expression sympathetic. "Just remember that gossip will always be there, especially in high school. People thrive on drama. What matters is how you and Kai feel about each other. Forget about what the others say."

His encouragement warmed her, yet doubts still lurked in her mind, fueled by her parents' concerns and the whispers echoing in the hall. "You're right, but I can't shake off the fear that my parents might reject him if they hear what people are saying."

"Have you talked to your parents about it since dinner?" Akira asked, his brows furrowing with concern.

She hesitated, the weight of uncertainty sitting heavily on her shoulders.

"Not yet. I'm still trying to figure out how to have that conversation without it turning into a confrontation."

"Why don't you plan a moment to sit down with them? Lay it all out on the table," Akira suggested. "If you want them to understand you and Kai, you'll have to find the courage to talk about it."

"Yeah, I guess." Just then, the bell rang, and students began to flood into classrooms, cutting their conversation short. "Thanks, Akira. I'll think about it."

As they parted ways, Mei's resolve began to waver. The sting of unexpected comments drifted back in reminders, creating a tempest of doubt around her heart. What if Kai was right but her parents held on too firmly to their beliefs? What if she lost them in the process of pursuing her happiness?

Classes dragged on, the ticking clock echoing steadily as Mei fought to concentrate. Every passing moment felt heavy with anticipation, and her thoughts continuously returned to the instability of her situation. Yet she held onto the belief that honesty would create a path forward.

After class, Mei met up with Kai at their designated spot—the small cafe where they had their first little adventure. The cozy atmosphere spread warmth in her heart as she spotted him waiting for her, already seated at their favorite table.

"Hey, beautiful!" he greeted, looking up with that endearing smile that always made her feel like the center of his universe.

"Hey!" She returned the smile, but with it came the weight of her earlier worries. As they exchanged pleasantries and ordered their usual favorites, her mind stewed over the conversations she needed to have.

After they settled into their drinks, Kai leaned in and asked, "How was your day? I hope the rumors aren't getting to you."

She sighed, the air heavy with the thoughts she had carried throughout the day. "They are. I overheard some girls talking about us in between classes. It's exhausting trying to ignore all the noise."

Kai's expression shifted, a hint of frustration crossing his face. "I can't believe they're still talking about it. Honestly, it shouldn't matter what anyone else thinks about our relationship."

"I know! It's just… hard not to let it affect me, especially since I care so much about what my parents think," she admitted, feeling the tears threaten to brim at the edges of her eyes. "I just need to confess to them how much you mean to me and hope they will see what I see in you."

"You will. You're incredibly strong, Mei," he said, reaching across the table to take her hand. "And I'll be right there with you when you do it. Whatever it takes."

His reassuring words and the warmth of his touch gave her a glimmer of hope, fortifying her spirit. "Thank you, Kai. Your support means everything. I'll talk to them this weekend; I have to."

They spent the rest of the afternoon wrapped in warmth and laughter, discussing the possibilities that lay ahead, each word stitching the threads of their connection tighter. But beneath her enthusiasm lingered the underlying fear that wouldn't let go, the apprehension rising with every laugh, a constant reminder of the challenge that awaited her.

As the sun began to dip, casting a soft golden hue across the cafe, Mei felt a shift in the air, a sense of impending revelation. Would the confrontation with her parents go as she hoped? Would Kai's support be enough to overcome the fears that had grown like weeds in her mind?

The next few days would hold the answers, but for now, surrounded by Kai's warmth and humor, she could focus on the moments they shared in the present. Each laugh, every playful tease, felt like a thread weaving their lives together—a tapestry of delightful memories that distracted her from the anxieties lurking in her periphery.

As the weekend drew near, Mei's resolve began to strengthen. She felt an anticipation bubbling within her—the excitement of her upcoming conversation with Kai's encouragement propelling her forward. Despite the doubts still lingering, she was ready to face her parents and have an honest conversation about her feelings.

On Saturday, as the sun rose warmly over Tokyo, Mei felt her heart racing in anticipation. She had spent the morning mentally preparing for this moment, rehearsing her thoughts and considering how to approach her parents without igniting tensions.

After breakfast, she finally mustered the courage to approach her mom, who was sitting in the living room absorbed in a book. "Mom, can we talk?" she asked, her voice steady but dripping with unspoken nerves.

Her mother set the book down and looked up, sensing the seriousness in her daughter's tone. "Of course, what is it?"

Mei glanced around, uncertain yet determined. "It's about Kai," she began, taking a deep breath to steady herself. "I really like him, and I know you were hesitant about him. I want you to understand how I feel."

Her mother's expression shifted, concern flickering across her features. "Sweetheart, you know we just want what's best for you. What do you think about him?"

"I think he makes me happy," Mei said firmly, her confidence elevated by her previous conversations with Kai. "He's kind and respectfull, and he genuinely cares about me. I want you to see him for who he is."

Her mother leaned back in her chair, thoughtfully considering her words. "I want to understand. Perhaps it would help if we all spent some time together. You know that."

"I'd like that," Mei replied, feeling a surge of hope. "Dinner, maybe? I want you to get to know him, to see how great he truly is."

Her mother nodded slowly, seemingly mulling over the idea. "Alright. We can plan something. But I just need you to promise to be honest with me about how you feel throughout this process."

"I promise," Mei said earnestly, feeling the tension in her chest begin to lift.

As they finalized their plans, Mei felt an exhilarating blend of excitement and apprehension. She texted Kai, filled with hope about telling him the news.

Mei: Guess what? My mom is willing to meet you! We're planning for dinner this Thursday!

Kai: Really? That's amazing! I'm excited! Let's make this dinner memorable!

Their exchange filled Mei with a thrill of possibilities, and as the day unfolded, she felt a surge of courage propelling her forward. Unbeknownst to her, however, whispers still floated like shadows among her peers, including a rumor that had begun heating up against her and Kai.

On Monday morning, as she approached the entrance to school, she caught snippets of conversations that sent waves of anxiety crashing against her. Students whispered and glanced her way, their voices laced with curiosity and judgment.

"Did you hear about Mei and Kai? Apparently, it's getting serious!" someone murmured, and other students giggled and exchanged knowing glances, soaking in the drama.

Each remark felt like a weight on Mei's shoulders, igniting her insecurities. Hadn't they just promised not to let the opinions of others dictate their feelings? But here she was, feeling vulnerable again, as if the entire student body were scrutinizing her relationship like a specimen under a microscope.

As she walked through the hall, the laughter around her felt sharp. She felt eyes following her, questions lingering in the air as she moved. A pang of fear gripped her heart. Would they ever see the goodness she saw in Kai, or was their judgment too strong to overcome?

Shaking off her unease, Mei managed to detach from the conversations, focusing on her classes and preparing for her upcoming dinner with her parents. Yet, the gossip persisted, permeating through everything. It was hard not to think about how others perceived her relationship.

During lunch, she sat with Akira, who noticed her distracted demeanor. "What's going on, Mei? You've seemed a bit off today," he asked, concern creeping into his voice.

"It's the rumors. I know I shouldn't let them bother me, but how do I not?" she sighed, feeling a mix of frustration and vulnerability.

"Listen, most people talk without knowing the full story. Just focus on what you feel and what's real," Akira advised.

Mei nodded, but as she looked around the cafeteria, she couldn't shake the whispers that seemed to claw at her confidence. Groups of classmates huddled together, stealing glances in her direction, their hushed tones and giggles echoing in her ears like a dark cloud descending over her moment of clarity.

"Do you think they're talking about us?" she asked, her heart heavy with uncertainty. "What if they're right about everything?"

Akira frowned at the surrounding conversations and leaned in closer to her. "Listen, Mei, don't let what others say affect your happiness. Most of them don't know anything about you or Kai. They're just looking for something to gossip about."

"Maybe you're right, but…" she trailed off, her eyes drifting toward a nearby table where a group of students was laughing, some pointing at her and Kai's empty seats. It stung to think that they could reduce what felt so beautiful to mere whispers and jokes.

Before she could delve deeper into her worry, the bell rang, signaling the end of lunch. "I know you're feeling the pressure, but focus on the positives," Akira said as they gathered their things. "You have a plan for dinner with your parents. That's a big step."

As they walked to their next class, Mei felt the weight of his words but remained anxious. What if the dinner didn't go well? What if her parents reacted badly to knowing about Kai, and then everyone at school found out? It was overwhelming, and the cloud of uncertainty hung over her, stifling the joy she had felt just days before.

When the afternoon classes ended, Mei's stomach churned in anticipation for dinner. As she left school, she clutched her bag tightly, the realization that she would soon have to confront her fears looming heavy in her mind.

Later that evening, after a whirlwind of preparing for dinner, she stood nervously in front of the mirror, adjusting her outfit yet again—her favorite blouse paired with a chic skirt that felt both comfortable and stylish. She wanted to appear confident, to reassure her parents that this was truly what she wanted.

When it was finally time, her heart thundered as she descended the stairs. Her parents were already seated at the dining table, the fragrance of homemade curry wafting through the air, combining with the comforting scents of home. They appeared calm, caught up in casual conversation, but the tension Mei felt was palpable.

"Are you ready for tonight?" her mother asked warmly, her eyes scanning Mei as she entered the room.

"Yeah, I think so," she replied, forcing a smile. She could feel her heart racing as the enormity of the moment sank in.

"Just remember, being open and honest is key," her father added, offering her an encouraging nod. "We want to understand your feelings, not judge them."

Mei nodded, grateful but still feeling the pressure mount. "Thanks, Dad," she said as she took a seat, glancing toward the door, anticipation mingling with anxiety.

A few minutes later, the doorbell rang, causing her stomach to flip. "That's him!" she blurted out, standing up abruptly. Her mother exchanged a glance with her father—him showing slight concern while her mother's expression reflected cautious optimism.

"Go ahead," her mother urged gently. "We're excited to meet him."

With a determined breath, Mei walked toward the door, her nerves bubbling over. She opened it to find Kai standing there, a bouquet of flowers in hand—vivid blooms that brought a bright smile to her face amid the apprehension.

"Hey! I thought these would add to a lovely dinner!" he beamed, presenting them to her.

"Wow, they're beautiful! Thank you!" Mei said, feeling the swell of warmth in her chest. But as her eyes shifted to his, she saw the slight hint of nervousness reflected in his gaze, mirroring her own feelings.

"Are you ready?" he asked, stepping inside as she stepped aside.

"I think so…" she responded, her heart fluttering with both excitement and anxiety. "My parents are just starting dinner."

"Then let's make a good first impression!" he said with a confident grin, and with that, they stepped into the dining area together.

"Hi, Kai! It's so lovely to finally meet you," her mother said warmly, standing to greet him with genuine enthusiasm.

"Thank you, ma'am. I'm really happy to be here!" Kai replied, his charm shining brightly despite his slight nervousness.

Mei watched as her parents welcomed him, hoping to see them warm to him. She could feel her heart racing, riddled with both anticipation and anxiety. She settled at the table, and they all began dinner, the atmosphere brimming with the enticing aromas of curry.

As they passed plates around and engaged in light conversation, Mei felt a tension in her chest slowly dissipate. Her parents were asking Kai about his interests, and he responded with charm and sincerity, sharing his love for art and music. His responses seemed to pique her parents' interest, and she felt a flicker of hope that they might see the wonderful person she had come to know.

"This curry is delicious," Kai said, taking a bite. "I love how the spices blend together. Mei always talks about how amazing your cooking is, but this is on another level."

Her mother's face lit up at the compliment. "Thank you! I've been experimenting a bit with the flavors. It's nice to know it's a hit with friends."

"Absolutely! You should see the curry back in my house; it can't hold a candle to this!" he laughed, and Mei couldn't help but smile at how easily they settled into conversation.

After some small talk about school and art, her father nodded appreciatively. "It's great to hear that you have such passions. Mei has always loved photography; it seems you both share a creative spark."

"Definitely! I think art and creativity bring people together," Kai replied enthusiastically. "I've loved sketching the cherry blossoms lately, and photography perfectly captures that beauty."

Her father exchanged a glance with her mother, who appeared interested but still slightly hesitant. Mei sensed the questions bubbling beneath the surface—a nagging worry that her parents harbored doubts about their relationship.

"Do you and Mei have plans to collaborate on an art project?" her mother asked, trying to draw out more about the connection they shared.

Kai seemed delighted by the question. "Yes! We're planning to explore the city together, discover new places, and document our experiences through art and photography."

"That sounds interesting," her father said, his tone probing. "But what about your studies? How do you balance both?"

"Schoolwork definitely comes first for me," Kai said, his demeanor earnest. "I've always believed that pursuing your passions can actually fuel your drive to excel in other areas, too. Having a balance is key."

Mei felt a swell of pride as she listened to him articulate his thoughts. He was charming and intelligent, and she hoped her parents would pick up on that. Yet, despite the seemingly easygoing dinner, the tension still lingered at the edges of her mind.

"What about Mei's future? Do you ever think about how it aligns with your plans?" her father asked, his tone careful but inquisitive.

The question hung in the air, the moment feeling pivotal. Mei felt her heart skip a beat, anxiety creeping in. Would Kai be caught off guard? Would he stumble over his answer?

Kai, however, responded with confidence. "Absolutely. I think it's important to support each other's aspirations. If we both stay focused on our goals and communicate openly, it could work out beautifully."

As he spoke those words, she saw her parents soften slightly, though there was still an undercurrent of concern in their brows. A faint glimmer of hope sparked within her—maybe they would come to understand.

"Of course, it's vital that both of you are aligned in your goals as you grow together. Relationships can be complicated," her mother said diplomatically, her tone still cautious.

Mei nodded, feeling the tension blend with determination. "I know that, and I'm grateful for your support," she added, looking between her parents and Kai. "It means a lot that we can have this conversation openly."

After a brief silence filled with contemplation, her father finally spoke. "We just want you to make sure you choose someone who respects our family values and brings out the best in you, Mei. It's important that someone appreciates your identity and background—someone who understands what family means."

Kai met Mei's gaze, and for a moment, she could see the resilience in his eyes. "I promise I will always respect Mei and what's important to her. I want to be that person," he stated firmly, his expression earnest.

As dinner came to a close, everyone seemed to mirror a sense of cautious optimism. The conversation shifted back to lighter topics, and laughter slowly filled the room again while Mei facilitated the easing of tensions, grateful for the rare moments of unity.

But as the evening ended and Kai prepared to leave, Mei felt a slight heaviness in her chest. She knew their conversation was just the beginning. The whispers at school and her parents' concerns still echoed in her mind.

"Thanks for dinner," Kai said, standing at the doorway and looking down at her with warmth. "I really enjoyed meeting your family. They're incredible."

"I'm glad they got to meet you," she admitted, feeling a mix of relief and lingering anxiety. "And thank you for being so fantastic. It means a lot."

As she stepped out into the cool night air, the brief moment of happiness they had shared hung like a delicate thread between them. Mei stood on the doorstep, watching Kai walk down the path, the weight of the evening's conversation starting to settle heavily on her shoulders again.

Once she closed the door, she leaned against it, her heart racing from the emotionality of the evening. It had gone better than she had expected, yet the reality of the world around them still gnawed at her. Would her parents really come to accept Kai? Would the ever-judging eyes of her classmates force her into a corner?

She slowly made her way to her room, feeling a medley of excitement and worry pulse through her veins. What she felt for Kai was undeniably real, and each encounter with him deepened her affection, yet the turbulent waters of judgment waited at every turn. She picked up her camera and scrolled through the photos she had taken with him, a soft smile breaking through her anxieties as she relived those moments.

In the days following their dinner, the swirling rumors at school intensified, making her feel like she was walking through a gauntlet of whispers and stares. Every time she caught a glimpse of students snickering and exchanging looks, her heart would lurch. Despite her best efforts to brush off their opinions, the insecurity crept back in, threatening to overshadow her happiness with Kai.

As Wednesday rolled around, she was sitting with Akira at lunch, trying to distract herself from the noise around her.

"Did you talk to your parents again?" he asked, concern lining his features.

"Not yet," she admitted, feeling the anxiety twist in her stomach. "I've been thinking about it, but I just don't know how to bring it up again."

"You have to be brave, Mei. You've confronted them once; you can do it again," Akira encouraged, giving her a supporting nudge. "You'll never know what they really think unless you push through the fear."

As he spoke, Mei felt a glimmer of encouragement ignite within her. Maybe it was time to take another step forward and discuss her feelings with her parents freely. With whatever emerged from that conversation, she hoped it would bring clarity and strength.

"Alright," she resolved, feeling determined. "I'll talk to them tonight."

Akira beamed, relief washing over his features. "Good! I'm rooting for you. Just know that I'm always here if you need anything."

Once they finished lunch, Mei left Akira and headed to class. But as she moved through the halls, she felt the familiar gaze of judgment following her—a reminder that gossip lingered like a shadow.

Throughout her afternoon classes, she couldn't focus. Each whisper echoed in her mind, taunting her insecurities. She steeled herself against the flood of concern, knowing that she had to confront her feelings head-on.

By the time the final bell rang, she felt a mix of adrenaline and determination surging within her. She left school, her feet moving quickly as she made her way home, rehearsing her conversation with her parents in her head.

That evening, the words she needed to share felt heavy on her tongue, but she knew it was time. She found her parents seated in the living room, engaged in a game of cards they often played together in the evenings.

"Can we talk for a minute?" Mei called out, her heart pounding as she approached them.

Both of her parents looked up, their expressions shifting from casual to concerned. "Of course, Mei. What's on your mind?" her father asked, placing the cards down.

Taking a deep breath, she scanned their faces, feeling the weight of her vulnerability. "I want to discuss Kai again."

Her mother set aside her cards, her gaze steady but careful. "Alright. What do you want to talk about?"

"I want you to understand how important he is to me," Mei began, her voice trembling but resolute. "I know you have reservations, but we've been developing a strong connection. And I believe it's real."

There was silence for a moment as her parents exchanged glances, their thoughtful expressions betraying the deliberate mental process behind their impending response.

"We want you to be happy, Mei," her father said finally, his tone supportive yet firm. "But you know our concerns. It's not just about you and your feelings; it's about the future and how this could affect your life."

"I understand," she responded, trying to convey her sincerity. "But I need to pursue what makes me happy. Kai respects me and my values. You will see that if you give him a chance."

"Have you thought about how he fits into our family?" her mother asked, searching her face. "We just want to protect you."

"I want to show you," Mei pleaded, her emotions bubbling to the surface. "I want you to meet him again—so you can see how wonderful he truly is. I believe that if you get to know him, you'll understand why I care about him so much."

Her mother and father exchanged cautious looks, and Mei felt a mixture of hope and anxiety gnawing at her. Was she asking too much? Was it too soon?

"Mei, we appreciate your enthusiasm," her father began slowly. "But we need to consider how this will affect you emotionally and socially—"

"Dad, please!" she interrupted, her voice rising slightly in frustration. "I'm not asking you to agree with everything right away. I just want you to see him for yourself, to understand what I see in him."

Her mother sighed, placing her hands together as she searched for the right words. "It's not that we don't want you to be happy, Mei. We're just worried about the complexities that can arise—"

"Complexities that won't matter if we just focus on the fact that we care about each other!" Mei replied, her heart racing as she leaned in, feeling desperate for them to understand. "I get that you want to protect me, but I want to live my life, to have my own experiences and my own connections."

"We understand that, but as your parents, our job is to look out for your well-being," her father said gently. "This is a big step, and we'd like to ensure that you're not hurt along the way."

"I'll take that risk," she responded, her heart pounding with determination. "Kai respects me and my values; he makes me feel seen and understood. If I hide this part of my life from you, then I'm not being honest with you—or myself."

Her mother looked thoughtful, and Mei felt a flicker of hope. "I see how passionate you are about this. That's why we want to approach whatever happens carefully."

After a moment of contemplation, her mother finally nodded. "Very well. We will give it a chance, but we expect you to communicate openly with us about how you're feeling as you go through this."

"Thank you!" Mei exclaimed, relief flooding through her. "I promise I'll be honest about everything. How about we set a dinner date with Kai this weekend? I want you to really get to know him."

Her father smiled faintly, appearing more accepting. "Let's see how that goes. We're willing to try, Mei."

As she left the room, a colossal sense of relief washed over her. She felt as if a heavy weight had been lifted, the apprehensions that had hung like clouds now beginning to disperse.

Later that night, she texted Kai with excitement about the chance to meet her parents again.

Mei: Great news! My parents are open to meeting you again for dinner this weekend!

Kai: Really? That's amazing! I'm excited to meet them again!

Her heart soared at the enthusiasm in his text, feeling the connection between them deepen once again.

As the days passed leading up to the dinner, however, Mei hoped she would remain resolute. She felt a surge of determination to showcase everything beautiful about their relationship but couldn't shake the anxiety of whether her parents would fully accept him.

Thursday evening arrived, and as she prepared for dinner, her heart raced with a mix of nerves and excitement. She chose a floral dress that reminded her of cherry blossoms—vibrant yet subtly elegant, hoping it would impress both Kai and her parents.

When the doorbell rang, her heart raced. She took one last deep breath, trying to quell the anxious thoughts swirling in her mind. "You can do this," she whispered to herself as she opened the door to find Kai standing there, holding a bouquet of fresh flowers in his hand—noticing how the colors slipped beautifully in with her chosen dress.

"Hey, you look lovely!" Kai beamed, extending the bouquet to her.

"Thank you! And thank you for the flowers—they're beautiful!"

His presence offered a soothing comfort, and as they walked to the dining area together, she felt the excitement bubbling back up, aided by the warm atmosphere within her home.

"Are you ready for this?" Kai asked, glancing at her with a mixture of support and concern.

"More than ever," she smiled, feeling a sense of determination surge within her.

As they entered the dining area, Mei's parents greeted Kai with warm smiles, and they settled into the familiar rhythm of dinner preparation. Mei felt a flurry of hope sparking inside her, eager for the opportunity to bridge the gap as they all came together once more.

As they began dinner, laughter and comments flowed easily. Mei felt encouraged watching Kai engage with her parents, sharing stories and learning about their lives with genuine interest. She could see her parents slowly warming up to him, the initial hesitations gradually fading with each shared laugh.

"This curry is fantastic!" Kai exclaimed after taking a hearty bite, his eyes lighting up. "You've outdone yourself, Mrs. Suki. I honestly can't get enough of it!"

Mei's mother beamed at the praise, visibly pleased. "Thank you, Kai! I'm glad you're enjoying it. I'm always experimenting with the spices."

"Any tips for someone who might want to try cooking curry at home?" Kai asked, and the conversation soon shifted into a delightful exchange about culinary techniques and family recipes. Mei watched as her mother took the lead, proudly sharing her culinary secrets, and a sense of warmth wrapped around the table.

Her father chimed in, "Eating together is such an important part of any family. Meals offer the perfect opportunity to bond and share stories."

"Absolutely," Kai agreed, still engaged in the conversation. "I think meals can be an expression of love, especially ones that take time and care to prepare."

Mei felt her heart swell at the sight of her parents enjoying the dinner, allowing themselves to see Kai for who he was: a thoughtful and respectful young man who genuinely cared for her. As they continued to talk, Mei slid in stories of her own—anecdotes of school and how she and Kai connected over art and creativity. Each shared story seemed to help her parents understand the depth of their bond better.

As the dinner progressed, Mei noticed a shift in the atmosphere. The underlying concern that had previously surrounded the table dissipated as laughter filled the air. The more they spoke, the more it seemed her parents recognized Kai for the kind-hearted person he was, rather than simply seeing their daughter's romantic interest.

With dessert approaching, a shared sense of camaraderie had settled between them all. Kai leaned back in his chair, addressing Mei's parents directly. "You both raised such a wonderful daughter. She has a unique perspective on life that I admire very much."

Mei felt a rush of gratitude toward Kai for his kind words, appreciating how he acknowledged her individuality. "Thank you, Kai!" she said, smiling brightly, while her parents exchanged approving glances.

As dessert—a delightful selection of mochi—was served, Mei became aware of the lightness in her heart. The atmosphere was reminiscent of a family gathering, filled with warmth and connection.

"Alright, enough about food and work! Let's dig into something fun. How about a karaoke challenge?" her father suggested playfully, his eyes glinting with mischief.

"You're on!" Kai shot back, enthusiasm radiating from him. "I love karaoke!"

"Looks like we've got a performer in the house," Mei's mother laughed, encouraging the playful suggestion.

Before Mei knew it, laughter erupted around the table, and her parents began to debate which songs to sing, coaxing each other into participating while Kai effortlessly jumped in with playful banter.

Mei felt warmth bloom within her, a wave of happiness washing over her. This was going better than she had dared to dream. Kai was charming, engaging, and genuinely connecting with her parents, fostering an environment of acceptance rather than resistance.

After several rounds of karaoke and shared stories about their singing skills—which varied from "professional" to "let's never speak of this again"—the atmosphere was undeniably light. The evening was a celebration, a blend of stories, laughter, and shared experiences that strengthened their connection.

Eventually, as the night came to a close, Mei felt a deep appreciation for both her parents and Kai. "Thank you for being so open tonight," she said, her voice filled with sincerity. "It means a lot to me."

Her father smiled, nodding thoughtfully. "We see how happy you are, Mei. As your parents, our priority is your happiness."

Kai's eyes met hers, and a silent understanding passed between them; he felt accepted, making the night feel even more special.

After Kai said his goodbyes, promising to text Mei later, she felt an exhilarating sense of hope filling her heart. They had turned a significant corner as a family; this evening proved that love could triumph over doubts and fears.

But as Kai walked away, Mei couldn't shake the faint whispers of rumor that still lingered in the back of her mind, a reminder that not everyone would understand their relationship. She knew challenges remained as they navigated their feelings, but she felt emboldened to face whatever lay ahead.

As the moon cast a soft glow over the night, Mei stepped back into her home, feeling lighter than she had in days. She had taken the steps to bridge the gap between her feelings and her family, and with Kai beside her, she felt ready to tackle any obstacles that might arise.

That night, she drifted into sleep, dreaming of cherry blossoms, laughter, and the light of Tokyo glimmering below her. In her dreams, she felt bold and free, exploring every corner of the city with Kai, hand in hand, their hearts intertwined through each shared adventure.

But when dawn broke, reality crept back in, bringing with it the weight of the outside world—a world where rumors pulsed through the hallways of her school like an infectious disease, threatening to undermine the happiness she had just begun to embrace.

As she prepared for the school day, she tried to shake off the remnants of anxiety that settled in her gut. Today was a new day, and she resolved to focus on herself, on Kai, and on what they were building together.

When Mei arrived at school, however, she could feel the tension in the air, a sharp contrast to the hope she had felt the night before. It was as if everyone was watching, waiting—with whispers hot on their lips. The laughter she heard in the hallways felt laden with familiarity, like a looming storm ready to break.

As she walked carefully down the crowded corridors, she overheard snippets of conversations that seemed to pin her to the wall. "Did you see them at dinner? So cringeworthy," one girl snickered, her voice dripping with mockery. "Mei thinks they're in a love story.Such a cliché."

"Totally. How can she even be with him? Their backgrounds are too different!" another voice chimed in, and Mei felt the harshness of ignorance like ice slicing through her insides.

The words echoed in her mind, stirring the insecurities she had thought were banished. She pressed her lips together, trying to maintain composure, but anxiety began to take a hold of her.

What if they were right? What if her parents couldn't accept her relationship with Kai?

Her heart pounded as the fear crept back in, igniting the worries she had felt since the first whispers of gossip emerged at school. When she spotted Akira in their usual spot, she hurried over, desperate for a moment of solace.

"Hey, how's it going?" Akira asked, his expression brightening upon her arrival, but there was a flicker of concern in his eyes that caught her attention.

"Not great. The rumors are getting worse," Mei admitted, her voice barely above a whisper as she slid into a seat beside him.

"Did you hear what people were saying?"

Akira frowned, looking around to ensure no unwanted ears were nearby. "I heard a few things. The gossip has definitely intensified since dinner, but remember, it doesn't define you or your relationship. Don't let their opinions shake your confidence."

"I know, but it's really hard sometimes," she sighed, feeling the weight of their judgment press down on her. "I'm worried about how this will affect things with Kai."

"Focus on what matters," Akira advised, a determined look in his eyes. "You and Kai have a real connection, and you need to give that room to grow. If you let these rumors dictate your feelings, it's only going to hurt you."

"Easier said than done," Mei muttered, taking a deep breath. "But I'll try. I just wish people could see him for who he is instead of what they think a different relationship looks like."

Akira nodded emphatically, his expression shifting to one of understanding. "People can be judgmental, but you should not let their ignorance define your happiness. Look at what you and Kai have built so far. That's what really matters."

As the day dragged on, Mei felt the whispers swirl around her like autumn leaves caught in a gust of wind. She could hear her classmates muttering about her and Kai, laughing as they passed. Each glance and comment weighed heavily in her chest.

Finally, as lunch approached, the tension seemed almost unbearable. Mei couldn't shake the feeling that her worries were amplifying the rumors. She needed to talk to Kai.

When lunchtime arrived, she bolted toward the courtyard where they often met, her mind racing with thoughts of how to address the ever-growing gossip. The open space offered a reprieve from the claustrophobia of the hallways, but her unease was still palpable.

As she reached their usual spot, she spotted Kai leaning against a tree, pulling out his sketchbook as he waited for her. He looked up and smiled, that familiar warmth swelling inside her. The sight of him made her heart skip a beat, a fleeting reminder of why she fought for this connection in the first place.

"Hey, you!" he called out, his face lighting up. "Ready to brainstorm ideas for our next adventure?"

Mei returned the smile, but a wave of anxiety washed over her. The whirl of rumors and whispers lingered in her mind, clashing with the warmth he brought into her life. "Kai, can we talk for a minute? I've been thinking a lot about what's been happening at school," she said, her voice trembling with the weight of what she needed to address.

"Of course! What's on your mind?" His concern was immediate, and as he stepped closer, the intensity of his gaze made her heart race.

"Things are getting a little… complicated," she admitted, her voice low. "I overheard some things that people are saying about us, and it's really getting to me. I just don't want to ruin what we have, you know?"

Kai frowned slightly, his brow furrowing in concern. "I get it. The gossip can be tough, especially when people don't know the real story. But you have to promise me that you won't let it affect how you feel. Our connection is what truly matters."

"But how do we defend it?" Mei felt the tears prick the corners of her eyes, her emotions threatening to spill over. "What if my parents change their minds? What if my classmates continue to doubt us? It's hard to just push it all away!"

"Let's chat about it. We can face this together," Kai said softly, tilting her chin up gently so their eyes met. "You're not alone in this, even if it feels overwhelming right now. We'll figure out a way to reassure your parents while also staying strong against the gossip."

Mei felt a surge of gratitude for his unwavering support as she nodded, trying to calm the storm brewing in her chest.

But as they continued discussing their feelings and the rumors, the fleeting moment of companionship was interrupted by a loud group of students walking nearby, their laughter echoing through the courtyard. Mei's heart sank as she recognized some familiar faces among them, all too aware of the message being traded in whispers.

"Look, it's Mei and her 'artistic' boyfriend! How romantic," one of the girls said, pairing her words with an exaggerated swoon response that ruffled Mei's confidence, like a chill in the air.

Kai's expression hardened as he glanced over at the group. Mei could feel the sting of humiliation creep in, and despite knowing they were being ridiculous, it still hurt.

"Let's not let them ruin our moment," Kai said, subtly squeezing her hand. "Focus on us."

She took a deep breath, trying to draw strength from him as she nodded. "Yes, let's just ignore them."

With a moment of resolve to push through the negativity, she turned her focus back to Kai. "Can we be proactive about how we handle this, though?" she asked, the gears in her mind spinning as she planned their next moves.

"Absolutely. Together, we've got this," he said, regaining the lightness in his tone.

The bell rang, signaling the end of lunch, sending students dispersing back into the building. Mei felt a flicker of determination; she wasn't going to let the rumors and uncertainty get the best of her.

As they walked in together, her heart flickered with newfound resolve. If they were going to tackle the challenges of their relationship head-on, they needed to be prepared to communicate openly and confront the judgments that awaited them.

After a long day filled with classes and the lingering weight of gossip, Mei returned home with Kai at her side. She felt her heart quicken with both excitement and apprehension as she realized the significant conversation that awaited her ahead—the moment of truth that could shape their relationship.

The time had come to reinforce her love for Kai, to showcase the beauty of their connection, and to stand against the doubts that seemed to circle them like vultures.

As they neared her home, Mei took a deep breath, clutching Kai's hand tightly. "This is it," she whispered.

"This is our moment," he responded, radiating support as they made their way inside.

Little did Mei know, the evening ahead would test their bond and challenge them in ways neither had anticipated. But with Kai by her side, she felt ready to face whatever storm lay ahead.

CHAPTER 9

A HEART'S DILEMMA

The evening settled over Mei's home like a heavy fog, and as she stood in the living room, her heart raced with anticipation mingled with anxiety. Kai sat beside her on the couch, his presence a comforting anchor, but the weight of the impending conversation loomed over them both.

Mei's parents had agreed to this discussion, but she could sense the undercurrent of tension swirling in the air. The living room, usually filled with warmth and laughter, felt stifled and heavy as if time itself held its breath.

"Are you ready for this?" Kai whispered, glancing at her with genuine concern. He gently squeezed her hand, grounding her amidst the whirlwind of emotions churning inside her.

"Honestly, I don't know," Mei admitted, her heart pounding. "What if they don't understand? What if they reject what I'm feeling and make it worse?"

"They have to see how much happiness you've found with me," Kai reassured her, his eyes steady and sincere. "But it's okay to be scared. Just remember that you deserve to express your feelings."

Taking a deep breath, Mei nodded, steeling herself for the conversation that lay ahead. She heard the sound of her parents' footsteps approaching, and her heart rate quickened. This was a pivotal moment. It was time to confront the fears that had haunted her since the beginning.

Her parents entered the room, their expressions a mixture of concern and curiosity. "Thank you for sitting down with us tonight," her mother said, her tone gentle but serious.

"We want to hear you out, Mei," her father added, settling back into his seat. "We know this is important to you."

Mei felt the pressure slam down, a cacophony of thoughts racing through her mind. She glanced at Kai, who offered her an encouraging nod, urging her to embrace her truth.

"Alright, here goes nothing," she muttered, taking another deep breath before speaking. "I want to talk to you about Kai and how I feel about him. It's not just a crush anymore; I really care about him."

Her mother glanced at her father, and there was a moment of silence, each uncertainty hanging in the air like a fragile thread. "Mei, sweetheart, we understand that you feel strongly about him," her mother began, carefully choosing her words. "But we've expressed our concerns about the complexities that arise from a relationship like this."

"Mom, I know. But please try to understand. Kai is an amazing person. He makes me feel understood, cared for, and accepted for who I am. He respects my values," she urged, pouring her heart into her words. "I want you to see that what we have is real."

Hesitation flickered in her parents' eyes, and Mei pressed on, driven by fear yet bolstered by the support of Kai beside her. "I've never felt this way about anyone. I want to explore this relationship, and I need your support."

"Mei, it's not that we don't care about your happiness," her father said, his voice steady but gentle. "We just want to make sure you're cautious about it. Relationships can be complicated, especially when family values are involved."

There it was—the familiar push and pull of traditional expectations clashing with her desire to chart her own course. "I understand that, but can't you see that I'm trying to live my life authentically? I don't want to hold back just because it's different from what you want for me."

Her mother opened her mouth to respond but paused, taking a moment to reflect. "We love you, Mei, and our worries come from a place of wanting to protect you. We just want to ensure that you're choosing someone who will be good for you in the long run."

"Are you saying you don't think Kai is good for me?" Mei's heart hammered in her chest as she struggled to suppress the tears threatening to spill. "I need you to see him for who he is, not just who society thinks he should be."

Her father leaned forward, his expression softening. "We want to see him as he is. But understand that it takes time for us to adjust to changes, especially when it comes to relationships. We've seen how strongly traditional values can influence experiences."

A sinking feeling settled over Mei again. It felt like no matter how compelling her argument, a part of her parents remained resistant, locked into their own beliefs about what love should look like. "Then help me understand. I'm being honest about my feelings and I want to honor you as my family. But I also want you to honor me in return."

"I am proud of you for being so brave and direct," her mother said, voice trembling slightly. "But we're worried about the obstacles you both might face."

"Worry shouldn't stop you from being happy," Kai interjected softly, his own concern evident in his eyes as he turned to Mei's parents. "I genuinely care about Mei, and I understand the complexities that come with relationships, especially one as public as ours. But I believe that if we approach this with honesty and open hearts, we can navigate whatever challenges arise together."

Her mother looked between Kai and Mei, visibly touched by his sincerity. "It's encouraging that you want to be there for Mei. We see that," she said, her voice softening just a little. "But have you thought about the weight of expectations both of you will be carrying? Not just from us, but from others as well?"

"I have," Kai replied earnestly, unwavering. "But what truly matters to me is Mei's happiness. This connection we have is real, and we're willing to face whatever comes our way."

Mei felt a swell of pride and appreciation for Kai's strength. He had supported her through many uncertainties, and his unwavering commitment was something she deeply valued. But her heart still wrestled with the contrasting feelings of hope and apprehension.

"Just think about what you're saying," her father cautioned, his expression serious. "It's easy to feel invincible in the beginning, but reality often complicates those feelings. Love requires sacrifice—sometimes it means making tough decisions."

"I understand that, but love also means believing in one another," Mei said, her voice gaining strength. "We're both ready to take on this journey. I'm not asking you to agree with everything, but I need your support as I navigate this path."

Her parents remained silent, contemplation etched across their faces. Mei felt the weight of their scrutiny as they processed everything, and she could sense the storm of emotions swirling beneath the surface.

"I just want you to promise me something," her mother finally spoke, her tone shifting to one of earnestness. "Promise that if this relationship becomes complicated, you'll both be honest with us about it. We want nothing more than for you to be happy. But happiness can come with challenges too."

Mei nodded, a solid wave of determination pushing her forward. "I promise, Mom. I want to be open with you both, no matter what happens. I want to navigate the complexities together. With Kai."

After a prolonged moment of silence, her father finally sighed. "Alright, I think we can give this relationship a chance. But we want to be involved; we'd like to meet again with no reservations, just honesty."

"Thank you!" Mei exclaimed, relief flooding her. "I'm so grateful for that."

As the evening progressed, the uneasy tension began to dissipate, leaving behind a tentative but genuine spirit of understanding. They engaged in lighter conversations, and for the first time, Mei felt as though she was bridging her two worlds: her parents' protective love and her willingness to assert her own desires with Kai.

Once dinner concluded, Kai stood to leave, sending Mei a bright smile, the kind that made her heart skip. Encapsulated in the warmth of their earlier exchange, she felt empowered to embrace the journey that lay ahead.

"Thanks for having me, Mr. and Mrs. Suki," he said respectfully, offering a polite bow. "I'm looking forward to getting to know you better."

As Kai waved goodbye and walked out, Mei felt both nervous and excited about the possibilities ahead. She was ready to stand firm in her truth, armed with the support of both Kai and her parents, willing to embrace the challenges together.

The following days at school were filled with a new sense of purpose. Though whispers still surrounded her, Mei found it easier to brush them off. After the confrontation, she felt renewed, propelled by the knowledge that her parents were beginning to open their hearts to Kai.

But with each passing day, she grew increasingly aware of the delicate balance they had to maintain—especially in an environment marked by rumors and pressures. She grew more determined than ever to show everyone the depth of her relationship with Kai would prevail despite the obstacles ahead.

As they walked through the school hallways together, their fingers intertwined, Mei felt the warmth of their connection thrive. Each moment spent with Kai solidified the hope in her heart that they could navigate the challenges together.

But unknown to them, external pressures would soon emerge, testing their bond and forcing them to confront deeper insecurities.

As they reached the weekend, a flicker of joy spread through Mei at the thought of their planned visit to the art exhibit. But the upcoming adventure was tinged with an anxious anticipation; whispers hung in the air like ominous shadows, preparing her for the storm that seemed poised to break.

CHAPTER 10

SUPPORTIVE FRIENDS

The weekend had arrived, and the day of the art exhibit dawned bright and clear. Mei felt a sense of anticipation bubbling within her, excited not only to immerse herself in the world of art but also to spend another meaningful day with Kai. It was a welcome escape from the tension and uncertainty of the past week.

She met Kai at the entrance of the exhibit, where the bright banner fluttered above them, announcing the show. He greeted her with his usual warm smile, and as they stood together, Mei realized just how much she cherished these moments shared with him.

"Ready to explore?" he asked, his enthusiasm infectious as he linked their arms, propelling her forward into the vibrant atmosphere of creativity and culture.

"Absolutely! I can't wait to see the exhibits," she replied, her heart buoyed by the thrill of their shared adventure.

As they stepped inside, the atmosphere overwhelmed her senses—a kaleidoscope of colors, sounds, and emotions swirled around them. Artworks adorned the walls, each holding a story and an expression of creativity that left her breathless. Mei felt herself getting lost in the intricacies of each piece, her heart alive with inspiration.

"Look over there!" Kai exclaimed, gesturing toward a canvas drenched in bold colors that depicted an abstract view of Tokyo at night. "What do you think?"

"It's beautiful," she marveled, her eyes tracing the brushstrokes and the emotions they conveyed. "It captures the city's vibrancy so perfectly."

As they wandered deeper into the gallery, Kagai enthusiastically discussed various pieces—how each artist conveyed their perspective and message, a reflection of how art connected them as humans. The shared passion and appreciation for creativity deepened their bond and allowed Mei to momentarily forget the worries of the outside world.

But as the day wore on, snippets of conversations from classmates pierced the blissful bubble they had created together. Paintings seemed to blend into whispers, and Mei caught wind of a few familiar voices in the corner of her mind.

"Did you see them together again? Who would have thought?" one voice mentioned, and though she tried to block it out, a sense of unease crept back in.

Eventually, after roaming through the exhibit, they took a break at a nearby café to grab refreshments. The scent of brewed coffee filled the air, a comforting aroma that helped settle Mei's racing thoughts.

As they sat across the table, sipping their drinks, she felt a familiar knot in her stomach tightening at the reminder of lingering rumors. "Kai, can we talk about something?" she began, unsure of how to voice the doubts that had begun to resurface.

"Of course! What's on your mind?" he responded, his expression grew serious as he leaned forward, waiting for her to open up.

"I love spending time with you, but sometimes the rumors at school… They're hard to ignore. It feels like no matter what we do, people are always going to judge us," Mei said, her voice laden with vulnerability.

Kai's brow furrowed in concern. "I don't want you to feel burdened by that. We can't control what people think, but we can choose how to react."

She nodded, appreciating his words, but doubt still lingered. "I just think it's unfair that we have to face this just because of what others believe. It makes me wonder if my feelings for you are worth the hassle."

Just then, Akira arrived, sensing the tension in the air as he slid into the seat beside her. "Hey, you two! What is with the heavy vibes?" he asked, casually reaching for a pastry.

"Just contemplating the complexities of high school rumors," Mei replied with a light sigh trying to mask her frustration.

Akira raised an eyebrow, his expression shifting to one of concern. "You can't let those whispers derail what you have! If you both care about each other, that's what matters. Real friends will support you, regardless of what others think."

"Thanks, Akira. I know I shouldn't let it get to me, but it's tough," she said, grateful for the reminder that some people truly understood—some would stand by her side without judgment.

"You've been dealing with a lot, Mei," he continued. "But remember the good memories and the fun moments you've had with Kai over the last few weeks. Those are what count. Concentrate on that joy instead of the toxicity."

Mei took a moment to reflect on his words as she watched Kai and Akira engage in playful teasing. She felt buoyed by the solidarity and unconditional support from her friends—a comforting reminder that she wasn't alone.

"I know we can face whatever lies ahead together," Kai said, breaking the moment of contemplation. "But if you ever feel overwhelmed, just let me know. We can tackle it as a team."

A sense of relief washed over her, and she felt her determination surge. "You're right, Kai. I want to focus on the positive moments we've created together. I'm ready to tackle whatever comes our way."

Kai nodded, a smile breaking across his face, and for a moment, the worry faded away. With Akira's presence adding to the buoyancy in the air, the trio shared stories, laughter exploding between them, their camaraderie radiating warmth and friendship.

After sharing jokes and analyzing the art pieces they had seen, Mei could feel the weight of insecurities begin to lighten. But deep within her, the underlying tension about the rumors still lingered, leaving her uncertain about the path ahead. She glanced at Kai, who was animatedly discussing an artwork, and the fondness she felt surged once more.

While they wrapped up their snacks and planned their next activity, Mei contemplated how much she relied on Kai and her friends for support—a realization that both warmed her heart and unsettled her. Could she truly navigate the upcoming challenges without external influences weighing on her decisions?

As they finished up, it was clear that Kai and Akira had both pulled her back from the brink of doubt. "Let's have a karaoke night next week!" Akira suggested, his eyes bright with enthusiasm. "We should give them something to really talk about!"

"I'm in!" Kai agreed, grinning. "The more outrageous, the better! Let's blow off some steam!"

As they stepped back out into the bustling streets, the comforting buzz of excitement hummed around them. Mei felt her spirit lift, bolstered by the support from her friends and the undeniable bond she shared with Kai.

Still, the undercurrents of doubt tugged at her. The whispers would not fade overnight. They lingered amid the laughter, reminding her of her vulnerability and the clashes she still had to face.

Later that evening, as she lay in bed, Mei's mind raced with thoughts of the upcoming dinner with Kai. She could practically hear the echoes of gossip—What will they say when they find out?

With every passing moment, she felt the gravity of her parents' expectations loom larger as she prepared to confront them again. A mixture of anticipation and fear washed over her.

What if they dismiss my feelings? What if I end up alone? The questions chased each other through her mind, each one amplifying the fear nestled deep inside her heart.

But then she thought of Kai—his warmth, his unwavering support, and the moments that had brought them closer together. She envisioned his reassuring smile, encouraging her to be brave.

"Tomorrow," she whispered to herself, "I'll speak my truth. I'll be bold and honest, no matter the outcome."

With that mantra in place, Mei closed her eyes, allowing the flickers of doubt to ebb away. She pushed aside the insecurities and placed her trust in the strength she gained from her friends and the blossoming connection with Kai.

The following day, a calm settled in her gut as she approached her parents again, bolstered by the strength of her conversation with Kai. She had spent the night contemplating her emotions and aspirations, feeling a renewed sense of hope.

When she finally found her parents in the living room, the moment felt defined, significant. She steadied herself, determined to express everything she needed to say.

"Mom, Dad," she began, her voice steady. "I want to talk about my relationship with Kai again. I need you to hear me out without any interruptions."

Her parents looked surprised but nodded, encouraging her to continue.

Gathering her courage, Mei shared her thoughts openly, wanting them to understand the depth of her feelings and the person who had genuinely impacted her life. She spoke about Kai and how he inspired her, igniting her passion and creativity, building a connection that transcended traditional expectations.

Just then, she could sense the tension in the room shift, her parents absorbing her words as they listened closely. But the questions that loomed behind their careful expressions were unspoken, leaving her wondering how they would respond.

As the conversation progressed, Mei poured out her heart, revealing her hopes and dreams. She fought against the remnants of fear that tried to cloud her confidence, and with each word, she felt a sense of resolution building within her.

But as she reached the conclusion of her heartfelt confession, a silence enveloped the room—an uncertain stillness that left her breathless.

Would they accept her feelings for Kai? Could they bridge the gap between their traditional values and her desire for love and happiness?

CHAPTER 11

A LOVING GESTURE WITH OBENTO

The week following Mei's conversation with her parents was a whirlwind of emotions—relief mingled with anticipation as she and Kai navigated the complexities of their budding relationship amidst the backdrop of their classmates' whispers. With each lunch they shared in the school courtyard, Mei felt herself growing closer to Kai, the connection between them deepening with every smile and laugh.

As Friday approached, Mei felt a flutter of excitement in her stomach. She had spent the week anxiously waiting for the weekend's celebrations of their bond—a chance to escape the chaos and focus on what mattered most.

On Friday morning, she received a text from Kai that made her heart race.

Kai: Morning, Mei! I made you something special for lunch today. Can't wait for you to try it!

Her heart swelled at the thought of him preparing something just for her. It was such a thoughtful gesture, and she couldn't help but smile at the sweetness of it.

Mei: You did? Now I'm even more excited for lunch! What is it?

Kai: A surprise! You'll find out!

As the clock inched toward lunchtime, Mei's anticipation grew. The sounds of laughter and chatter echoed around her, but her mind was focused solely on the moment she would share with Kai. She could practically feel her heart drumming in her chest, enthusiasm bubbling with every passing second.

When the lunch bell finally rang, she hurried outside, eager to see him. The courtyard was alive with students, and as she spotted Kai waiting under a tree, holding a colorful lunch box, her heart fluttered.

"There you are!" he grinned, his eyes lighting up when he saw her. "I was starting to think you'd forgotten about me!"

"Never!" she replied, her spirits lifting at the sight of him. "What do you have for me today? I can't wait to see!"

Kai walked forward, presenting the obento with a flourish. The box was beautifully arranged, each item delicately placed to create a vibrant masterpiece of flavors—a mix of traditional Japanese elements with a twist.

"Ta-da! I thought I'd surprise you with a homemade obento. I included a little bit of everything," he said, opening the box to reveal fluffy rice molded in the shape of a heart, tender slices of chicken katsu, colorful sautéed vegetables, and fresh fruit.

She gasped, her heart swelling at the thoughtfulness of his gesture. "This is amazing, Kai! You actually made this?!"

"Yep, all by myself!" he said, genuine pride shining in his eyes. "I hope you like it."

Sitting down together on the grass, Mei felt an overwhelming sense of gratitude flood her. "I love it! It's so beautiful," she said as she took a piece of katsu, sensations of warmth and affection blooming within her as she savored the flavor.

"How does it taste?" he asked, watching her expectantly.

"It's incredible! Seriously, this is restaurant quality," she replied, her eyes sparkling. "You've officially spoiled me for life."

Kai laughed, his cheeks flushing slightly with pleasure at her enthusiasm. "I'm glad you enjoy it! I wanted to do something special for you, especially after everything you've been dealing with."

The warmth of his words enveloped her, igniting feelings she had long kept at bay. With every bite, she felt the love and effort he had poured into this meal. The obento was not just food; it encapsulated the essence of their relationship—thoughtful, nurturing, and full of care.

"Thank you for this," she said sincerely, looking into his eyes. "It really means a lot to me, especially with everything going on."

"I'm always here for you, Mei," he said, a soft smile gracing his lips. "No matter what. We'll tackle everything together."

As they continued to eat, sharing food and stories, Mei's heart swelled with appreciation. Each laugh, every shared glance, ignited the bond they had forged over the past weeks, and she realized how much she had come to cherish him.

But amid the warmth radiating from their connection, the weight of her insecurities occasionally flickered at the edge of her mind. What if their love couldn't withstand the judgment of others? But with Kai beside her, she felt strong and determined.

After they finished lunch, they decided to take a stroll through the nearby park, enjoying the pleasant breeze. The blooming flowers around them reflected the happiness in Mei's heart, and as they walked hand in hand, she felt a deep sense of love for Kai—a realization that this was where she wanted to be.

Under a blooming cherry tree, Mei paused, taking in the beauty around them. "It's a perfect day," she mused, glancing at Kai, who was gazing back at her with a warmth that melted her heart. The soft pink petals danced in the breeze, showering them like confetti, and she felt as if nature itself was celebrating the connection they shared.

"It really is," Kai replied with a smile, stepping beside her. "And I can't think of anyone I'd rather spend it with."

Caught in the spell of the moment, Mei felt a rush of feelings surging inside her. Here they were, two souls interwoven beneath a canopy of blossoms, and she couldn't help but feel that what they shared was blossoming into something beautiful.

"Thank you again for the obento," she said sincerely, looking into his eyes. "It reminded me of how much love you put into everything you do."

"I just wanted to show you how much you mean to me," he said, his voice low and sincere. "You've brought so much into my life, and I wanted to give back a little of that joy."

She felt her heart flutter at his words, and she could sense a deeper connection forming—a bond that transcended the fun, laughter, and memories they were building together. "You've definitely given me a lot of joy. I'm so grateful for you."

"I'm grateful for you too, Mei." He took a step closer, the warmth radiating between them. "I've never felt this way with anyone before. It's like you see me for who I am, and I can be myself around you."

Her breath hitched in her throat, the intensity of his gaze sending shivers down her spine. In that moment, she knew that whatever challenges lay ahead, they had something genuine that deserved to be nurtured.

With the petals swirling around them and the warm sunlight framing their figures, something shifted, a magnetic pull drawing them closer together. Kai reached for Mei's hand, intertwining their fingers as he leaned in slightly.

"May I?" he asked softly, pausing as he read her expression, seeking permission.

She nodded, heart racing as she prepared for what felt like a moment suspended in time. It seemed the world faded around them, the rhythm of the city dulled to a quiet hum as they stood together beneath the blossoms.

In the soft embrace of the cherry tree, their lips met gently—a whisper of a kiss that woke every nerve in Mei's body. A surge of warmth flooded through her, filling her with affection as the fleeting touches deepened into something more passionate.

The kiss felt alive, as if it was a promise—a shared understanding of the feelings that had grown between them. As their lips parted, they held each other's gaze, their breaths mingling in the warm air, love shimmering in their connection.

"I've wanted to do that for such a long time," Kai confessed, a soft blush creeping to his cheeks as he brushed a strand of hair behind Mei's ear.

"Me too," she said, feeling elated and enchanted. "It felt perfect."

"Let's make the most of today," he suggested, his eyes brightening with excitement. "We can explore more of the park or take photos under the blossoms. I want to capture this moment with you."

"Definitely!" Mei beamed, feeling lighthearted as they wandered down the path. The air was rich with the fragrance of flowers and the laughter of other families enjoying the sun. They stopped at spots that caught their eye, capturing the beauty of the park amidst the fickle challenges they would face together: their playful moments, their affectionate smiles, and their newfound intimacy.

But as they spent the day exploring and laughing, shadows of doubt flickered at the edges of Mei's mind. She couldn't quite shake the feeling that the world outside still posed challenges, and despite the joy that Kai brought her, she knew their relationship would be put to the test.

As they walked alongside the picturesque pond, its surface reflecting the blue sky above, Mei made a quiet decision. "Kai," she began, her tone serious, "can we talk about the challenges we might face? The gossip? My parents' expectations?"

"Absolutely," Kai replied, his expression shifting to one of earnest attention. "I'm open to discussing anything you want, Mei."

She took a deep breath, prepared to confront the realities surrounding them. "I love what we have, but I know that not everyone sees it that way. I want us to be resilient against the pressure from school and even from my family. I just need to know that we're both on the same page."

Kai nodded, understanding etched on his features. "I promise I'm in this with you. We just need to keep communicating openly about our feelings. Ignoring the challenges won't make them disappear; facing them together will help us grow."

Feeling a surge of gratitude, Mei let out a deep breath, the tension in her shoulders easing slightly. "Thank you, Kai. It means a lot that we can have these discussions. You really are my rock."

Kai smiled, tilting his head slightly, making him look even more endearing against the backdrop of blooming cherry blossoms. "And you're mine. We'll tackle everything that comes our way, together."

With a newfound sense of determination, Mei nodded in agreement. It felt reassuring to have someone like Kai by her side, someone who understood the intricacies of her heart, someone willing to delve into the complexities of their relationship with her.

"Let's promise to always check in with each other, no matter what," she said, her voice steady. "I need to know that we can communicate openly about our worries and feelings."

"Deal," Kai said, holding out his pinky finger, a playful sparkle in his eye that reminded her of all the joy they had shared.

Mei smiled and wrapped her pinky around his, sealing their promise. Just then, a gentle breeze swept through the park, carrying with it the sweet scent of cherry blossoms. It felt as if nature itself was celebrating their vows—an unspoken assurance that they would navigate whatever challenges lay ahead.

"Now, let's take advantage of this beautiful day!" Kai said, his enthusiasm breaking through their more serious moment. "We still have more to explore and capture!"

As they wandered further into the park, Kai pointed out various spots that caught his eye, stopping frequently to snap candid pictures of Mei, capturing the joyous light in her eyes. With each click of the camera shutter, the lightness in her heart grew, reminding her of how special this connection already felt.

After spending hours immersing themselves in the vibrant beauty that surrounded them, they finally settled under another blossoming tree, where golden sunlight filtered through the petals, creating a magical atmosphere.

"This," Mei said, tilting her head back to let her thoughts spill free, "has been one of the best days I can remember."

"Same here," Kai agreed, laying back against the soft grass and stretching his arms out, basking in the sunlight. "And it's not over yet! We still have the karaoke night to look forward to."

Oh, the karaoke night. While the thought of it sent tinges of joy through her, it also reignited the flickers of anxiety about how classmates would react. She shrugged it off, reminding herself that she would face all the challenges together with Kai.

"Right! I can't wait to see what songs you pick!" she responded, trying to refocus on the excitement of the shared adventure.

"But I totally expect you to pick something embarrassing," he teased playfully, a mischievous grin spreading across his face.

"Oh, I might have a few songs in mind! Just wait and see," she teased back, playfully nudging him with her shoulder.

They spent a little longer basking in the sunlight, the laughter flowing easily, the worries of the outside world feeling distant, if only for a while. With the warmth of the day wrapping around them, Mei felt her heart swell with happiness.

But beneath the happiness lay a current of tension—her parents' concerns and the rumors still loomed like shadows, waiting to assert themselves. No matter how perfect this day feels, the reality still awaits, she thought.

As they packed up to leave, Kai turned to her, his expression serious yet filled with warmth. "I want you to know I'm with you through every twist and turn. No matter what anyone else says, I care about you, and I want to be by your side."

"Thank you, Kai," she said softly, feeling the weight of her feelings flood over her in an envelope of warmth. "That means more than you know."

With their hands intertwined, they walked back toward where they had parked, ready to take on the evening's karaoke adventure. Mei felt renewed spirit, buoyed by the connection they'd strengthened that day.

But as the thoughts of the evening ahead loomed like a distant cloud on the horizon, she reminded herself to take it one step at a time. No matter what challenges may arise, she would face them head-on, surrounded by the support of her friends and the warmth of her love for Kai.

As the sun began to set, painting the sky in breathtaking hues, Mei's thoughts turned toward the karaoke night ahead and the looming uncertainty of facing the gossiping eyes of her peers. Despite her confidence, the pressure began to brew quietly beneath the excitement.

The evening would not only be a test of her resolve but also a chance to cement her bond with Kai publicly, showing everyone that they were more than just whispers in the wind.

As they approached the karaoke venue, the neon lights flashed above them and the sounds of laughter and music welcomed them in.

"Let's have some fun!" Kai exclaimed, his infectious energy radiating through the air. He pulled open the door, and as they stepped inside, the vibrant atmosphere enveloped them—a mix of colorful lights, excited chatters, and the familiar hum of karaoke melodies spilling out from various rooms.

Mei took a moment to absorb it all, feeling a wave of excitement mix with a flutter of nervousness in her stomach. The venue buzzed with energy, and she felt the warmth of Kai's hand squeeze hers, his presence reassuring her as they ventured further inside.

"Are you ready to unleash your inner star?" he teased, flashing her a playful grin.

"Only if you promise to keep me from embarrassing myself too much," she joked back, trying to shake off the anxieties creeping in about the potential judgment from their peers.

"Don't worry—I'll make sure to choose the most epic duet for us! We'll be legends in this place!" Kai replied dramatically, egging her on.

They approached the registration desk to pick their songs, and Mei felt the buzz of anticipation spiral. She could hear snippets of people singing in the distance, some nervous but others belting out tunes with confidence.

"Alright, let's make a plan," Kai said, flipping through the songbook as if orchestrating the perfect performance. "I'll start with something easy, and then we can throw in a duet!"

He settled on a catchy pop song to kick things off, and when it was their turn, Mei's heart raced as they stepped onto the stage. The lights dimmed slightly, and the spotlight focused on them, amplifying her nervous energy.

But as the music began to play and Kai launched into the opening lines, she felt a wave of excitement swell inside her. He was animated, losing himself in the performance as he engaged the audience around him, and before long, his buoyancy spread to Mei.

Fueled by the thrill of his enthusiasm, she joined in, singing along, and for that moment, the doubts and worries faded away. The crowd began to cheer them on, laughter interspersing their performance, lifting Mei's spirits higher with every beat.

As they finished the song, applause echoed around them, and Kai looked over at her with a triumphant gleam in his eyes. "See? You're a natural!"

"That was so much fun, Kai!" Mei laughed, the adrenaline coursing through her. It felt like they had solidified a new chapter of their connection, one rooted in shared experiences and joyful expressions.

After a few more songs—each one carrying with it bouts of laughter—Kai leaned in closer as they sat at the table between performances. "How are you feeling?"

"Surprisingly good! I can't remember the last time I felt this free," she admitted, the weight of the day's anxieties seeming to diminish in the warmth of their shared moments.

As they prepared for their next karaoke performance, Mei's earlier apprehensions resurfaced, even as she cherished the connection they were creating. What if the rumors intensified after tonight? Would they still be able to enjoy moments like this in the face of everything else?

Just as those thoughts began to cloud her mind, two classmates approached their table. Mei recognized them, and her heart sank slightly.

"Hey, Mei! Nice to see you out having a good time," one girl chimed in, her tone almost mocking.

"Yeah, we heard you and Kai singing," another one added, smirking. "Honestly, we didn't think you had it in you!"

"Thanks?" Mei replied, her initial joy diminished by the undertone of judgment in their words. She could already feel her cheeks flushing as whispers swirled just beyond her control. "It's just karaoke."

"Sure! A lot of people are talking about you two," one of them said, her eyebrows raised. "What a surprise, huh? Does your family know you're dating someone outside your race?"

The comment stung, and Mei's heart sank at the reminder of the judgments that still hovered over them. She hesitated for a moment, feeling the undercurrents of insecurity and doubt swell within her.

"Why does that even matter? We're just having fun," Kai shot back, a protective edge in his voice.

"Just saying what everyone else is thinking," the girl retorted, unfazed. "Not everyone thinks it's a good idea, you know."

Mei swallowed hard, her stomach churning as the words hung heavy in the air. It felt as if the whispers had materialized into a tangible weight, threatening to crush the happiness she had built alongside Kai. Her parents' doubts and the gossip around school suddenly felt more real than before.

"Let's go sing again," Kai suggested, his voice firm and clear, wanting to deflect the tension. He stood, extending his hand toward Mei, and she took it, grateful for his unwavering support.

As they made their way back to the stage, the noise of the crowd faded just a little, and Mei focused on the thrill of performing rather than the gossip that lingered. Kai's hand felt warm and reassuring in hers, a silent reminder that they were a team facing the world together.

When they reached the microphone, she took a deep breath, her heart still racing from the previous encounter. She glanced at Kai, who was radiating confidence, and it reignited her own excitement. With the music starting, they threw themselves into the next song, a lively duet that echoed in the walls of the karaoke venue, filled with energy and joy.

As they sang, Mei felt the weight of judgment lift, buoyed by the connection they shared on stage. She poured her heart into the performance, her laughter mixing with the music, and as the crowd cheered them on, a sense of belonging washed over her once again.

With every note, the rumors felt a little less pressing, the cheers of their classmates momentarily drowning out the whispers of doubt. Kai's presence anchored her, pulling her into the moment, and together they created a vibrant bubble filled with laughter and music.

After their performance, they stepped off stage, exhilarated and breathing heavily. "That was amazing! You completely rocked that!" Mei exclaimed, her eyes shining with excitement.

"You were incredible too!" Kai said, his enthusiasm infectious. "We should definitely do that again!"

As they returned to the table, Mei felt a renewed sense of camaraderie envelop them. But before she could relax completely, she saw the same classmates from earlier hovering nearby, their presence a sharp reminder of the undercurrent of gossip.

"Nice performance, you guys," one girl said, her tone dripping with sarcasm. "You definitely have the crowd's attention, but do you think it's enough to make everyone forget?"

Mei's heart sank at the jab, and she fought to maintain her composure, reminding herself of the strengthened bond she and Kai had just solidified through their performance. "We're just having fun," Kai replied, his voice steady, his gaze unwavering as he faced the group. "That's what karaoke is all about."

"Right," the girl scoffed. "But fun doesn't change the fact that people are always going to talk. Just be careful."

"I can handle it," Mei shot back, feeling emboldened by Kai's presence. "We're not here to please anyone else. We're here to enjoy ourselves."

"Sure, whatever you say," the girl shrugged, a smirk playing at the corner of her lips. They turned and walked away, leaving Mei and Kai in an atmosphere thick with uncertainty.

Kai squeezed her hand under the table, grounding her once again. "Don't let them get to you. They're just trying to provoke a reaction," he said softly.

"I know," Mei replied, still feeling the sting of judgment. "But it's hard not to think about the implications. What if they end up affecting what we have?"

Kai's expression shifted to one of sincere understanding. "We can't let others dictate our happiness. What we have is real, and we need to trust that."

"Yeah, I'll try," she said, nodding resolutely, determined to shake off the creeping doubts.

The remainder of their time at the karaoke bar bubbled with laughter and playful teasing, even as whispers from their classmates faded into the background. With each song they sang and every shared smile, the bond between them blossomed, reaffirming her hope and beliefs.

By the end of the night, Mei felt victorious, ready to face the world outside the venue. They stepped into the cool night air, hand in hand, the tension of the day lightening significantly with each step.

As they walked toward the subway, the city pulsed with a life of its own— a lively symphony that mirrored the excitement and uncertainty of their relationship. They chatted animatedly about their favorite songs, while Mei began to contemplate the ultimate challenge that lay ahead: facing her parents about Kai once more.

"Let's make a pact," Kai suggested as they neared the train station. "When you talk to your parents again, I'll be there to support you—no matter what, I promise."

"Thank you," Mei said, squeezing his hand. "This means everything. I wish I could shake off the worry, but I know having you with me will help."

"Then let's make plans to tackle it together—and we'll celebrate afterward, sound good?"

She smiled, feeling the warmth of his words wrap around her like a hug. "Definitely. Whatever happens, we'll face it together."

As they boarded the train, the city lights danced outside the window, twinkling like stars against the darkening sky. Mei felt the rhythmic sway of the train as it moved, bringing a sense of calm to her racing heart. With Kai beside her, the worries of the day began to dissipate, replaced by the familiar warmth that blossomed in her chest.

"Can you believe we did that?" she said, laughter bubbling up as the adrenaline from performing still lingered. "Karaoke was so much fun!"

"Absolutely! We need to make this a regular thing," Kai replied, his eyes shimmering with delight. "Next time, we'll tackle a duet that will really blow everyone away!"

"Deal! But only if you promise to lead the way," she teased, nudging him playfully with her shoulder as they settled into their seats.

As the train glided smoothly through the dark tunnels, Mei took a minute to appreciate the comfort of Kai's presence, grateful that they could share these moments together. She felt her confidence growing, knowing that they would face her parents' scrutiny hand in hand, and with that thought came a wave of assurance.

"Hey, maybe we can do a mini photoshoot after dinner," she suggested, glancing at him with a soft smile. "I want to capture tonight—our first karaoke adventure."

"Great idea! We'll create a montage of our memories together," he said excitedly. "I think it'll be a blast!"

The conversation flowed seamlessly between them, filled with joy and laughter, but Mei couldn't help but feel a slight twinge of apprehension as the anticipation of dinner with her parents loomed closer. As they approached her stop, the excitement and nerves collided within her.

The subway doors opened with a soft ding, and they stepped out onto the bustling street, the city alive around them. However, as they walked toward her house, the atmosphere shifted, the weight of the upcoming conversation pressing heavily on her mind.

"Are you ready?" Kai asked, sensing her mood change. He looked at her with genuine concern, his touch a comforting anchor against her swirling thoughts.

"More than ever," she replied, her voice steady, though the apprehension still flickered within her. "I know this is just part of our journey, but I can't shake off the feeling that it'll be a turning point for us."

"We'll take it one step at a time," he encouragingly reassured her. "No matter what happens, I'm here for you, and together we can work through it."

As they approached the entrance of her home, Mei's heart raced, the moment of truth palpable in the air around them. "Thanks for standing by me. I'm really grateful," she said, taking a deep breath.

"Always," Kai replied, his unwavering confidence giving her a final push of courage.

With a gentle squeeze of his hand, Mei opened the door, stepping into the warmth of home, turning to find her parents already seated at the dinner table, awaiting her return. The atmosphere felt charged with anticipation, and she could sense that tonight was going to be pivotal.

"Welcome back," her mother said softly, her eyes scanning them with curiosity. "Ready for dinner?"

"Yeah," she replied, feeling the determination surge within her. She glanced at Kai, who offered an encouraging smile, silently promising his support.

As they sat down, Mei's heart raced as she prepared to voice her feelings and hopes, knowing it was time to confront the doubts and fears directly, not just for her relationship with Kai, but for the authenticity of her own heart.

This moment would shape everything—their relationship, her bond with her parents, and the pathway ahead. As she took a deep breath and summoned her courage, Mei steeled herself for the conversation that would pave the way for new beginnings.

CHAPTER 12

THE FAMILY GATHERING

The atmosphere in the dining room was thick with anticipation as Mei took her seat at the table. Her parents were seated across from her, warm but slightly cautious; she could see the remnants of their earlier concern lingering in their eyes. Kai settled in beside her, offering a reassuring smile that bolstered her courage.

"Thank you for having me over again," he said, breaking the ice as he gestured toward the food on the table, a beautifully arranged spread of dishes. The aroma of home-cooked curry filled the air, a familiar scent of love and care that wrapped around Mei like a comforting blanket.

"Of course, Kai. We're glad you could join us," her father said, nodding warmly, a hint of approval flickering behind his gaze.

As they began to serve the food, Mei felt her stomach twist with both excitement and apprehension. This dinner was more than just a meal; it represented a tentative understanding between her parents and the boy who had become so important to her.

"So, how has school been?" her mother started, trying to create a bridge within the conversation, a genuine smile spread across her face as she focused on Kai.

"It's been good, thank you! I'm really enjoying my art classes and getting to explore new styles," Kai said, his passion evident in his tone. He and Mei exchanged glances, the warmth of their connection flowing silently between them.

"That's great to hear." Mei's father leaned forward, appearing genuinely interested. "Art can play a huge part in developing one's perspective. What kind of projects are you working on?"

Mei felt a sense of relief; her parents were engaging with Kai, wanting to know him better, and she found herself softening under the warmth of familial hope. Watching them interact, she felt the tension around the table begin to ease as Kai animatedly spoke about his latest sketching techniques and inspirations from local art, captivating her parents' attention.

Every positive exchange drew Mei in deeper, gradually melting the fear that had settled within her. Laughter bubbled up, permeating the dining room as stories were exchanged and Kai continued to charm her parents with his authenticity.

However, as dinner progressed, Mei found her own anxiety creeping back in—every lingering glance her parents exchanged felt heavy with unspoken thoughts. There was still a realization that they had their reservations, and she sensed that apprehension lingering, as if they were teetering on a precipice.

After a tasty dinner full of lively conversation, her father finally broached a more serious topic. "Mei, I appreciate you bringing Kai into our home, but I hope you understand that this relationship, like any relationship, comes with its challenges. Have you two talked about any of these challenges or complications?"

Mei froze for a moment, caught off guard. She had hoped the dinner would breeze through without apprehensive questions. "We've talked a little," she replied. "But we want to focus on putting our energy into enjoying what we have right now."

"Understandable," her mother said gently. "But it's important to consider how others may view this relationship, especially given your cultural backgrounds. We just want to ensure you're prepared for the potential difficulties."

The knot in Mei's stomach tightened again, tension creeping back. "I understand you want to protect me," she said, her voice steady but edged with vulnerability. "But this is about my happiness. I want to be honest about my feelings—because Kai makes me happy."

Kai interjected, his tone calm yet determined. "I care deeply for Mei, and I promise to support her through any challenges we face. I want to get to know her culture, her family values; that's important to me."

Her mother exchanged a glance with her father, their concern evident. "It will take time to navigate these differences," her father stated, his voice measured. "We simply want the best for you, Mei."

Mei took a deep breath, feeling a surge of bravery. "And I want you to see Kai for who he truly is. He values me, respects my family, and makes me feel seen. That should count for something."

For a moment, the room fell silent, the air thick with tension as her parents processed her words. The lingering uncertainties hung in the atmosphere like a heavy fog, and Mei could feel her heart pounding loudly in her chest.

"Then let's take the time to get to know one another," her father suggested slowly, breaking the silence, his expression softening slightly. "Perhaps a family outing would help us see the connection you two share."

Mei's heart swelled with hope, appreciating her father's willingness to consider that option. "I'd love that," she said, glancing at Kai, whose bright smile mirrored her own enthusiasm.

"Great! This is a step in the right direction," Kai added, his eyes gleaming. "I'd be honored to spend more time with you all."

As the evening drew to a close, Mei felt a swell of gratitude and relief wash over her. The conversation had unfolded in a way she had hoped for—a cautious yet sincere willingness from her parents to understand her relationship with Kai better. Though there would be challenges ahead, they had taken a significant step toward acceptance.

"Thank you for dinner, Mrs. Suki. It was delicious," Kai said, standing and offering a respectful bow to Mei's mother.

"Thank you, Kai. You're welcome back anytime," her mother replied, a genuine smile lighting up her face. It felt like a victory, and Mei couldn't help but feel proud of the progress they had made as a family.

As they left, the cool evening air greeted them, wrapping around them like a soft blanket. Mei took a deep breath, savoring the moment—the sweet scent of the night mixed with the lingering warmth from dinner and the hope that now filled her heart.

"I can't believe that went so well," she said, turning to Kai, whose expression reflected shared excitement. "I was so nervous!"

"See? You did great! Honestly, I'm impressed with how you handled everything," Kai replied, his praise invigorating her spirits. "It's not easy to confront family traditions and expectations, but you showed incredible strength."

"Thanks! I couldn't have done it without you by my side." She smiled brightly, her heart swelling with warmth at his support.

As they strolled through the streets of their neighborhood, the ambiance felt lighter, buoyed by the progress they had made. The laughter of children playing nearby and the distant sound of music filled the air, and Mei felt a renewed sense of possibility blooming within her.

"I'm so glad we're taking this journey together," Mei said, squeezing his hand as they walked.

"Me too," Kai said, his tone serious yet tinged with enthusiasm. "And who knows? Maybe your parents will surprise you even more as they get to know me."

"Let's hope so!" Mei replied, laughter spilling effortlessly between them. "I'd love for them to change their perception."

When they finally reached the park, they found a bench beneath a sprawling cherry blossom tree, the blossoms shimmering gently in the soft evening light like scattered dreams. They settled in, the moment feeling perfectly serene—just the two of them surrounded by the beauty of the blossoms.

"I've been thinking about all the places we want to explore together," Kai said, looking up at the floating petals. "There are so many hidden gems in this city."

"Exactly! I want to capture as many moments as we can," she agreed, her excitement rekindling. "I've always wanted to find more unique spots for photography, things that showcase the spirit of Tokyo."

"Then let's make that our mission. We'll become the ultimate exploration duo!" Kai exclaimed, his eyes sparkling with enthusiasm.

Mei couldn't help but giggle at his exuberance, feeling the deep connection they shared grow with every word. "I love that idea. We'll document everything together. But right now—" she paused, taking in the beauty surrounding them, "let's just enjoy this."

They shared stories, laughed, and talked about everything under the cherry blossom tree, the worries of the week fading into the background. As the stars began to twinkle above them, Mei reveled in the comfort of Kai's presence, feeling grounded by his steadfast support.

Yet, as they found themselves leaning closer under the branches, the heartwarming intimacy was interrupted by the sudden chime of Mei's phone. Her heart sank as she saw a text notification—one from a school group chat that she and Kai had both been a part of.

Anonymous: Did you hear? Mei and Kai are a thing now. How hilarious!

Laughter and emojis flooded the chat, a wave of snickers that felt like a slap in the face. The joy they had just built now felt fragile, shattered by the harsh words and careless judgments floating in that digital world.

Kai glanced over at her, having caught the tell-tale expression on her face as she read the message. "Hey, don't let it get to you. They're just trying to get a rise out of you," he said gently, his tone reassuring.

"I know, but it hurts. I just got to a good place with my parents, and now I have to deal with rumors swirling around school." Mei said, frustration bubbling up as she felt the pressure mounting.

In that moment, the evenly balanced joy of the day wavered. The shadows of doubt crept back, echoing her fears about acceptance from not only her family but also her classmates.

"I can't believe people would stoop so low," Kai said, shaking his head. "We're stronger than their attempts to bring us down, Mei."

His unwavering confidence reignited a flicker of resolve within her. "You're right. I won "...I won't let their opinions define what we have," Mei said, taking a steadying breath.

"Exactly!" Kai encouraged, squeezing her hand gently. "What matters is that we both know how we feel about each other. We can't let the negativity of others overshadow that."

As they sat beneath the blossoming sakura tree, Mei could feel the petals falling softly around them, creating a serene atmosphere that reminded her of the beauty of their connection. Yet, despite Kai's encouragement, the whispers and skeptics from school continued to nag at the back of her mind.

"Maybe we should show them how happy we are together," Kai suggested suddenly, a spark of mischief lighting up his eyes. "How about we post a picture on social media of us at the cherry blossoms? That would definitely get them talking!"

Mei laughed at the idea, picturing the expressions on her classmates' faces if they saw her radiantly happy beside Kai. "Do you really think that would help?" she asked, the thrill of rebellion flowing through her.

"Why not? It's a way to confidently claim what we have! Besides, you've got a better chance of showing them the truth of our relationship rather than just letting them gossip," he reasoned, his energy infectious.

"Okay, let's do it!" Mei agreed, feeling the adrenaline rush of anticipation. They snapped a few joyful pictures together, capturing their smiles beneath the pink blossoms. As they reviewed the images, she felt a thrill spark between them—knowing the power of their connection made them radiant against the backdrop of nature.

They posted the picture with a caption that reflected their bond, infusing a sense of pride and confidence into each word.

Mei: Celebrating friendship and love under the cherry blossoms!

After hitting send, Mei felt a mix of excitement and nervousness course through her. "What if people react badly?" she asked, her smile fading slightly as she contemplated the possibilities.

"Then that's on them," Kai replied confidently. "What matters is that we love and support each other. Let them talk while we keep making memories and enjoying our time together."

As they sat together, gazing at the vibrant lights that twinkled throughout the city, Mei felt as though she was finally stepping into her truth—a truth that embraced Kai while honoring her family. Yet the impending conversations with her parents still hung in the air, an undeniable weight that she needed to address.

As the evening faded into night, they decided to continue celebrating their relationship with a karaoke night. Laughter bubbled between them as they navigated song choices and teased each other about past performances. The joy of the moment helped push away any lingering doubts.

But as they entered the karaoke venue, Mei felt the familiar tension resurface just before they joined their classmates inside. She took a moment to breathe, reminding herself of the resolve she had found. Amidst the laughter and the energy of the crowd, she sought comfort in Kai.

"Are you ready for this?" he asked, sensing her apprehension, a knowing look in his eyes.

"I am," she replied, feeling a mix of excitement and anxiety. "No matter what, I have to do this for us."

As they filed into the karaoke room, the atmosphere vibrated with the sound of their peers having fun. The energy teetered on the edge of wild and carefree, but Mei noticed whispers beginning to swell as some of her classmates spotted her and Kai.

"Oh look, it's the new couple!" one girl announced, laughter trailing behind her words.

Mei felt a wave of heat flush her cheeks, but Kai stood tall beside her, pulling her closer, a fierce protectiveness radiating from him. "Let's show them how much fun we can have," he said, lifting his chin slightly, his confidence unwavering.

As they took the stage, heartbeats synchronized, the music began, and the worries faded momentarily into the background. When they sang, the audience clapped along, and Mei focused on Kai, the powerful connection between them defying the judgment from others.

Completely lost in the moment, laughter bubbled over once more as the crowd cheered them on. The whispers faded into the distance, drowned out by the music and excitement.

It was finally time for their final song, and as they harmonized, Mei felt the euphoria wash over her, pushing back against the lingering doubts. This was her truth—this connection with Kai—and she would embrace it, no matter the challenges awaiting her daily.

As their performance concluded, cheers erupted, momentarily drowning out the whispers of doubt in the room. In that joyful celebration, Mei felt galvanized, buoyed by the realization that love, real love, was worth the struggle.

Later that evening, they stepped outside into the crisp night air, the city flickering with lights and possibilities. With the hum of excitement still echoing in their hearts, Mei felt a rush of exhilaration as they walked hand in hand down the illuminated streets.

"I can't believe how much fun that was!" Mei exclaimed, her cheeks flushed from the joy of performing, the positive energy wrapping around them like a warm hug. "You really brought your A-game tonight!"

Kai chuckled, his eyes bright with enthusiasm. "You were the star of the show! The way you sang made me feel like we could take on the world!"

Mei felt a lightness in her heart, the burdens from earlier fading into the background. Yet, the reality of her parents' expectations loomed at the edge of her mind, reminding her that despite the joy, challenges still awaited.

"Hey, can we take a moment to just soak this in?" Kai suggested, stopping at a small bridge overlooking the shimmering reflection of the city lights on the water.

"Absolutely," she agreed, stepping up beside him, breathing in the crisp air. They gazed out over the landscape, the view sprawling before them like a beautifully crafted canvas.

In the backdrop of the vibrant skyline, Kai turned to her, his face softening. "I really appreciate everything we've experienced together lately. It's been special."

Mei's heart swelled at his words. "It has been. I want to cherish every moment," she said earnestly. "But I know we need to confront the challenges ahead—especially with my parents."

"Let's take it one step at a time," he said, his tone steady and reassuring like an anchor against her concerns. "I'll be here to support you through any conversations you need to have."

She nodded, grateful for his unwavering presence. "I know it won't be easy, but I want to appreciate what we have, regardless of whatever else is said."

As the cool breeze rustled the trees around them, Mei felt the beginning of clarity forming—a sense of resolution would help her face the complexities of the world around her.

They stood together, leaning against the railing, lost in their own thoughts. The connection between them felt palpable, and Mei felt invigorated by all that lay ahead. She realized that no matter the challenges and the whispers, what they shared was more significant.

"After meeting your parents, I feel like we've turned a corner," Kai said, breaking the comfortable silence. "We can be strong together and face any doubts others have."

"Yes," Mei replied, a soft smile growing on her lips. "I believe we can navigate through it all, and I'm ready to take this journey with you."

As they finished admiring the view, the reality of their circumstance began to seep back in. They still had to tackle the judgments of their peers and the complex weight of tradition that surrounded their relationship. But within her heart, Mei felt empowered to approach it with Kai by her side.

"Let's celebrate our victory tonight," Kai declared, his energy reigniting. "Ice cream, maybe? We can make it a real adventure!"

"Definitely!" she replied, laughter spilling over, waking her spirit back up. They knew life outside awaited, filled with possibility and joy.

As they made their way toward their next destination, Mei felt the beauty of the moment wrap around her—the sights, the sounds, and the laughter they shared. She glimpsed the cherry blossoms that continued to bloom in her heart, excited to embrace the challenges ahead, bolstered by the strength of their bond.

With every step, they moved toward the future together—hand in hand, ready to unfold the next chapter of their story.

CHAPTER 13

THE BREAKTHROUGH BY THE SEA

The sun hung high in the sky, its rays reflecting off the gentle waves lapping at the shore as Mei and Kai made their way to the beach. Excitement buzzed in the air, intertwined with the invigorating scent of saltwater, making Mei feel as if the world was opening up for them. It was the perfect day for a getaway, a brief escape from the swirling rumors at school and the weight of family expectations.

"Isn't it beautiful?" Mei exclaimed as they stepped onto the sandy beach, her spirits soaring with the sight of the sparkling ocean stretching out before them. Families dotted the shore, laughter ringing out as children built sandcastles and splashed in the shallow waves.

"Absolutely. I can't wait to feel the sand between my toes!" Kai said, his laughter infectious as he kicked off his shoes. Mei watched him, a smile growing on her face. His enthusiasm for life made her heart swell—the joy he radiated was a reminder of their shared connection.

They settled on a soft patch of sand, laying out a colorful beach blanket that Mei had packed. As they sat together, the warmth of the sun enveloped them, and Mei felt a relaxed ease wash over her—a stark contrast to the heaviness of the past week.

Taking a deep breath, she leaned back and let the sound of the waves lull her into a state of tranquility. Kai turned to her, a playful glint in his eyes. "Ready for some beach games?"

"Absolutely! What do you have in mind?" she replied eagerly.

"How about a game of frisbee? I brought one along," Kai suggested, pulling the brightly colored disc from his bag.

"Sounds good to me!" Mei said, playfully accepting the challenge. They raced along the shore, the frisbee soaring through the air as they shouted encouragements and laughter at each other's antics.

Each toss brought them closer, the playful competition serving as a balm for their insecurities. For those moments, the worries about school gossip and familial pressures melted away as they simply enjoyed each other's company.

After playing for a while, they flopped down onto the blanket, breathless and giggling. "I think we need a break before we pass out from all this activity," Mei said, wiping the sweat from her brow.

"I'd say that's a pretty solid plan," Kai agreed, leaning back and stretching out. The sun bathed him in golden light, and Mei couldn't help but admire the way his contentment radiated from him.

"C'mon! Let's go for a swim!" he suddenly suggested, sitting up with a spark of excitement in his eyes.

"Are you serious? Right now?" she asked, a thrill coursing through her veins at the thought of plunging into the cool water.

"Absolutely! It'll be refreshing, and we can cool off after all that running around," he replied, standing up and offering his hand to her.

She took it, feeling the familiar rush of electricity between them as they raced toward the waves. The moment they entered the water, a laugh escaped her lips as the cooler ocean splashed against her skin, invigorating and freeing.

Once they were submerged to their waists, Mei turned to face Kai, who was grinning broadly. The world around them faded, and in that moment, the connection they shared felt as vast as the ocean itself.

"See? Isn't this amazing?" he shouted above the sound of crashing waves.

"It is! I can't believe we waited this long to do this!" she laughed, feeling a sense of joy wash over her. They splashed each other playfully, laughing as they ran through the waves, the sunlight sparkling on the water creating a magical atmosphere.

After some time, they finally stopped, breathless from laughter and splashing. They floated on their backs, letting the gentle waves rock them as they gazed up at the blue sky. The vastness of the sea wrapped around them, and for the first time in a long while, Mei felt truly free.

"I'm so happy we came here," she said softly, taking a moment to soak in the experience. "This is exactly what I needed."

"Me too. Being here… with you… it reminds me that life is about cherishing the connections we have," Kai replied, his voice grounding her amidst the sea's ebb and flow.

For a moment, silence fell between them, filled only by the soothing sounds of the ocean. A rush of emotion washed over Mei as she turned to him, the warmth of the sun adding to the glow of their connection.

"You've changed my perspective, Kai. I truly feel like I can be myself around you. This moment… it encapsulates everything we've built."

Kai turned to her, looking deeply into her eyes, and Mei felt the intensity of his gaze penetrate her heart. "I'm glad you feel that way because you deserve to live your truth, Mei. No matter what anyone else thinks, you have every right to pursue your happiness."

His sincerity hung in the air between them, making Mei's heart race. The warmth of the sun and the gentle rocking of the waves felt like a protective embrace, cradling them as they shared this intimate moment. She felt her resolve strengthening under his unwavering support.

"I want to embrace that courage you see in me," she admitted softly, her breath catching as she continued to gaze into his eyes. "I'm ready to confront the judgments and live authentically, especially when it comes to what we have."

Kai smiled, a radiant light sparking in his expression. "That's my girl. Together, we can face anything. We'll build our own path, no matter the obstacles."

Feeling the tide of emotions surge within her, Mei felt a rush of affection. "Thank you for always believing in me and making me feel free to be myself. You really mean so much to me."

"I feel the same way," he replied, his voice filled with warmth. "You inspire me to be better, to explore more, and to embrace life fully."

Caught in the raw beauty of their vulnerability, Mei felt a pull, one that urged her to step closer. The world around them faded into a soft blur as she leaned her forehead against his, feeling a cascade of warmth envelop her. It was an unspoken understanding, a shared connection that seemed to bond them together amidst the waves.

In that enchanting moment, she felt the desire surge within her to close the distance further. Their lips met again—a soft, tentative kiss that quickly deepened, ignited by the raw passion and affection that had been building between them. The taste of saltwater mixed with warmth filled her senses, and as they kissed, it felt as though the universe had aligned perfectly, as if everything around them had taken a step back to allow this moment to exist.

When they finally pulled apart, breathless and giggling, the thrill of the kiss lingered in the air like a soft echo, sending shivers down her spine.

"Wow," Kai breathed out, his eyes sparkling as he looked at her. "That was… amazing."

Mei smiled, feeling elated from the shared kiss, her heart fluttering with joy. "I can't believe how right that felt."

"Neither can I. Here we are, just floating in our own little world," he said playfully, gesturing toward the expansive sea that sparkled under the sun. "Let's make tonight memorable and capture it all! How about we take some pictures by the shore?"

"Great idea!" Mei replied, the excitement bubbling within her once more. As they moved to gather their belongings, she felt lighter, buoyed by the love and connection that enveloped her.

After a delightful afternoon filled with laughter and poses against the backdrop of the ocean, they basked in the satisfaction of their playful photo session. Kai set up the camera on a nearby rock, capturing candid moments as they splashed water at each other, side by side on the beach.

Eventually, as they wrapped up their outdoor adventure, Mei checked her phone, noting it was getting late. "Maybe we should start heading back," she suggested, glancing at Kai, who looked content but a hint of sadness crossed his face.

"Yeah, but I'd much rather stay here with you," he replied, a soft sigh escaping him. "I can't believe how perfect this day has been. Moments like this remind me of how essential it is to embrace happiness when we can."

Mei nodded in agreement. "I wish we could bottle up this feeling and carry it with us forever."

"Let's keep creating moments like these—wherever life may lead us," he suggested, his words striking a hopeful chord in her heart.

As they made their way back toward the parking area, they walked hand in hand, relishing the peace and joy that lingered in the air.

But as they finally reached the parking lot and prepared to head home, the ominous weight of reality flickered at the corners of Mei's mind again, reminding her of the judgments and insecurities still lingering. The whispers from school, the gaze of classmates, and her parents' reservations came flooding back, threatening to overshadow the beautiful day they had just filled with magic.

As they climbed into the car, Mei could feel her heart pound with both excitement and apprehension. The challenges ahead loomed larger than ever, and she knew that the time for honest conversations was approaching again.

"Hey," she said, stealing a glance at Kai as they backed out of the parking spot. "Can we talk about what's next for us? I want to be prepared for whatever comes our way."

"Of course," Kai replied, his expression shifting to one of focus as he navigated the car onto the road. "What's on your mind?"

Mei took a deep breath, gathering her thoughts. The lingering excitement from their enchanting day began to blend with the worries she had carried back from school. "I think we both know that the gossip and the pressures from our classmates won't just disappear. I want to talk about how we can face those challenges head-on."

"I've been thinking the same thing," Kai said, glancing at her as they drove. "It's important to address these situations together, especially with you opening up to your parents about our relationship."

"Right," Mei responded, her confidence wavering slightly. "But what if we can't navigate it? What if external judgments or misunderstandings start to pull us apart?"

Kai's brow furrowed as he thought. "Look, all we can do is stay true to ourselves and what we feel for one another. If we let the opinions of others dictate how we feel or how we act, we risk losing the authenticity of what we have."

Mei nodded, appreciating his unwavering perspective, but anxiety still quivered in her chest. "I just want us to be prepared for anything. I know you support me, and that means the world. But I want to ensure that the pressure doesn't drive a wedge between us, especially when people keep bringing it up."

"Let's promise to communicate openly," Kai suggested, his tone growing serious as he focused on the road ahead. "If you ever feel overwhelmed or if there are moments you doubt us, I want you to tell me. We'll tackle it together."

"Definitely," she agreed, encouraged by his strength. "I just hope my parents stick to what they agreed on after getting to know you better. I don't want any misunderstandings to emerge."

"They'll see how happy you are with me. I believe in that," Kai said confidently. "But we just need to be patient. It takes time to break down perceptions that others hold, especially when it comes to love and relationships."

As they drove on, Mei felt a surge of hope gripping her heart. Kai's reassuring words blended with her ambitions for their future, echoing the promise they had made with each other. She could almost visualize a life where they could explore every possibility together, liberated from the weight of judgment.

When they finally arrived back in her neighborhood, the familiarity of home enveloped them like a warm embrace. Kai parked the car, and as they sat in the vehicle, the moment felt charged with tension, anticipation, and a shared understanding of what lay ahead.

"Tonight is the beginning of a new chapter, isn't it?" Mei said, her voice laced with both excitement and apprehension.

"It is," Kai replied, his eyes reflecting determination. "No matter what happens with your family or what anyone else thinks, you and I will face this together."

She looked at him, the warmth of his gaze giving her the courage she needed. "Thank you for always being my rock."

With that encouragement in mind, they stepped out of the car and walked toward her house. The air was filled with the promise of new beginnings, yet the weight of uncertainty still lingered at the edges of Mei's thoughts.

As they entered the house, her heart raced with the knowledge of what was coming. Would her parents be receptive again? Could they see past their traditional beliefs to truly understand the love she had for Kai?

Once in the living room, Mei's parents looked up from the couch where they were watching TV. They greeted her and Kai, sincere yet slightly reserved. She could feel their watchful eyes, searching for signs of how the evening would unfold.

"Hey, Mom, Dad," Mei said, summoning her resolve as she stepped forward. "Can we talk for a moment? It's about Kai and me."

Her parents exchanged glances once more, and she sensed their curiosity mixed with underlying concern. "Of course, what's on your mind?" her father asked, placing the remote aside.

Taking a steadying breath, Mei glanced at Kai, feeling the pulse of anticipation and anxiety quivering in her chest. This was the moment she had been preparing for, and she vowed to approach it with honesty and openness.

"I want to talk about our relationship again. I know things aren't always straightforward, but I need you to see how important Kai is to me…"

As she began to speak, the evening loomed ahead like a pivotal turning point, where love, family, and the truth of her heart would collide in the most meaningful way.

CHAPTER 14

THE ART OF CONVICTION

The days following Mei's heartfelt conversation with her parents passed in a blur of anxious anticipation. Though her parents had agreed to give her relationship with Kai a chance, she couldn't shake off the uneasy feelings swirling in her chest. The underlying tension about acceptance loomed over her like a shadow as she considered how to bridge the gap between her world and her parents' expectations.

Meanwhile, on the other side, Kai was not one to shy away from a challenge. He had taken it upon himself to create something special—a project that he hoped would help Mei's parents see him in a new light and appreciate their connection without the constraints of societal judgments. It was a gesture of love and conviction, and he wanted to show her parents that he respected Mei and where she came from.

On a bright Saturday morning, Mei received a text from Kai that made her heart race with excitement.

Kai: Hey, Mei! I'm working on something special for your parents. Can't wait to show you later!

Curiosity bubbled inside her. What could he be up to? She remembered how passionate he was about art, and the thought of him putting effort into something that could ease her parents' reservations made her heart swell with admiration.

A few hours later, Mei met Kai at the café where they often hung out. She walked in, excitement bubbling within her, and found him already seated at their favorite corner table, a sketchbook open in front of him.

"Hey!" she called, sliding into the seat across from him. "So, what's this surprise you mentioned?"

"Well," Kai began, a glimmer of mischief in his eyes, "I've been working on something inspired by you and your family. I think it might help convince them that our love is worth embracing."

He flipped the pages of his sketchbook, revealing a series of beautifully drawn illustrations. The first was a depiction of the cherry blossoms swaying in the wind—a symbol of beauty and transience that held significant meaning for both Mei and her parents. It was vibrant, with intricate details capturing the delicate petals and the energy of spring.

"Oh, Kai, this is stunning!" Mei exclaimed, her heart swelling with pride at his artistic talent. "You captured the blossoms perfectly."

"There's more," he said, turning the page. The next illustration was a layered scene featuring Mei and her family, gathered together under the cherry blossoms, framed by Tokyo Tower in the background. It encapsulated the essence of their connection—joy, warmth, and a sense of unity.

Tears pricked the corners of Mei's eyes as she took in the artwork. "This is so beautiful. I can see how much thought you put into it," she said, her voice thick with emotion.

"I wanted to create something that represents not just our love but also your family," Kai explained, looking intently at Mei. "I thought this could resonate with them. It's like an invitation to understand our journey together."

"I love it! You've truly captured what it means to blend our worlds." Her heart swelled with admiration for his thoughtfulness. "I can already imagine how my parents will react! This is going to show them how genuine we are."

Kai's eyes sparkled with excitement. "I was thinking that we could present it to them at the family dinner. I want them to see what I see in you, and this represents that perfectly."

Mei felt a rush of warmth for him, appreciating his effort to connect with her family. "Are you sure? What if they don't respond well?"

"We'll cross that bridge when we come to it. What matters is that we put ourselves out there, no walls between us," he said confidently, squeezing her hand across the table.

"You're right," she said, feeling encouraged by his conviction. "I can't thank you enough for this. It means so much to me—and I know it will resonate with my parents."

As the time went on, they discussed their strategies for the dinner, the best ways to frame their relationship, and how to showcase Kai's artwork more prominently. Mei felt a renewed sense of optimism, a driving conviction that this moment could solidify their connection.

After a few hours spent planning, they left the café hand in hand, and Mei felt lighter, determined to face her parents once again, this time armed with a beautiful reminder of the love and connection she shared with Kai.

When Monday came, Mei felt jittery as she approached class, the excitement of the upcoming dinner mingling with nerves. The whispers at school still floated around, but she was ready. She had Kai by her side, and his unwavering support became her shield against the judgment of others.

As the evening of the family dinner arrived, Mei helped prepare the dining area, laying out the table carefully, wanting it to feel special. She could sense the bubbling tension in her stomach as she and Kai finished setting everything up.

"Are you ready?" he asked, placing his hand on Mei's shoulder, grounding her as she stood amidst the bustling kitchen, setting the final touches on the dining arrangement.

She turned to him, taking in his warm smile, feeling a sense of calm wash over her. "I think so. I mean, I have to be, right?" she replied with a nervous laugh, her heart racing as she prepared for the conversation ahead.

"You've got this, Mei. Just remember to breathe. It's about honesty, and your parents want to see you happy," Kai encouraged, his tone reassuring and steady.

Taking a deep breath, Mei nodded, feeling a flicker of determination rise within her. "Okay, let's do this."

They moved toward the dining table, where her parents had already set the delicious dishes they had prepared—a fusion of traditional recipes with some modern twists—and Kai's carefully crafted obento artwork stood proudly on display. The combination of familiar scents made her heart swell with appreciation.

As they exchanged glances, the doorbell rang, causing her stomach to flip with nervous energy once more. "That's them," she whispered.

"Ready?" Kai asked again, his voice warm and sincerely encouraging.

"Yes." With a final nod for confidence, Mei opened the door to find her parents standing there, their expressions soft and welcoming as they greeted Kai.

"Good evening! Thank you for coming," her mother said, giving just a hint of warmth as they entered.

"Thanks for having me again," Kai replied, bowing slightly in respect as he carried the artwork toward the dining room. With Kai stepping into her home, Mei felt a surge of gratitude that he was there to share this moment with her.

Dinner kicked off smoothly, the atmosphere enjoying a mix of casual conversations and laughter as the food was served. Mei felt the warmth of her parents' hospitality wrap around them, even as she sensed their cautious eyes on Kai.

As they shared the meal, conversation flowed naturally, with Kai charmingly engaging with her parents. They discussed their interests and exchanged stories, the initial skepticism from her parents gradually lightening as they began to see the genuine warmth in Kai's demeanor.

"So, Mei has told us how passionate you are about art," her father said, probing a bit deeper. "What inspires your work, Kai?"

"I find inspiration in the everyday moments around me—how people interact, the beauty in nature, and even places like Shinjuku Gyoen with its cherry blossoms," Kai explained, glancing at Mei and offering a smile. "I love capturing emotions that resonate with people."

"That's beautiful," her mother remarked, a hint of admiration creeping into her expression. "You have a way of expressing feelings that can connect deeply with those who see your work."

While the conversation continued to build a bridge of understanding, Mei still felt the anticipation of the moment she had been waiting for—the moment to present Kai's artwork, to showcase their love in the hopes of garnering their approval.

Eventually, as the laughter and conversation mellowed following dessert, Mei cleared her throat, courage rising from within. "I wanted to share something with you both," she began, glancing at Kai, who offered her an encouraging smile. "Kai and I have something special, and I'd like to show you."

Her parents exchanged curious glances, and Mei felt the weight of their expectation settle upon her. With trembling hands, she carefully lifted the cover from Kai's obento artwork, revealing the intricate sketches that embodied her feelings and the connection she wanted them to understand.

"This is a piece Kai created, inspired by our relationship and the beauty of our connections—both in art and culture," she explained, her heart racing as she unveiled his talent.

As her parents leaned closer, examining the artwork, Mei felt a surge of pride swell within her as she listened to their reactions. "This is truly remarkable, Kai," her mother said, a genuine smile spreading across her face.

"Yes! The detail is incredible," her father added, nodding appreciatively. "You've captured the essence of these moments beautifully."

Mei's heart soared at their responses. It was a breakthrough—a sign that her parents were beginning to understand the importance of what she and Kai shared.

"What's more is that this artwork represents who we are becoming," Mei said, her voice filled with conviction. "It symbolizes the joy we find in one another and the strength we gain together."

Kai's eyes shone with admiration, a warmth spreading in the room as her parents took it all in. For the first time, Mei felt a sense of approval radiating from them, and it gave her hope that they could navigate the complexities of love and acceptance.

As dinner wrapped up, the atmosphere felt transformed. Mei could see her parents' perceptions slowly begin to shift, allowing room for acceptance and understanding.

After Kai said goodbye and promised to text her, Mei felt an exhilarating rush of triumph. As she closed the door behind him, she leaned against it for a moment, allowing the reality of the evening to wash over her—a beautiful culmination of her hopes, challenges, and a tentative embrace of her relationship with Kai.

"Did everything go alright?" her mom asked, stepping into the living room with a curious expression.

Mei turned to her parents, her heart swelling with gratitude. "It went really well! Kai showed you all his artwork, and I think you both genuinely liked it."

Her father nodded thoughtfully. "We can see how much you care for each other. I still believe that these relationships can be challenging, but if there's mutual respect and understanding, then we'll be supportive."

Mei felt a wave of relief wash over her. "Thank you for being open to getting to know him. I appreciate that you're starting to see how wonderful he is."

"There's a long way to go," her mother replied, her smile warm but cautious. "But as long as you communicate with us, we're willing to listen."

As the evening mellowed, the weight of anxiety lifted, leaving Mei feeling lighter. The day had marked a significant step forward, and she knew that with each moment, their connection deepened.

"I'm going to head to bed," Mei announced, a sense of accomplishment infusing her every word. "Thank you for dinner—and your support. I love you both."

"We love you too, Mei," her father replied, his voice filled with sincerity.

As she walked up the stairs, hope bloomed anew inside her heart. Tomorrow held its own possibilities, but she felt ready, and the next chapter of her journey with Kai was beginning to materialize.

When she lay down, she pulled out her phone, anxiously wanting to hear a message from Kai. After scrolling through her notifications, her heart leaped when she saw a text come in.

Kai: Hey! I'm really glad I got to meet your parents tonight. I enjoyed it!

Mei: Me too! It was a big step, but I think they're starting to understand us. Thank you for being amazing!

Kai: Always! Let's keep building those memories together!

As she drifted off to sleep, the echoes of their shared adventure filled her mind, painting her dreams with vibrant colors of hope and love.

The following week passed in a blend of anticipation and excitement. Each day at school felt different, as if the air had shifted—classmates still gossiped, but Mei had a renewed confidence that fortified her against the negativity. She relied on Kai's unwavering support, buoyed by their shared experiences and the openness between them.

Finally, the weekend arrived, and they planned to visit a nearby beach, looking forward to savoring another day of each other's company. As they made their way to the coast, Mei felt a swell of joy blooming inside her—another opportunity to solidify their connection.

Once they reached the beach, the waves kissed the shore, and the sun cast down a golden hue over everything. It was a perfect day, and Mei couldn't wait to dive into the ocean with Kai.

"Ready for another adventure?" he asked, his excitement infectious as they spread their blanket on the warm sand.

"Always! But first, we have to get through the small talk," Mei replied playfully, her anxiety momentarily forgotten in the embrace of the sea and sun.

As the day unfolded, they splashed in the waves, laughed, and built a sandcastle together—a representation of their bond and the intricacies of their relationship. Together, they felt invincible, free from judgment and surrounded by the beauty of nature.

Later, as they sat comfortably on their blanket, listening to the ebb and flow of the ocean, Mei turned to Kai, feeling the warmth of the sun wrap around them.

"Kai," she said, her voice softening, "I just want you to know how much I appreciate your support and kindness. It means a lot to me, especially with everything I've faced this past week."

He smiled back at her, his eyes shining with sincerity. "Mei, I'll always be here for you. We're a team—no matter what."

As the sun began to dip lower in the sky, casting a warm golden glow over the beach, Mei felt the moment crystallize in her heart—the bond they shared solidifying with each passing adventure, promising endless possibilities ahead.

But with the beauty of the evening came conflicting emotions, reminding her of the challenges that still lay ahead. The balance between her love for Kai and the lingering doubts of others was intricate, a tangled web formed from insecurity and fear.

"Whatever happens next, let's promise to keep being honest with each other," Mei said, trying to quell the storm swirling inside her.

"Absolutely," he agreed, leaning closer. "Honesty is key. We'll be open about how we're feeling as we face the challenges together. Trust me; I want you to feel secure in this."

Mei nodded, comforted by his unwavering support. "Thank you for being so understanding," she said, feeling a soft blush spread across her cheeks. The peace of the beach—the rhythmic sound of the waves and the warmth of the sun—created a comforting backdrop for their conversation.

As they sank back into the warmth of the sand, the playful energy around them ignited their spirits. They talked about everything, from dreams of future adventures to their favorite music, forging deeper connections through shared laughter.

Eventually, as the sun dipped lower, casting golden hues across the sky, Mei noticed Kai flipping through a sketchbook he had brought along. "Hey, I wanted to show you something I worked on recently," he said, a hint of excitement in his voice.

He flipped to reveal a series of sketches depicting scenes from the beach they were currently enjoying—waves crashing against rocky outcrops, children playing in the sand, and the sunset glowing behind the horizon. Each sketch captured the essence of the moment and the joy they had experienced together.

"Wow, these are incredible, Kai!" Mei exclaimed, her eyes wide with admiration. "You've really captured the spirit of this place."

"I'm glad you think so. I really wanted to document our day together," he said, a shy smile crossing his face. "I hoped it would remind us both of this adventure and how we've grown closer."

The gesture stirred something deep within Mei, igniting her affection and admiration for him. "It's so thoughtful," she said sincerely. "You always find ways to make our time together special. You really are talented, and it means a lot to me."

"Thanks, Mei. It helps me connect with my emotions," Kai shared, his gaze dropping for a moment. "And now, it helps me connect with you."

Feeling a rush of affection, Mei leaned closer to him, resting her head on his shoulder. The warmth of the moment wrapped around them, creating a perfect space for intimacy and understanding.

"It's amazing how much I've learned about myself since meeting you," she whispered, closing her eyes and letting the peaceful sounds of the surf wash over her. "You've opened my eyes to what it means to cherish the connections we build."

Kai glanced down at her, his expression shifting from playful to serious. "I feel the same way. Being with you has encouraged me to be brave and explore both my art and my emotions."

Mei's heart swelled as she listened to his words, but as the sun dipped below the horizon, painting the sky in vibrant purples and reds, a pang of worry pierced through her joyous mood. What if the storm of judgment returned? What if all this happiness was fleeting?

She pushed the thoughts aside as Kai gently turned her chin to face him, locking eyes. "Let's make a promise to keep this openness between us. No matter what happens with our families or others, I want us to communicate honestly about everything."

"Absolutely," Mei said, her voice soft but resolute. "It's important to me that we do that."

Feeling the moment shift, the air thick with unspoken emotions, they shared another gentle kiss—this one filled with sweetness and promise, reaffirming the bond they had nurtured.

Pulling back slightly, Mei looked into Kai's eyes, the glow of twilight reflecting the warmth they shared. "Whatever the challenges we will face, I believe we can overcome them together. You make me feel strong."

"And I'll always be here to support you. We're a team," he replied, quiet determination radiating from him.

With the stars beginning to twinkle above, they spent the remaining moments encapsulating their laughter and love, capturing the memories they were creating and the growth of their relationship.

But as they packed up the blanket and headed home, Mei couldn't shake the nagging doubts that lingered in the back of her mind. The upcoming conversations with her parents, the whispers from classmates, and the precarious journey of love still lay ahead.

That night, as Mei lay awake in bed, she resolved to tackle whatever challenges awaited her. She thought of how Kai had captured both her heart and her journey through his art, reminding her that love was worth standing for.

The next day held the potential for both joy and conflict—a day that could redefine everything she had hoped for with Kai.

A Love Heist

CHAPTER 15

THE MISUNDERSTANDING

The following week began with a ripple of excitement in the air as Mei prepared for another lunch date with Kai. After their beautiful day at the beach, their bond had deepened, and she felt a sense of hope blooming in her heart. But as the weekend slipped into the busy routines of school life, the old worries about her relationship lingered like shadows, waiting for an opportunity to resurface.

As she navigated through the hustle and bustle of the school corridors, whispers and glances from other students buzzed around her. Despite the warmth and confidence she had found with Kai, the nagging specter of gossip refused to fade entirely. Just when she had almost banished her worries, the universe had a way of reminding her just how fragile it all felt.

At lunch, they found their usual spot under the sprawling tree in the courtyard, the sunlight filtering through the leaves above, creating playful patterns on the ground below. Mei was particularly excited to share a new photo she had taken of the cherry blossoms after their beach trip, eager to keep the joy of their connection alive.

"Hey, check this out!" she exclaimed as she pulled out her phone, ready to share the image with him.

Kai leaned in closer, the warmth of his presence washing over her. "Wow, that's stunning! You really have an eye for capturing those moments, Mei." His admiring gaze made her heart flutter, and she felt a rush of happiness.

"Thanks! I think we should have many more photo adventures together," she suggested, already planning their next outing in her mind.

But just as they began discussing potential spots to visit, Mei noticed a group of girls from her class snickering nearby, casting glances in their direction. Her heart sank as she overheard snippets of their conversation.

"Did you see that? I heard they're pretty serious," one girl said, her tone dripping with sarcasm. "She's just looking for attention, dating someone like him."

Another girl chimed in, "Yeah, her parents are just going to love that. Isn't it, like, so embarrassing?"

Mei felt her stomach twist as the laughter rang in her ears, the familiar sting of judgment piercing her confidence. For a moment, she felt paralyzed, the bubble of joy that had surrounded her and Kai popping like a soap bubble in the midst of harsh reality.

"What's wrong?" Kai asked, noticing the sudden change in her demeanor, his voice laced with concern.

"I-I just overheard some girls," she stammered, the panic rising in her chest. "They're talking about us again, saying things that really hit hard."

Hurt flickered across Kai's face, and Mei felt a wave of guilt wash over her. "You don't need to worry about what they think," he said firmly, trying to reassure her. "They don't know anything about us."

"I know that!" Mei replied, a mix of frustration and fear choking her words. "But I can't help but wonder—what if they're right? What if I'm being naïve?"

"Mei—" he started, but before he could finish, the lunch bell rang, and students scrambled to their feet, their chatter filling the air and drowning out their conversation.

As they both stood, Mei's mind raced with confusion and anxiety. The whirlwind of feelings turned into a storm, causing her to draw away just as Kai leaned in for a comforting touch. Without realizing it, she began to retreat, her heart thudding in apprehension.

"I—I'll see you in class," she mumbled, walking away quickly, ignoring the way Kai's expression fell with concern.

The sudden panic clawed at her heart, and as she moved through the sea of students, she couldn't shake the feeling of potential loss looming over her. What if their relationship was fragile? What if their bond couldn't withstand the weight of others' judgments?

As the afternoon dragged on, Mei found it difficult to concentrate in her classes. Her thoughts kept drifting to Kai—his laughter, his encouragement, and the way they had shared their dreams together. She felt torn between the love she had for him and the insecurities expressed by her classmates.

Replaying the day's events in her mind, the whispers of doubt began to morph into an obsession. What if I lose him? What if everyone else is right? The fears that had been simmering beneath the surface began to rise like a tidal wave, drowning out the joy she found in their connection.

After school, as the final bell rang, Mei gathered her things with urgency, determined to find Kai and clear up the misunderstanding. But the weight of anxiety crippled her resolve, and as she headed toward the parking lot, she caught sight of him laughing with a group of friends, a genuine smile spreading across his face.

Her heart ached at the sight of him, but she felt panic grip her throat. What if he thought she didn't want to be seen with him anymore? What if he believed the rumors had gotten to her, that she was distancing herself because of their differences?

Without thinking it through, Mei spun on her heel and hurried in the opposite direction, her stomach twisting with regret. She had to clear her mind before facing him—before risking the chance of them miscommunicating and creating distance that she didn't want.

She found a quiet alcove in the school's courtyard, away from the prying eyes of classmates. Leaning against the cool stone wall, she tried to catch her breath. Why did I let their words affect me? she chastised herself. Every time she thought she was confident in her feelings for Kai, the insecurity reared its ugly head.

"Mei?" Kai's voice startled her, pulling her from her spiraling thoughts as he stepped around the corner, his eyes wide with concern. "Is everything okay?"

Panic surged through her; she could see the confusion and worry etched on his face. "I… I just need a minute," she stammered, forcing a laugh to disguise her anxiety.

"Talk to me," he urged, stepping closer. "Don't retreat away from me. Whatever is going on, we can face it together."

His insistence ignited a flicker of hope, making Mei's heart flutter and her resolve break. "I'm sorry, it's just—everything feels overwhelming," she admitted, unable to hold it in any longer. "I overheard what some classmates said, and I let their words get to me."

"I know people can be insensitive," he said, his voice steady and warm. "But what do they know about us? About our feelings?"

"Exactly! And yet, I still worry. I fear their judgment will push us apart," she confessed, feeling the pressure in her chest constrict her voice. "What if my parents don't understand? What if their expectations drive a wedge between us?"

Kai stepped closer, and this time, he wrapped his arms around her, pulling her into a gentle embrace. "Mei. Listen to me." He held her tightly, and she could feel the steady beat of his heart against her. "What we have is real, and I want you to feel secure in that. Don't let the noise from others cloud your view of what we've built together."

Mei leaned into him, letting his warmth envelop her as she felt the tension begin to dissolve. "But what if their opinions matter more than I want them to?" she murmured.

"They don't matter," he breathed against her hair. "What matters is that we support each other and communicate. If your parents start acting distant again, we tackle it. If the rumors get louder, we face them head-on. You're not alone in this."

With every word he spoke, Mei felt her worries begin to shrink as if his unwavering confidence was a lifeline pulling her back toward surface. "You're right. I need to trust that we can go through this together."

"I'm not going anywhere," he said, leaning back to look in her eyes. "We've made it through so much already. I'm committed to making this work, and I want you to feel the same."

With a newfound sense of clarity, Mei nodded, the resolve within her feelings reignited. This isn't just a phase; it's something real, worth fighting for.

"Let's navigate this together," she said, her voice stronger now. "I need your support just as much as you need mine."

"Always," he promised, his eyes sincere and full of affection. "Now, are you ready to show the world how amazing we are together?"

Mei laughed, her heart lightening. "Let's do this. But first, we need to get through the rest of the day!"

With their hands entwined, they stepped out of the alcove, returning to the world with renewed strength. As they walked through the halls, the murmurs still buzzed around them, but this time, Mei felt equipped to face whatever came their way.

Their resolve would be tested in the days to come, but with Kai beside her, she believed they could overcome any obstacle. Together, they would navigate the complexities of their relationship and the scrutiny of others, forging ahead into uncharted territory—where love and courage intertwined, promising to blossom even amidst doub

CHAPTER 16

EXPLANATIONS UNDER THE STARS

As the week progressed, the weight of gossip and scrutiny began to seep into the cracks of Mei and Kai's relationship. Despite their shared moments of laughter and warmth, each passing day brought with it new whispers that threatened the bond they had built.

Mei felt a growing tension in her chest, a mixture of anxiety and fear that clung to her like a shadow. Despite the resolve she had found, the murmurings around school were relentless. It seemed every new day brought fresh rumors—comments about their relationship rippling quietly through the hallways, punctuating her interactions with others.

"Did you hear?" a classmate would say, and though she tried to ignore the taunts, the sting of their words crept into her heart, each moment exacerbating her insecurities.

On Friday evening, after a particularly exhausting day, Mei found herself at their favorite park once again. She had invited Kai for what she hoped would be a chance to reconnect away from the noise. The warm summer air enveloped them as they walked under the canopy of trees, the evening sky deepening into shades of indigo.

"Thanks for coming out tonight," she said, shifting her gaze to the starry sky dotted with shimmering points of light. "I needed some time to think and breathe."

"I did too," Kai replied, glancing sideways at her. "It's good to get away from everything and just be with you."

As they found a small clearing, they settled on the grass, the soft blades tickling their legs as they reclined back and gazed at the stars. The peacefulness of the night resonated, yet Mei could still feel a slight tension that hung in the air between them.

"Kai," she began, her voice steady but edged with vulnerability, "I've been feeling a lot of pressure lately. The rumors, the whispers— everything… it's making me question things."

"I've felt it too," he admitted, turning his head to meet her gaze directly. "But I don't want to let them affect what we have. What matters is that we care for each other."

"I know that," Mei said, her heart racing as she searched for the right words. "But it's hard when other people seem to think they know our relationship better than we do. It's frustrating."

"That frustration is valid," he agreed. "But we have to find a way to navigate that together. I don't want you to feel like you're alone in this—because you're not."

His words resonated deeply within her, and as she looked into his eyes, filled with sincerity, she felt her worries begin to dissipate. "You make it easier to breathe. I feel strong with you," she confessed, letting herself lean closer.

"Mei," Kai continued, his voice softening. "I want you to know that no matter what others say, my feelings for you are real. I'm not going anywhere. We'll face whatever comes our way, together."

With every word, Mei felt the weight of the world lift slightly. The connection they shared was not defined by others but rather by the authenticity of their love—a love that promised to weather the storms surrounding them.

"I'm sorry if I've let my insecurities get in the way of our time together." Mei said, her voice wavering. "I never want to jeopardize what we have. You mean too much to me."

"I'm glad you're being honest," he replied, moving a little closer, so their arms brushed against one another. "Doubt is just as powerful as love when we're together, and we need to fight against that."

Beneath the shimmering stars, the tension from earlier began to dissolve, replaced by the warmth of shared understanding. Mei turned her head to watch the stars twinkle in the expansive sky, awash with feelings of contentment.

"You know," she said softly, "when I look up at the stars, I feel like there's so much more out there waiting for us—so many adventures we could experience together."

"I feel that too," Kai replied, matching her awe. "These stars, they're like the stories we're creating—each twinkle a memory, a moment to cherish."

Caught up in the moment, Mei felt the beauty of it all. "Whatever happens… I want us to keep creating our own stories, no matter what challenges we face."

"Now that's a promise I'm willing to keep," he said, his gaze locking onto hers with intensity. "Let's make every moment count."

And as they leaned closer, enveloped in the warmth of the night, they took a moment to simply be with each other—two souls connecting under a blanket of stars, ready to face the uncertainties together.

As the gentle breeze wrapped around them, Mei felt the love she held for Kai reaffirmed, the spark of their bond igniting a flame of hope for the journey ahead. The challenges they would face were undeniable, but in this moment, under the vastness of the night sky, she realized that together they could weather any storm.

"I really enjoy moments like this," Mei said, glancing over at Kai. "Just us, away from all the noise and distractions."

"Me too," he agreed, his voice low, grounded. "It's nice to have a space where we can just be ourselves."

The stars twinkled overhead like glittering diamonds on velvet, and as they sat in comfortable silence, Mei felt a sense of clarity wash over her. The tensions she had previously experienced began to dissipate, and in its place, a profound certainty emerged.

"I want to protect this between us," Mei finally said, her voice steady. "And I know that means I have to be honest with myself and my feelings."

"I want that too," Kai replied, shifting slightly to look at her directly. "We've built something special, and I don't want fear to jeopardize it."

He reached for her hand, intertwining their fingers once more, the warmth of his touch grounding her in the realization that they were in this together. The heartbeat of the city beneath them faded, replaced by the intimacy of the moment, and as she gazed into his eyes, Mei felt an unshakeable bond forming—a connection that transcended the noise of their surroundings.

"I can't help but feel grateful for you," she said softly, squeezing his hand. "You're so open and understanding, and it means everything to me."

"I feel the same about you," he responded, a hint of a smile breaking through. "You're brave for wanting to speak up about your feelings and face your fears."

Mei took a deep breath, feeling the weight of her emotions surge within her. "We've navigated so much in such a short time. I want to continue to embrace this, no matter what."

"I promise we'll face it all together," Kai said, his gaze unwavering, a mixture of determination and affection lighting up his features. "We'll explore those hidden places of happiness together."

Emboldened by Kai's conviction and the magic surrounding them, Mei leaned in closer. It felt as if the world had shifted, drawing them into a cozy bubble where only they existed. Her heart raced, and she could feel the spark igniting between them again.

"I've loved every moment that we've shared," she whispered as Kai gently brushed a strand of hair behind her ear. "And I want to keep discovering more—about you, about us."

Just then, an unexpected commotion broke the serenity of the evening. A group of rowdy classmates from school ambled through the park, their laughter ringing through the night like harsh bells.

"Oh look, there's Mei and her—friend," one of the girls jeered, her voice dripping with sarcasm. "How romantic under the stars!"

The comment stung, and Mei felt her face flush as a wave of embarrassment washed over her. Kai shifted, standing a little taller beside her, the protective instinct radiating from him. "Can you not?" he called out, his tone firm, defensive.

"Oh, what? Is the great artist now a bodyguard?" one of them said with a mocking chuckle, and the entanglement of whispers began to ripple through the nearby group.

"Come on, let's just enjoy ourselves," another voice chimed in, reinforcing the mocking tone as laughter erupted.

In that moment, isolation crept in around Mei, masking the bond they had just shared under the stars. The whispers felt heavy, smothering the joy she had found, igniting the insecurities that lay dormant.

Overwhelmed, she turned to Kai, a mixture of panic and longing swelling up inside her. "I'm sorry... I didn't mean for this to happen," she said, biting her lip, feeling the weight of the moment shift.

"Don't apologize for who you are or who you choose to love," Kai replied sternly, holding her gaze with unwavering intensity. "This is our moment, and we can't let them take that away from us. We're here together, and that's what matters."

Mei felt her heart swell with gratitude for his unwavering support, yet doubt gnawed at her. Would their love withstand the noise of judgment? Would she always worry about how others perceived them?

"We'll get through this," Kai reassured, a soft smile breaking through the tension on his face. "Let's keep focusing on us and on every incredible moment we create, regardless of the noise around us."

With that, he took her hand, intertwining their fingers in solidarity once more. The warmth of their bond reignited her resolve, reminding her of the strength they could manifest together. Despite the whispers and the doubts swirling around them, Mei felt a renewed determination to honor their connection and not let others dictate her feelings.

"Let's just enjoy the rest of the night," Kai said, his voice steady. "They can say what they want. We know what's true between us."

Mei nodded, taking a deep breath as she let the tension begin to fade. "You're right. I don't want to let them ruin this moment. We were having such a good time."

"Exactly," he replied, leaning closer, a playful smile dancing on his lips. "How about we head back to the karaoke spot later? We'll drown out their voices with our own!"

Mei couldn't help but laugh, feeling light again as they began to stroll through the park, the sounds of nature filling the spaces between them. The earlier abrupt confrontation began to shift into a memory, and she focused on the beauty of the night—the stars twinkling like diamonds above them, the gentle rustle of leaves in the breeze.

They found a quiet bench overlooking the park, where the faint glow of the city lights painted the horizon. As they sat, Mei leaned into Kai's side, their shoulders touching comfortably. In this moment of tranquility, she allowed herself to relax into the connection they had built, feeling safe in his presence.

"I love coming here," she said softly, glancing up at the stars. "It makes me feel like anything is possible."

"Me too," Kai replied, his voice low and heartfelt. "There's something magical about being under the stars, isn't there? It feels like all the worries below just fade away."

She turned to Kai, her heart full of affection. "You're right. It's like the universe is reminding us how small our struggles are compared to the beauty around us."

Kai looked at her, his gaze contemplative. "Speaking of beauty... I know we're facing rumors and challenges, but it still doesn't change how I feel about you. You deserve to go after what makes you happy without fear."

Encouraged by his words, Mei felt emboldened to stand firm in her emotions. "You make me feel brave enough to do that," she admitted. "I know it won't be easy, especially with the way people talk, but I want to embrace our relationship fully."

"Then let's do it," he said, his expression full of determination. "Together, we'll show everyone the real us. We'll make our own story."

As the night deepened, Mei felt the warmth of connection enveloping her, the comfort of knowing that their bond was strong enough to withstand anything life threw their way. They continued to talk about their dreams, their favorite music, and their aspirations, each topic drawing them closer while weaving the fabric of their relationship tighter.

Eventually, they shared a blanket under the stars, listening to the soft sounds of the city around them. Mei looked at their intertwined hands resting on the blanket, feeling a sense of peace wash over her as the fear of judgment receded into the background, replaced by the joy of being together.

"Hey, can I show you something?" Kai asked as he reached into his bag. He pulled out a sketchbook filled with his recent drawings, flipping through the pages with excitement. "I've been working on capturing what our time together means to me. Here, look!"

Mei leaned closer, her eyes wide as she took in the sketches he had created. Each piece reflected moments they had shared—laughter at karaoke, quiet moments under the cherry blossoms, and their time at the beach. Each drawing was imbued with emotion, radiating the vitality of their connection.

"Wow, Kai, these are incredible!" she exclaimed, her heart swelling with admiration. "You capture everything so beautifully. It makes me feel like I'm reliving those moments all over again."

"I wanted to make sure you understand how much you mean to me," he said, looking at her with an intensity that set her heart racing. "This is my way of expressing that."

The vulnerability in his eyes ignited a fire within her, pushing her insecurities to the periphery and reminding her of the love they shared. "Thank you for sharing this with me," she said, reaching out to trace her fingers gently over one of the sketches. "It means so much to see how you perceive our time together."

As they sat under the stars, surrounded by the warmth of their connection, Mei realized just how powerful their love had become. It wasn't impervious to challenges, but it was strong enough to endure whatever rumors and judgments lay ahead.

And in that moment, the clarity she had sought arrived—instead of fear or uncertainty, there was only a sense of profound understanding and love. The world around them faded as they sat together in contentment, surrounded by the beauty of the night and the magic of their blossoming relationship.

"Mei," Kai said softly, pulling her attention back to him. "I know things might get hard, but no matter what happens, I'm committed to you. I mean that with all my heart."

Tears of gratitude pricked at the corners of her eyes, and she couldn't help but meet his gaze, the warmth of his words igniting a fire within her. "I'm committed to you too, Kai. I want to embrace this relationship for all that it can be."

As they leaned in closer, the moment felt like a turning point—the culmination of their journey so far, a promise of what was yet to come.

Time seemed to stand still, the stars above twinkling like tiny affirmations of their love.

But as they shared a tender kiss, Mei's heart was momentarily pulled back to the reality of their circumstances. The worries about her parents' acceptance and the chatter from classmates threatened to creep in again.

"I wish I could be more carefree," Mei confessed, breaking the kiss and searching Kai's eyes for reassurance. "But it's hard when there are so many opinions swirling around us."

Kai brushed his thumb against her cheek, his gaze steady. "Mei, don't let their whispers drown out what we have. It's precious, and we need to protect it. People will always talk, but that doesn't dictate our reality."

Feeling buoyed by his conviction, she nodded, allowing herself to bask in the love and support he radiated. "You're right," she said, her voice gaining strength. "We'll keep navigating this together. I can't let fear dictate my happiness."

As they continued to talk, the sky shifted from dusk to a deep blue, revealing countless stars twinkling brightly above. The universe felt alive, and she couldn't help but think that perhaps it was a sign—a reminder that they were meant to be on this journey together.

"I want to make more memories with you," Mei said, her heart fluttering at the possibilities that lay ahead. "Every adventure feels like a new chapter just waiting to be written."

"Then let's make a pact," Kai suggested, a glint in his eye. "No matter what happens, we promise to cherish every moment we share, both the good and the challenging ones."

"Agreed!" Mei said, wrapping her pinky around his in their familiar sign of commitment. "Together, we can create a story that's uniquely ours."

As she settled into her thoughts, she felt a wave of warmth overcome her anxiety. With Kai by her side, things seemed more manageable, every challenge feeling surmountable if they tackled it together.

When they finally made their way back to the car, the anticipation of their next adventure filled the air. Mei glanced over at Kai, his energy vibrant and infectious, fueling her own excitement.

"I can't wait for all the memories we'll make," she said, letting hope wash over her like the gentle waves of the ocean.

"Neither can I," he replied, his expression serious yet playful. "And I promise I'll always bring my best self to this relationship."

As they drove through the twinkling lights of Tokyo, Mei realized that while the road ahead might be bumpy, she felt ready to embrace every twist and turn. With Kai by her side, the future felt bright, alive with possibility and love.

The clarity she had found beneath the stars, combined with Kai's unwavering support, made her feel invincible. She closed her eyes for a moment, breathing in the scent of blossoms and dreams—from this point forward, she was ready to forge her path, hand in hand with the boy who had captured her heart.

CHAPTER 17

FOLLOWING DREAMS TOGETHER

The following week was marked by a sense of renewed energy and inspiration for Mei and Kai. Following the heartfelt conversations they had shared under the stars, both felt invigorated to pursue their individual passions while nurturing the budding relationship that had taken root between them.

Mei found herself diving deeper into her photography, driven by the memories of their recent adventures and the encouragement Kai had given her. Every moment spent with him fueled her creativity, inspiring her to explore new techniques and stories to capture through her lens. In return, Kai dedicated himself to refining his artistic style, infusing his sketches with the vibrant emotions he felt while spending time with Mei.

One sunny Saturday morning, they decided to meet at their favorite café, a cozy nook filled with art and culture. The café buzzed with energy that matched their own, the mixed aromas of coffee and freshly baked pastries wafting through the air. As they found a table by the window, Mei felt the weight of excitement lift her spirits, perfectly aligned with the promise of the weekend ahead.

"Ready to plan our next adventure?" Kai asked, his voice bright as he pulled out his sketchbook. "I want to know what you've been dreaming about lately."

"Absolutely!" Mei replied, her heart racing with excitement. "I've been thinking a lot about capturing the hidden beauty within the city. There are so many unique places that people overlook."

"Like what?" he asked, his curiosity piqued.

"Well, there's an old shrine hidden in this alleyway near my neighborhood that I've been wanting to photograph. I think the contrast between the historical architecture and the modern streets could create a striking image."

"I love that idea!" Kai responded, his enthusiasm mirroring her own. "I could sketch the shrine while you take photos. It'll be a great way for us to experience it together while each of us documents our perspective."

Their eyes sparkled with excitement as they began brainstorming their next outing, feeding off each other's energy. "And there's that market on the weekend where local artists showcase their work. We could go there too!" Mei suggested.

"Yes! We could pick up some inspiration, meet new artists, and maybe even do a mini-interview segment with them about their art. It will help us grow as creatives!" Kai proposed, his passion radiating.

"I love that idea! Maybe I can feature some of their work along with my photos," Mei said, her mind racing with possibilities. "We can really develop our skills together."

As they continued to plan, the discussion shifted to their broader aspirations. Mei felt an urge to express her hopes, wanting to share everything that had been blossoming within her. "You know, I'm considering applying for a photography workshop this summer. It could help me refine my techniques and expand my portfolio."

"Do it! That sounds incredible! You'd be so amazing in that environment," Kai encouraged, leaning back in his chair with an approving smile.

"But what if I'm not good enough? What if I don't measure up?" she said, unease creeping in.

Kai shook his head. "Don't think like that. You are good enough. You have a unique perspective and talent. Plus, being in a workshop will help you grow and gain valuable feedback. It's an opportunity to challenge yourself."

His words ignited a spark of courage inside her, and she let out a deep breath, sensing that he believed in her. "You're right. Maybe this is the push I need to take my photography seriously."

"Absolutely! And whatever you decide, I'll be there supporting you. Just like I want to grow too; I've been considering taking my art to the next level as well," Kai admitted. "I want to hold more exhibitions and maybe even showcase our collaborative work."

"Your art deserves to be seen! The way you capture emotions is extraordinary, and I want the world to see it too," Mei affirmed, feeling empowered by his aspirations as much as her own.

Encouraged by each other's dreams, they continued discussing their visions for the future and how they could inspire one another. They felt invincible, two artists vying for growth and connection while supporting one another in their respective journeys.

After hours of planning and dreaming, they finished their coffees and packed up to leave, buzzing with creativity and anticipation. "Let's take this weekend to explore, document, and share experiences; we can pour our hearts into our art," Kai proposed.

"Definitely! I can't wait to see what we create together," Mei said, a sense of purpose brightening her spirits.

As they strolled through the city streets, the sun began to set, painting the sky in rich, warm colors. Mei felt the weight of her worries lift more with each passing moment, bolstered by the knowledge that she and Kai were both committed to pursuing their dreams while nurturing their budding relationship.

"Together, we'll create something beautiful," she said, the optimism flooding through her, intertwining seamlessly with the excitement radiating from Kai.

"Yes! I can already imagine the pieces we'll produce," he replied, his eyes bright with inspiration. "We'll capture our adventures and experiences, and maybe even share them with others through an exhibition one day."

The thought of showcasing their combined creativity filled Mei with enthusiasm. She felt that their journey wasn't just about her growth but about carving a space where they could share their love for art and each other with the world.

As they wandered through the bustling streets, the sun dipped lower, casting a golden hue across the radiant cityscape. "Look at how the light hits the buildings!" Kai exclaimed, pulling out his phone to capture the moment. "This is a perfect opportunity for you to take a picture!"

Mei smiled and set up her camera, framing the scene. She took the shot, feeling the energy of the moment flow through her, the world bursting with life as people moved like a dance within the urban symphony.

"Let's try out the new spot you mentioned later!" Kai chimed, his excitement infectious. "We can grab some dinner afterward—I want you to show me what Tokyo's food scene has to offer!"

"Definitely! I know just the place!" Mei said, enthusiasm bubbling within her. "There's a little restaurant I've been dying to take you to—it's famous for its ramen."

A shared adventure awaited, and as they continued walking, the conversation flowed effortlessly, punctuated by laughter and the thrill of new experiences. Each moment felt rich with potential, making Mei's heart flutter at what was to come.

As they approached the bustling ramen restaurant, the tantalizing aromas wafted through the air, pulling them inside. They chose a small booth and ordered an array of dishes to share, eager to immerse themselves in the varieties of flavor and culture.

"This smells amazing!" Kai exclaimed, his eyes lighting up as the steaming bowls arrived at the table. "I can't wait to dive in."

The warmth of the ramen filled the air, and as they dug in, the flavors exploded in their mouths, washing away any remnants of worry. They shared bites and recommendations, playfully encouraging each other to try new things. Mei loved seeing Kai's expression transform with each taste—his genuine reactions reminding her of how alive he made her feel.

"Every bite is better than the last!" he said, grinning from ear to ear. "I'm glad you introduced me to this place."

They settled into their meal, the warmth of the food and their connection creating a cozy ambiance that enveloped them.

"Thank you for pushing me to take risks with my art and career," he said suddenly, pausing while lifting his chopsticks. "You inspire me to follow my passion."

Mei felt her cheeks heat at his words. "You inspire me too, Kai. Seeing your dedication and creativity has encouraged me to embrace my dreams."

As they completed their dinner, Kai's expression shifted to one of determination. "Let's promise to keep this momentum going. We can support each other as we pursue our passions and artists."

"Absolutely," Mei agreed, feeling empowered by the idea of not only pursuing her dreams but doing so alongside someone who understood her completely. "We'll encourage each other and share our experiences—I want us to grow together."

With the promise of their future lingering between them, they finished their meal and walked back out into the street, filled with the warmth of their connection and the pleasant aftertaste of the delicious ramen.

As they reached the park that evening, surrounded by the glowing city lights, they decided to find a quiet spot to sit and talk about their artistic aspirations.

"Let's use this time to set some goals for ourselves," Kai suggested, sitting down on a bench that offered a perfect view of the sparkling Tokyo skyline.

"That sounds perfect," Mei replied, excited at the idea of visualizing their dreams together.

They settled in, the vibrant lights reflecting off their faces, and began discussing what they hoped to accomplish as individuals and as partners. With every spoken word, they began to map out a future filled with art, exploration, and the commitment to nurturing their connection.

But as the evening deepened, a shadow of doubt began to tiptoe back into Mei's mind. The earlier rush of excitement was tempered by the realities of the whispers surrounding them—the concerns about her relationship with Kai. Would their love be strong enough to endure the obstacles ahead?

With determination bubbling within her, Mei felt ready to address those fears, now more than ever. They would navigate this together, supporting one another through the challenges life would present.

"Together, we can conquer anything," she declared, her voice filled with conviction as she turned to him. "I truly believe that."

Kai looked at her with admiration. "I believe that too, Mei. Nothing can dim the flame we've ignited." As they sat beneath the shimmering city lights, Mei felt a profound sense of connection with Kai—a bond that shimmered like the stars above them. "Let's keep nurturing our dreams and support each other no matter what."

"Definitely," Kai said, squeezing her hand with warmth. "We'll create a space for both our artistic expressions. And any obstacles we face, we'll tackle together."

Feeling emboldened by his conviction, Mei turned to the skyline. "I can imagine it now—showcasing our work, the experiences we capture together, and sharing them with the people we love."

Kai's eyes glinted with excitement. "Maybe we can do a joint art exhibit one day, featuring your photography alongside my sketches."

"That sounds amazing!" she exclaimed, the prospect of their future igniting a flutter of joy. "I'd love to share our journey with everyone!"

As they continued to brainstorm ideas and highlight their aspirations, Mei felt the unease that had lingered in her chest began to dissipate. The laughter and familiarity they shared transformed the insecurities that once weighed her down into stepping stones leading toward their growing connection.

But as the evening began to drift into night, Mei recalled the whispers from earlier, the doubts that still clung to her thoughts. Would their resolve be enough to withstand the pressures and scrutiny from others?

"Hey," she said, a shadow of hesitation creeping back as she turned serious. "What if we encounter more resistance from classmates? Or if my parents change their minds after seeing the buzz at school?"

Kai met her gaze with a fierce determination. "Absolutely. We can protect our relationship and the joy we share. No matter what the world thinks, we have each other, and that's what truly matters. Remember, we made a promise to be open and communicate about our feelings. If anything arises, we'll confront it together."

Mei felt a swell of gratitude for his unwavering support. "You're right. I can't let doubts pull us apart."

As they made their way home, hand in hand, the comforting warmth of Kai's confidence and love filled her heart, pushing away the lingering worries she had been clinging to. The night felt alive with possibilities, and each step felt lighter, infused with hope for what lay ahead.

Once they reached her front door, Mei turned to face Kai, her heart racing with excitement. "Thank you for today. You've given me a renewed sense of purpose."

Kai smiled, a tender warmth in his eyes. "I'm proud of you, Mei. We're in this together."

As he reached to kiss her gently on the forehead, they lingered for a moment, basking in the connection they had forged. It was a sweet act of affection, and though the world outside still posed challenges, in that moment, it felt like nothing could ruin the bond they shared.

Stepping inside her home, Mei felt a sense of completion as the door clicked behind her. She had taken significant leaps toward her goals, and with Kai's unwavering support, she felt strengthened. But deep down, the external pressures still loomed, a reminder of the challenges that awaited her.

As she laid down that night, the warm embrace of her dreams quietly washed over her, allowing her to reflect on everything they had discussed. Tomorrow held new possibilities, and she felt ready to face it all— emboldened by love and the knowledge that together, they could confront whatever came their way.

CHAPTER 18

THE CHARMING RIVAL

The air was electric as Mei entered school the following Monday, the thrill of the weekend's adventures with Kai still fresh in her mind. Their heartfelt discussions and burgeoning love had added a vibrant layer to her life, and she felt optimistic as she navigated through the bustling hallways. But that optimism was soon met with the sharp sting of surprise.

As she settled into her seat in class, a handsome new face caught her attention. He was tall, with wavy dark hair and a confident demeanor that exuded charisma. Mei's gaze followed him as he sauntered in, effortlessly attracting the attention of her classmates, who whispered and giggled among themselves.

"Who's that?" Mei asked quietly, turning to Akira, who sat beside her, eyebrow raised at the newcomer.

"Oh, that's Yuki." He leaned closer, a hint of intrigue in his voice. "He's an exchange student from a school in Kyoto. I've heard he's quite the charmer."

Mei's stomach knotted slightly as she observed the way Yuki interacted with the other students. He had a magnetic presence, captivating anyone in his vicinity with his charming smile and laid-back attitude. It was impossible to ignore the buzz of excitement that followed him wherever he went.

When she caught Yuki's eye across the room, he smiled at her, a confident grin that sent a flutter through her heart. She smiled back politely, trying to shake off the unexpected feeling of intrigue.

As the period carried on, she couldn't help but notice how he seemed to gravitate toward her, joining her group during lunch. "Mind if I sit here?" Yuki asked, flashing his disarming smile. "I've heard great things about you."

Mei felt a mixture of flattery and awkwardness at his attention. "Um… sure," she replied, glancing subtly at Kai, who sat a few tables away, his expression unreadable.

As the lunch hour passed, Yuki regaled her classmates with stories of his travels and experiences in Kyoto, speaking with such ease that everyone hung on his every word. Mei could sense Kai's presence grow tense, a subtle shift in the air between them as the lunch crowd's laughter became focused on Yuki's charm.

"Have you tried the cafes here? I hear they're incredible," Yuki said, turning to Mei with genuine interest. "I'd love to check some out and capture the city's atmosphere with my camera."

Mei felt a tug of guilt. While she appreciated Yuki's attention, her heart belonged to Kai. "Actually, I have one in mind! My favorite cafe has the best matcha lattes and great photo spots!" she said, trying to steer the conversation back to their shared interests.

"That sounds great! Maybe we can go there together sometime," Yuki suggested, flashing another charming smile that made Mei blink in surprise.

Feeling the heat rise to her cheeks, she glanced briefly at Kai, who was now watching from a distance, his expression clouded with a mixture of frustration and disappointment.

"I mean… yeah, it would be fun, but I usually go with my friends," Mei replied cautiously, trying to maintain a balance between being polite and protective of her relationship with Kai.

As Yuki continued to engage with her and the table, Mei noticed Kai stand up, making his way toward their group. "Hey, can I cut in for a second?" he said, glancing at Yuki with a hint of tension. There was a possessive edge to his tone that heightened Mei's anxiety.

"Of course!" Yuki responded cheerfully, but she could sense the shift as the energy around them became charged with unspoken rivalry.

Once Kai took a seat next to Mei, the dynamic changed immediately. His presence filled the space—a surge of warmth and strength that reminded her of the bond they shared.

"Hey, how's it going?" Kai asked casually, though Mei caught the slight edge in his voice as he looked at Yuki.

"It's going great! Just talking to Mei about the cool spots in the city," Yuki replied, unfazed. He flashed a confident smile, oblivious to the undercurrent of tension beginning to bubble.

"Sounds like fun," Kai said, his tone friendly but protective. "Just so you know, Mei and I have plans this weekend to check out some projects together."

Mei felt a flicker of gratitude at Kai's instinct to stake their claim, but at the same time, she sensed her own insecurities creep in. Would Yuki's charm sway her friends and classmates to question her relationship with Kai?

"So, you two are working together?" Yuki said, raising an eyebrow as if assessing the dynamics between them. "That's cool. Collaboration is key, especially in art."

"Yeah, definitely," she said, trying to project confidence despite the feeling of insecurity lurking just beneath the surface. "I value Mei's creativity, and we work really well together."

Kai leaned in, the protective instinct woven into his demeanor. "We have some exciting projects lined up, and I believe our collaboration will produce some amazing results."

Mei felt warmth against the chill of uncertainty that had crept in with Yuki's presence. She appreciated Kai's support, yet felt the stirrings of jealousy bubble just beneath the surface, pooling at the edges of her mind. What if Yuki's charming demeanor drew her friends' attention away from Kai? What if her classmates began to question her choices again?

"Sounds like a solid plan," Yuki said, unfazed. His confidence radiated in a way that made it difficult for Mei to ignore. "I'm really interested in photography too. Maybe you could show me some of your work sometime, Mei?"

"Sure!" she replied, feeling a twinge of guilt as she denied the pull to indulge in Yuki's interest, hoping to bring the focus back to Kai. "But I actually have plans to go to a photography exhibit first with Kai. We're working together on that."

Kai glanced at her, relief flickering in his eyes for a fleeting moment, but the smile on his face faltered when he looked back at Yuki. "As Mei said, we have our projects, but it'd be cool to hang out with you and exchange ideas one day."

"Definitely," Yuki replied with an easy smile, though Mei noticed a glimmer of rivalry in his gaze.

The conversations continued, drifting in and out of various topics. Yet the tension remained, simmering just beneath the surface. Mei could feel Kai's subtle changes in mood; his humor was slightly strained, and she recognized the jealousy that crept into the edges of his smiles as the lunch wore on.

As the bell rang to signal the end of lunch, Mei felt a mixture of relief and dread. The kindness that Kai had shown her was strong, but she could sense his growing displeasure toward Yuki's undeniable charm. Every smile Yuki shot in her direction felt like a challenge—a reminder that a rival had emerged.

After the class, as they walked together, a heavy silence settled between Mei and Kai. "Are you okay?" she finally asked, breaking the tension. "You seemed a bit off during lunch."

"I'm fine," Kai said, his tone clipped, though she could tell it was anything but. "It's just… frustrating. I don't like how Yuki was flirting with you in front of everyone."

"It was just casual conversation!" she replied, feeling defensive. "He's friendly, and I didn't mean to encourage anything."

"I know that," Kai said, his voice softening slightly but still carrying a hint of pain. "It's just…it makes me feel anxious, especially when everyone's gossiping about us."

Mei nodded slowly, understanding. "I get it, Kai. I care about you, and I want to navigate through these rumors together. But I also want to be friendly without letting others dictate how I interact with people."

"Then let's make sure we're always communicating about how we feel, even when things get complicated," he said, his tone growing more collected. "I want us to face these challenges together without letting others come between us."

"Absolutely," she replied, feeling a sense of warmth return as they walked hand-in-hand through the school grounds, determination settling within her. "I promise we'll keep our connection strong no matter what happens. I want you to trust me."

As the days passed, the tension surrounding Yuki remained, aggravating Kai's jealousy and prompting frustrating conversations between them about the gossip that circulated through school. Mei found herself torn—wanting to keep her friendship with Yuki intact while simultaneously nurturing the beautiful connection she had forged with Kai.

Finally, she resolved to tackle her feelings head-on. One afternoon, as she sat in the courtyard, absorbed in her photography, she spotted Yuki approaching her. Determined, she steeled herself to communicate openly.

"Hey, Mei! Just wanted to check in. How's everything going?" Yuki said cheerfully.

"It's going well, thanks," she replied, trying to keep her tone light while feeling a twinge of apprehension. "I've been taking a lot of photos lately—experimenting with different lighting and angles."

"That's awesome! I'd love to see some of your work," he said, leaning against the table.

Feeling both intrigued and cautious, Mei decided to let him know her intentions. "I appreciate your interest, Yuki, but I thought I should clarify something. I just started dating Kai, and I want to make sure we keep the focus on what's real."

His expression shifted slightly, a flicker of surprise crossing his features. "Oh, I didn't realize. I'm sorry if I overstepped. I just thought we were all friends here."

"We are friends!" Mei reassured him, feeling the tension ease a little. "But I need to be clear that my relationship with Kai is important to me. I hope you can understand."

Yuki regarded her with a pensive expression. "I get it. I didn't mean to make you uncomfortable or create any drama," he replied, his tone sincere but carrying a hint of charm. "It's just that I find you really interesting, and I thought we could get to know each other better."

Mei hesitated, a mix of flattery and concern coursing through her. "I appreciate that, but I'm serious about my feelings for Kai. It's not just a fling; it means something."

"Fair enough. I can respect that," he said, nodding slowly. "I just didn't want you to think that I was trying to intervene or anything. I'm all about making friends, not stepping on toes."

"Thanks, Yuki. That means a lot," she said, feeling a cautious relief—but shadows of doubt still lingered. "I hope you can understand that I want to focus on my relationship with Kai. It's hard enough with all the gossip around school."

"No hard feelings, Mei. I'll back off and let you two figure things out," Yuki responded, offering a friendly smile.

"Thanks," she nodded, appreciating his willingness to respect her boundaries. But the encounter had sparked an unsettling awareness—a realization that the rumors surrounding them might not only come from students.

As the school day progressed, her mind wrestled with the lingering effects of Yuki's charm. Although he had promised to respect her relationship with Kai, she felt threatened by how easily he garnered attention and admiration from those around them. The fear of losing Kai to someone like Yuki simmered beneath her concerns, pushing her insecurities to the forefront.

When the final bell rang, Mei met Kai outside, and a wave of relief washed over her as their eyes met. "There you are! I was just about to text you," he said, a broad smile lighting up his features.

"Hey! I was just talking to Yuki," she began, needing to address the encounter.

"Oh? What did he want?" Kai asked, his expression shifting slightly as he sensed a hint of tension.

"He wanted to check in and clarify that he wasn't trying to come between us. He said he just thought we could be friends," Mei explained, watching Kai's expression carefully.

"That prick," Kai said under his breath, frustration clouding his features. "I don't trust him."

"I know, but he said it wasn't like that. I think he genuinely wants to be friends with everyone," Mei said, feeling the tightness in her chest return. "But it's making it hard for me to ignore the rumors when I see how easily he fits in. His charm feels like a threat, Kai."

"I get it," Kai replied, his voice tight with tension. "But you shouldn't compare us. I care about you in a way that means so much more than just being a casual friend. I wish everyone could see that."

Mei's heart ached at his frustration, recognizing how deeply he felt about the situation. She reached out to hold his hand, feeling the warmth and familiarity reassure her. "I know how much you care, and I want everyone to see that too. I'm with you in this, and I'm not going anywhere, Kai."

"I hope you know I'm not trying to make you feel uncomfortable or threatened by him," he said, the sincerity in his voice piercing through her insecurities.

"I trust you." Mei took a deep breath, grounding herself in that feeling. "This is about us, and the bond we're building together."

As they walked through the bustling school lot, Mei felt a flicker of determination. "Let's focus on our next adventure. We can push through the doubts and show everyone the strength of our connection. We have what counts."

"Exactly," Kai agreed, his mood lifting as they moved forward in conversation. "In the next few weeks, we'll make so many memories that it'll drown out whatever noise is out there."

As they climbed into the car, Mei felt the weight of the world shrink as warmth surrounded her. The conversations they shared strengthened their bond as if building an unshakeable foundation, equipping them for whatever lies ahead.

As they set out for their next destination, the sky opened up above them with beautiful hues of pinks and purples, offering the promise of a bright future filled with love, adventure, and creative spirits.

Later that weekend, as they arrived at the photography exhibit they had been looking forward to, the spark of excitement reignited. The two young artists stepped into the venue, lights twinkling around them amidst a buzz of creativity and inspiration that filled the air.

Together, they wandered through the galleries, capturing the essence of each piece of art in their minds and on camera. Mei felt a rush of excitement with every photograph she took; the different styles and techniques inspired her, making her heart swell with possibilities as they delved deeper into the exhibits.

"Look at this one!" Kai exclaimed, pointing at a striking photograph of a bustling Tokyo street at twilight, vibrant colors contrasting with the soft glow of neon signs. "The way the artist captures movement, it almost feels alive!"

Mei nodded, already framing the piece through her lens. "It's incredible! The use of lighting is phenomenal. I can only imagine the stories behind each person captured in that moment."

As they moved through the exhibit, they shared thoughts and discussed their dreams, their excitement deepening with each piece they saw. Mei felt the connection between them grow even stronger; being surrounded by creativity and inspiration heightened her appreciation for the journey they were both embarking on.

When they reached the final gallery, a series of photographs depicting serene landscapes caught Mei's eye. She was drawn to a breathtaking shot of the sea at sunrise—soft waves lapping at the shore bathed in golden light, the tranquility radiating from the image.

"Wow," she breathed, stepping closer to examine the photograph, appreciating the craftsmanship and emotion that flowed from it. "This is beautiful. I want to capture moments like this."

"Let's recreate it," Kai suggested, enthusiasm igniting in his voice. "We'll find our own spot by the water someday! Just the two of us."

A smile broke across Mei's face. "I'd love that!" she said, envisioning the sunrise at the beach, capturing the moments with him.

The atmosphere began to shift subtly as they lingered on this thought, a promise underscoring the air. The whispers of doubt began to fade, replaced with the possibilities that lay ahead, filled with adventures yet to be experienced together.

As they exited the exhibit, the warm glow of evening beckoned outside. The city buzzed with life, and the anticipation of what came next filled Mei with excitement. She felt alive with the vibrancy around her, and her heart was lighter, ready to embrace every challenge.

But as they made their way back to the parking lot, her thoughts turned back to the rumors and the attentiveness of classmates. Would they still allow themselves to enjoy these moments without the judgment of others weighing them down?

Just as they reached the car, they turned a corner and encountered Yuki once again, who was flanked by a group of friends. Seeing them together, his expression shifted to one of smug amusement. "Well, well, if it isn't the artists in action. Still painting the town with creativity, I see," he remarked, a smirk on his face.

Mei felt her stomach churn at the sight of him and the tension rising. Kai's grip tightened around her hand, and he stepped slightly in front of her, positioning himself protectively. "What do you want, Yuki?" Kai asked, his voice steady yet firm.

Yuki shrugged, clearly enjoying the moment. "Just thought I'd see how you two are doing. Heard you were out and about today—nice to see you haven't been held back by all the, well, noise."

Mei felt the heat rise in her cheeks, the anxiety tugging at her as she met Kai's protective gaze. "We're just enjoying ourselves," she said, trying to sound confident amidst the pressure. "And trying to ignore the rumors."

"Good luck with that," Yuki said with a dismissive tone, flashing an infuriating smile. "You know they won't just disappear."

With that, he sauntered off, laughter echoing from his friends as they continued down the path, the tension hanging heavily between Mei and Kai.

"Are you okay?" Kai asked, concern etched across his face as they stepped away from the loitering group.

"I'm fine—just frustrated," she responded, feeling the knot tightening in her stomach again. "Why does he have to make everything so difficult?"

"Because he thinks he can," Kai said, his tone deepening with frustration. "But don't let him get to you. What matters is us, not what he or anyone else thinks."

Taking a deep breath, Mei felt the anxiety start to rise again but reminded herself of the strength they shared. "You're right. But it's hard not to feel pressured."

As they drove home, the weight of their earlier encounters lingered in the air. Mei's mind wrestled with thoughts of the challenges ahead, the burden of rumors still fresh in her mind.

Arriving home, she felt both exhausted and hopeful. The day had been filled with joy, but the specter of doubt still lingered. Thoughts of how to solidify her relationship with Kai amidst all the external judgment pulsed through her mind.

As she stepped inside, the comforting aroma of her mother's cooking wafted through the hallways, calming her racing heart. But beneath that comfort lay the unease of the upcoming dinner—the meal where she'd have to navigate the delicate dance of her relationship with Kai while facing her parents' concerns head-on once more.

"Hey, Mei! How was the exhibit?" her mother called from the kitchen, her voice filled with warmth and curiosity.

"It was really good! I had fun," Mei responded, forcing a smile as she set her bag down. It was true, but the reality of her struggles weighed heavily in the air.

"Did you take lots of photos?" her father asked, stepping into the hallway.

"Yeah, I did! I'll show you later," she said, her heart fluttering with enthusiasm. She wanted to share her passion with them, hoping it would help bridge any remaining gaps in understanding.

But as she headed toward the kitchen, the thoughts of Yuki's smirking face and the whispers in the halls crept back in, clouding her mind with insecurities once more. Would her parents still worry about her choice to date Kai after hearing the gossip? Would they see Yuki as a better option simply because he fit the mold of what they traditionally expected?

"Mei! Are you okay? You seem a little distant," her mother noted, noticing the shift in her demeanor.

"I'm fine, just thinking about school," she replied quickly, knowing that the last thing she wanted was to lay this burden on her family.

After dinner, Mei retreated to her room to process everything. She pulled her camera from her bag and scanned through the photos she had taken at the exhibit. With every click, memories of joy and connection flooded back, but the warmth of those moments was stifled by the bitterness of doubt.

Just then, her phone buzzed—a text from Kai lighting up the screen.

Kai: Hey! Just checking in. How's your evening?

A rush of warmth filled Mei at the sight of his message, the reminder of how solid and caring he was cutting through the fog of her worries.

Mei: Hey! Dinner went well, and the exhibit was amazing. Just feeling a bit overwhelmed. Some things happened today…

The response came quickly.

Kai: I'm here if you want to talk about it. Remember our promise about communicating?

Mei felt a swell of affection for Kai as she typed back, needing his reassurance.

Mei: Yuki was at the exhibit today, and he's been making comments that have gotten under my skin. I'm worried about the rumors and how they might affect us.

Kai: Don't let him get to you. You're strong and incredible. We can face these rumors together!

Mei's spirits lifted slightly.

Mei: You always know what to say. Thank you for being my rock. I really appreciate you.

She put her phone down and let the weight of her thoughts begin to untangle. Despite Yuki's comments, she knew that her relationship with Kai was built on a foundation of trust and love, and she had to believe that would shine through the darkness of gossip.

As the moonlight spilled through her window, illuminating her room, Mei felt the resolve crystallize—she would stand firm in the face of adversity, with Kai beside her. They would navigate the complexities together and embrace their connection, no matter the challenges that lay ahead.

The next day at school, Mei decided to confront her classmates about the rumors. She held her head high, determined to reclaim her narrative and express the truth of her feelings for Kai. As she entered the bustling hallway, her heart raced, but this time it was fueled by resolve.

With a mix of nerves and excitement bubbling within, she spotted a group of friends crowded together, including Yuki. As apprehension flickered in her

chest, she approached them, ready to voice her truth and draw a line against the whispers.

"Can we talk?" Mei said firmly, locating her gaze on Yuki. They needed to hear her out, and she wasn't going to hold back any longer. All the support she felt from Kai fortified her courage, priming her to stand up for the love she cherished.

CHAPTER 19

STANDING UP FOR LOVE

Mei stood at the entrance of the bustling cafeteria, her heart pounding in her chest as the midday rush of students flowed around her like a tide. The laughter and chatter felt overwhelming yet electric, the air thick with anticipation. Today was the day she would confront the rumors swirling around her relationship with Kai, words that had felt like thorns in her side for too long.

Taking a deep breath, she spotted Yuki and his friends across the room, gathered around a table, the same skeptical expressions lingering on their faces from the last encounter. The moment she made eye contact with Yuki, he smirked—an expression she could no longer tolerate.

With Kai by her side, she felt a flicker of strength bolster her resolve. "Are you ready?" he asked, sensing the determination etched across her features.

"I think so," Mei replied, clenching her fists to steady her nerves. "It's time to set the record straight."

Together, they approached Yuki's group, and as they drew closer, a mix of tension and anticipation hung in the air. The chatter quieted slightly as they noticed her presence.

"Hey, Mei! You look serious. What's up?" Yuki called out, his tone casual but dripping with insincerity.

The others looked on, curiosity piqued, and Mei felt the heat rise in her cheeks as all eyes landed on her, but she pressed on, the warmth of Kai's hand offering her confidence. "We need to talk about the rumors that have been circulating around school about Kai and me."

"Oh? Is this about your little romance?" one girl chimed in, smirking as the rest of the group stifled laughs. Her words felt like daggers, pricking at Mei's insecurities.

"Yes, it is," Mei said, her voice steadying as she pushed through the discomfort. "I want to clarify that my relationship with Kai is important to me. What you're saying is hurtful and, frankly, unnecessary."

Yuki raised an eyebrow, feigning surprise. "Look, we're just surprised to see you two together. It's a little… unexpected, given your backgrounds."

Mei felt the tension ripple through Kai as he stepped forward, standing protectively beside her. "What does that even mean?" he asked, his voice firm but calm. "Why should anyone judge what makes Mei happy based on assumptions about differences?"

"Yeah, it's not like anyone else has a say in our relationship," Mei added, feeling Kai's confidence bolster her resolve. "I respect my family, and I expect friends to do the same. This isn't about race or background; it's about love."

Yuki smirked, clearly enjoying the spectacle. "Look, we're just saying what most people think. You can't expect everyone to get on board with it, especially when it's not conventional."

"Love is not about convention," Kai shot back, a protective fire igniting within him. "It's about connection, understanding, and the respect we have for one another. If you can't see that, then maybe you should take a moment to reflect on your own perspectives."

The cafeteria fell silent, the weight of Kai's words hanging in the air, and Mei felt pride swell within her. She glanced around, and for the first time, she spotted a few classmates who were nodding in agreement, silently supporting them from the sidelines.

"Mei is brave for owning how she feels. That's what matters," one girl finally said from another table, and Mei felt encouraged by the scattered support.

"Exactly! We all should celebrate love, regardless of background," another student chimed in, and a wave of murmured agreement swept through the room.

Realizing the tide was beginning to shift against the negativity, Mei pressed further. "I'm proud of my relationship with Kai, and the joy he brings into my life is undeniable. So if you continue to spread these rumors, you're not just misjudging me, you're misunderstanding love."

As she spoke, confidence surged through her, the supportive voices around her lifting her spirit higher. Though she knew not everyone would understand, this moment allowed her to reaffirm her dedication to Kai without yielding to doubt.

"Why don't we all just move on?" Yuki said, masking his irritation with a casual tone, perhaps sensing that the crowd was beginning to turn against him.

"Agreed," Kai added, holding Mei's hand tighter as they stepped back. "We're here to live our lives, not be under a microscope for everyone else's entertainment. If people are going to talk, they might as well say something meaningful."

With that, Mei and Kai turned to walk away, leaving behind murmurs of shock, confusion, and reluctant admiration. As they exited the cafeteria, their fingers still entwined, a sense of strong relief washed over Mei, washing away the remnants of doubt and fear.

"I can't believe we actually did that," Mei said, her pulse racing as they navigated through the halls toward the exit. A sense of exhilaration mixed with disbelief coursed through her. "I was so nervous, but I can't tell you how good it feels to stand up for what I believe in."

Kai smiled, a spark of pride illuminating his face. "You were incredible, Mei. I knew you had it in you."

The warmth of his praise flooded her with confidence. "I just wanted to show everyone how real this is—how real we are. I don't want others' opinions to dim what we've built."

"Exactly! And look, a few of your classmates are clearly on board with us. That helps!" Kai said as they stepped out into the fresh air, the sunlight spilling over them and wrapping around them like a warm embrace.

As they walked together, a sense of relief washed over Mei. The pressure that had felt so heavy moments ago began to lift, replaced by a rush of hope and determination. "I'm so grateful to have you by my side. I couldn't have faced them without your support."

"Mei," Kai said, stopping to face her, "this is just the beginning. We're going to keep supporting each other, no matter what happens. I'm with you through thick and thin."

They shared a soft smile, the bond they had cultivated feeling even more substantial after facing the day's challenges together. It was as if they had weathered a storm, hand in hand, and emerged stronger on the other side.

Later that afternoon, they decided to treat themselves to a small celebration, stopping for bubble tea at a nearby shop, letting the stress melt away with each sip. The bright colors and playful atmosphere of the shop added to the joy bubbling inside them.

"Here's to us," Kai said, raising his drink with a charming grin. "And to all the adventures we will continue to have together."

"To us!" Mei echoed, clinking her cup against his, feeling the energy of hope surge as they settled in at a cozy table by the window.

As they sipped their drinks, laughter and playful banter flowed freely, drawing Mei further into the moment. But even amidst the joy, a thread of worry still tugged at her heart.

"Do you think my parents will really come to accept this?" she asked, the question lingering in her voice. "It's so important to me, but I still feel that tension hanging in the air."

Kai paused for a moment, his expression thoughtful. "I think it's going to take some time, Mei. But the fact that they've agreed to meet with me shows that they're willing to be open. That's a good sign."

"I hope so," she said, gazing out of the window as the world buzzed around them. "I just want you to see how beautiful this connection is. I want them to see it too."

"Just be patient with them. It's a journey for everyone involved," Kai reassured her, his tone soothing. "We'll handle it together, step by step."

As they finished their drinks, she felt fueled not only by the sugar but also by the encouragement that came from knowing they were aligned in their feelings and commitment to one another.

Later that night, as they parted ways at the train station, Mei turned to Kai, feeling the swell of emotions rise again. "Thank you for today. You really made me feel empowered to speak up."

"I'll always be here for you, Mei," he said, looking deeply into her eyes. "Whatever comes next, we'll face it together."

With a lingering kiss on her forehead, they exchanged smiles before parting ways, the promise of the future shimmering brightly on the horizon.

As she made her way home, Mei felt a renewed sense of purpose. The challenges awaiting her were still present, but she felt ready to embrace them, fortified by the love and support that she and Kai shared.

Tomorrow would bring new challenges, and she resolved to face them with the same courage she had shown today. Whatever the world threw at them, she was determined to hold onto the light they had cultivated, confident in their shared journey of love and understanding.

CHAPTER 20

THE BEAUTY OF ACCEPTANCE

The days following Mei's confrontation with her classmates dragged on, yet she felt a newfound sense of resilience. Each morning, she stepped into school with Kai by her side, their hands intertwined like a shield against the whispers and rumors that hung in the air. No longer were the opinions of others dictating her happiness; she had come to embrace her relationship with unwavering confidence.

As the week progressed, Mei felt the weight of uncertainty about her parents slowly lifting. They had agreed to a family outing with Kai, giving her hope that things were beginning to shift. Deep down, she could sense that her parents were starting to see the positive influence Kai had on her life—how he brought her joy, creativity, and a sense of purpose.

The day of the family outing arrived, and Mei was a bundle of nerves and excitement as she prepared to head out. She chose a cheerful sundress adorned with colorful flowers, a reminder of the happiness that bloomed in her heart whenever she thought of Kai.

When her family arrived at the designated meeting spot—an art festival showcasing local talents—she saw Kai waiting under a vibrant archway, the sunlight dancing across his features. His warm smile and delighted wave sent a rush of happiness through her.

"Hey! You look amazing!" he beamed as she approached, taking in her radiant appearance. "Are you ready for an adventure?"

"More than ever!" she exclaimed, feeling her spirit lift with his infectious enthusiasm.

As they entered the festival, they were greeted by a whirlwind of colors, sounds, and scents. Stalls showcasing various art pieces lined the pathways, bands played lively music, and the air filled with laughter and conversation.

"Let's see what we can find!" Kai said, pulling her along, their hands still linked. Mei felt an invigorating sense of freedom wash over her as they strolled down the bustling lanes, sharing thoughts and impressions on the art they encountered.

As they wandered, Mei caught glimpses of her parents nearby, observing them interact with other families and art vendors. There was a certain ease about them today, and she noted their smiles exchanged with those around them, a hint of openness emerging that hadn't been present before.

"Look at that painting!" Kai exclaimed, pointing at a vibrant canvas that depicted a busy Tokyo street, full of life and color. "We should definitely take a photo with it!"

"Sure," she replied, her cheeks lighting up with enthusiasm as they stood before the artwork, capturing the joyful moment with her camera.

As they took turns posing, Mei felt an urge to turn back and see how her parents were reacting. When she glanced over, she saw them standing together, watching the two of them with looks of cautious admiration.

"See, they're enjoying the atmosphere," Kai said, noticing her gaze. "I think they're starting to appreciate this side of you—of us."

Mei felt a warmth cresting in her chest—perhaps this was the moment they would come to see Kai for the incredible person he was.

After meandering through more stalls, they finally stopped at one highlighting canvas art from a local artist. The vibrant pieces depicting scenes of community life and family resonated with Mei deeply. She approached the display, lost in thought.

"Here's something that really speaks to me," she turned and said to Kai, pointing at a piece that represented a blossoming tree encircled by families.

"Absolutely. It captures the essence of togetherness beautifully," he replied, admiration sparkling in his eyes as he stood beside her, looking at the piece.

Just then, her parents walked up. "What do you think of that piece, Mei?" her father asked, genuinely curious.

"It's about families coming together and supporting each other, just like how art does," she replied earnestly, glad to include her parents in the conversation.

"It really is a striking piece," her mother remarked, examining the artwork closely. "The colors and emotions... it's like their connection to each other is palpable."

In that moment, Mei could see the cogs turning in her parents' minds—how they were beginning to recognize the importance of togetherness, acceptance, and support, both in art and relationships.

After some discussion about the artwork, Mei's parents moved to the next stall, and she and Kai stepped aside.

"Do you think they're starting to understand?" Mei asked, her voice filled with hopeful uncertainty.

"Definitely," Kai replied confidently. "You were brave in your conversations with them, and it seems like they're starting to see how happy you are with me. They're willing to open up."

As the festival unfolded around them, the joyous atmosphere filled Mei's heart. She felt lighter, buoyed by the love that surrounded her, and as they continued exploring the festival together, both the whispers from classmates and her previous doubts began to fade into the background.

Kai's positive influence had begun to ripple through her life, bridging the gap between her worries and the burgeoning happiness she found in their relationship. As they explored the art festival, Mei immersed herself in their surroundings—each painting, sculpture, and piece of art reflecting the vibrancy and emotion that resonated so deeply within her.

"Let's check out that pottery booth!" Kai said, pointing toward a colorful display across the courtyard. "I've always wanted to try my hand at making something like that."

"Me too!" Mei exclaimed, the enthusiasm bubbling to the surface. "Maybe we could take a class together and make our own pieces!"

They made their way to the pottery booth, where they eagerly browsed through the array of ceramics. The artisans spoke passionately about their work, explaining the techniques behind their creations. Mei felt a spark of inspiration ignite within her, awakening the creative side that thrived on exploration.

"Look at this one!" Kai held up a beautifully crafted ceramic bowl adorned with intricate designs. "This would be perfect for holding treats at home."

Mei nodded, admiring the craftsmanship. "And think of the stories behind each piece; they carry so much emotion and energy. Just like the art we've been talking about."

As they continued to wander, she caught her parents out of the corner of her eye, engaged in a lively discussion with another couple. The ease of their interactions made her heart swell; maybe they truly were beginning to open their hearts and minds.

"Let's get our parents some food and bring it over," Kai suggested, noticing Mei's gaze. "It might give us an opportunity to bond even more as a group."

"Great idea!" Mei replied, the thought of sharing a meal fostering an optimistic sense of hope.

Together, they made their way to a local food vendor, collecting a variety of snacks that showcased the cultural fusion of the festival. They selected savory dishes, sweet treats, and everything in between.

As they approached her parents, carrying the bounty of food in both arms, Mei felt a blend of nervous anticipation and excitement. "We thought you all might want to share some snacks with us!" she announced, a smile gracing her face.

Her parents turned, surprised but pleased as they accepted the offerings. "Thank you, Mei! This looks delicious," her mother said, her eyes twinkling as they began to sample the dishes.

As they gathered around a nearby table adorned with artful decorations, the atmosphere brightened. The conversation deepened as they bonded over food, laughter, and shared stories. Mei felt a sense of warmth envelop her, the earlier tension melting away under the weight of connection and understanding.

"So, Kai, what are your plans after school?" Mei's father asked, genuinely interested. "Do you have ambitions for your art?"

"Yes, I'd love to hold exhibitions and workshop my techniques," Kai answered, his enthusiasm palpable. "I believe art can forge connections, and I want to share that experience with others."

"Impressive," her father remarked, nodding appreciatively. "It's clear you have a passion for it. Mei speaks highly of your work, and it's nice to see someone dedicated to their craft."

Mei watched as a subtle smile crept onto her mother's face, clarified approval beginning to shine through. Could it be that they were starting to see Kai for who he truly was?

The conversation flowed, mixing laughter and storytelling as the families shared their experiences—revealing common ground and bridging gaps. Kai's easygoing nature fostered a sense of familiarity that Mei had hoped for, opening her parents' hearts a little wider.

As the festival continued around them, a broader understanding began to unfold. Mei could sense the warmth growing around the table, the differences that had once felt daunting now serving as a backdrop to a beautiful tapestry they were creating together.

"Thank you for including us in this," her mother said earnestly, her tone genuine. "It's nice to see you both like this, enjoying each other's company."

"Of course," Mei replied, glancing at Kai, whose face lit up at the compliment. "I really wanted you to get to know each other. It means a lot to me."

As the sun began to set, casting a golden hue over the event, Mei felt hope swell deep within her. The bond they had fostered that day felt strengthened as they all shared food, laughter, and a promise of new beginnings.

However, as they wrapped up their meal and prepared to explore more of the festival, Mei felt the weight of lingering insecurities creep back in. The struggle to maintain that balance between love and societal judgments was still present, and while her parents had become more accepting, there remained a feeling of uncertainty about navigating the outside world.

But with Kai by her side and her parents tentatively embracing this new dynamic, Mei felt empowered to take the next step toward embracing her identity as a person in love.

As they walked through the festival, the sun setting gently on the horizon, Mei felt a warmth radiating from the growing acceptance around her. The laughter, the vibrant colors of the art booths, and the sweet scent of food created an atmosphere of joy and possibility, paving the way for a brighter future.

"Let's check out that booth over there!" Kai exclaimed, pointing toward a display featuring handmade crafts. The idea of exploring further with her parents alongside them filled Mei with excitement.

"Sure!" Mei said, her spirits lifting as they moved together. The connection formed through laughter and shared experiences began to create bonds that felt unbreakable.

As they approached the booth, the local artisans proudly displayed their work—ceramics, paintings, and textiles reflecting the culture and creativity of the community. Mei's heart swelled as she watched her parents engage with the artists, asking questions and sharing their own experiences. It was heartwarming to see them genuinely interested, fostering an understanding that transcended their initial reservations.

"This is incredible!" her mother said as she picked up a delicately crafted vase. "I love how the artist uses color—there's so much emotion in their work."

"I think it's a great way to connect with the community," Kai added, stepping closer to join the conversation. "Art brings people together and helps us appreciate our differences."

Mei glanced at Kai, feeling gratitude for how effortlessly he connected with her parents, serving as a bridge between their worlds. The atmosphere around them hummed with potential, and she felt deeper affection blossoming for him.

After exploring the crafts booth, they continued to wander through the festival, stopping at various displays and immersing themselves in the artistry surrounding them. The more they shared, the closer they felt as a group, allowing themselves to open up and embrace the evolution of their relationships.

When they paused to watch a local dance troupe perform, the electric rhythm of the music swelled in the air, filling the space with joy and excitement. Kai stepped closer to Mei as they clapped along to the beat, the movement of the dancers igniting even more energy within her.

"This is amazing," she said, leaning against him, feeling a sense of safety she relished. "It's like the whole city is celebrating creativity."

"And love," Kai added, glancing down at her with a tender smile. "I think that's what art really embodies—capturing moments of connection."

The truth resonated deeply with Mei, and she found herself lost in the moment. As the performance drew to an uplifting conclusion and the audience erupted into applause, Mei tightened her grip on Kai's hand, feeling a surge of power in their connection.

As dusk settled in, the festival took on a magical feel. Strings of lights illuminated the pathways, casting a warm glow over everything. The soft scent of nearby food vendors wafted through the air, mingling beautifully with the laughter and chatter of those around.

"Let's capture this moment," Kai suggested, pulling out his phone. "One last photo to encapsulate the joy of the day."

Mei grinned, positioning herself next to Kai under the twinkling lights. They smiled widely at the camera, laughter dancing in their eyes as Kai snapped the picture.

"Perfect!" he exclaimed as he reviewed the shot. "This is going to be one of my favorites."

Mei felt her heart swell with pride and joy as they continued to take pictures, capturing the essence of the day—the connection between them, the acceptance blossoming in her parents' hearts, and the beauty of community they were all beginning to embrace.

As they prepared to head back home, Mei felt grateful for the day and reflective on the strides they had made. Maybe her parents were beginning to understand that love, in all its forms, was worthy of celebration, just like the art around them.

Once home, Mei shared the pictures with Kai, their laughter filling her room as they viewed the memories they had created together. But the lightness of the day encouraged her to address the shadows still lingering.

"Thanks for today," she said, her heart full of gratitude. "I really feel like my parents are starting to come around—and I can't wait to explore more together."

"I had a blast! And just remember, whenever you feel the pressure or doubt, I'm always here for you," Kai promised, his eyes earnest and warm.

They shared a lingering glance, a recognition of the connection they had forged amidst the chaos of fear and judgment interwoven into their journey.

But as the night deepened, a shadow of uncertainty flickered in Mei's heart once more, a reminder of how fragile their love felt against the backdrop of gossip and scrutiny.

Tomorrow loomed ahead, carrying with it the rising tide of tension that often accompanied the complexities of love.

CHAPTER 21

THE GRAND TANABATA FESTIVAL

The Grand Tanabata Festival had arrived, an event celebrated throughout Japan that brought together the hopes and dreams of the community under the twinkling night sky. As the streets filled with anticipation and vibrant decorations, Mei felt a blend of excitement and anxiety swirling within her. This festival was a beautiful opportunity to celebrate connections—love, friendship, and dreams—but it came with the underlying weight of her ongoing struggle for acceptance.

From the moment she stepped outside, wearing a light summer kimono adorned with delicate cherry blossoms, Mei knew the day would be special. The fabric felt soft against her skin and carried with it the sweet memories of her growing relationship with Kai.

Stalls adorned with colorful streamers and lanterns lined the streets, creating a festive ambiance that mirrored the joy Mei felt around her. The tantalizing aroma of festival food wafted through the air, combining with the laughter of families gathering to celebrate the night ahead.

"Wow, I can't believe how festive everything looks!" Kai remarked as they walked hand in hand through the bustling streets, his excitement infectious.

"It really is magical! The decorations are breathtaking, and it feels like the entire city is alive with joy," Mei replied, her heart swelling with happiness. She glanced around, taking in the laughter and the crowded stalls filled with people, each enjoying the festivities.

Mei and Kai stopped at a stall selling colorful tanzaku—small pieces of paper on which festival-goers write their wishes and hang them from bamboo branches. A thoughtful idea sparked in her mind, igniting a flutter of determination within her.

"Should we write our wishes?" she suggested, motioning toward the vibrant tanzaku. "It's a perfect way to express what we hope for our future."

"Absolutely! I love that idea," Kai responded enthusiastically. They selected bright papers in shades of pink and blue, and as they found a quiet spot in the festival grounds, they sat down to write their wishes.

Taking a deep breath, Mei pondered what her heart desired most. Thoughts of love, acceptance, and the beauty of her relationship with Kai danced in her mind, and she could feel the urgency swell within her.

Eventually, she wrote:

I wish for our love to grow stronger, for my family to accept Kai and for us to face the world together, no matter what challenges arise.

She felt a warm flush in her cheeks as she penned her thoughts, pouring her emotions into each stroke of her pen. Once she finished, she looked over at Kai, who was scribbling down his own wish, a focused expression on his face.

"What are you wishing for?" she asked, curiosity bubbling within her.

Kai looked up at her, a grin spreading across his lips. "I wrote that I wish to create beautiful art with you and to cherish every moment we share, building memories that last a lifetime."

Mei felt her heart flutter at his words, the sincerity behind them resonating deep in her soul. "That's perfect," she said, her voice filled with emotion. "Let's hang our wishes together."

They found a beautiful bamboo tree already adorned with tanzaku, bright wishes fluttering in the breeze. As they hung their pieces side by side, a sense of hope enveloped them. Standing there, together, they felt like their dreams had intertwined—a testament to their love, their aspirations, and the bond they were forging.

"Okay, now let's stand back and make a photo with our wishes—this will be a memory," Kai suggested, excitement lighting his features.

As they posed under the bamboo, holding their tanzaku, Mei felt a surge of joy swell within her. The moment felt monumental—a celebration of love shared, obstacles confronted, and dreams pursued together.

Later, as they wandered through the festival, taking in the sights and sounds, Mei's heart felt full and alive. They sampled delicious street foods, played games, and soaked in the joyful atmosphere as laughter and music filled the air. The vibrant colors and twinkling lights surrounded them, reminding Mei of the beauty of life unfolding.

But as the night progressed, the whispers of insecurity about her relationship still lingered in the back of her mind. She couldn't help but think of the challenges that lay ahead, particularly the staunch traditional expectations of her family.

"Do you ever wonder if people will ever really accept what we have?" she asked, her voice gentle as they paused to watch a dance performance nearby.

Kai turned to her, his expression forthright and sincere. "I think acceptance takes time. What we have is real, and over time, people will come to understand that love can exist across boundaries. What we're building is worth defending."

His confidence bolstered her spirits, momentarily pushing aside the turbulence of doubt. As they continued to embrace the warmth of the festival, Mei felt the cherished bond of connection growing stronger.

As the night sky deepened and fireworks lit up the horizon, she felt something shift within her—a burgeoning sense of hope and clarity. Each explosion of color across the sky felt like a celebration not just of Tanabata, but of her and Kai's journey together—a declaration that love could persevere despite judgment and challenges.

Standing side by side with Kai, surrounded by families and friends, Mei gazed up at the vibrant display. The brilliant lights echoed the determination she had recently stirred in her heart, reminding her that love was something worth pursuing.

With each firework burst, she felt her insecurities fade just a little more, replaced by an unwavering conviction. "Look at that!" she exclaimed, pointing towards the sky as a particularly brilliant firework lit up the night. "It's so beautiful!"

Kai turned to her, a playful smile spreading across his face. "Not as beautiful as you!"

Mei blushed at his compliment, warmth blooming in her chest. "You're just saying that to make me smile."

"Okay, maybe that's partly true," he admitted, chuckling softly. "But seriously, you light up every moment we're together, and I'm grateful I get to share tonight with you."

As the fireworks continued to pop and shimmer overhead, Mei felt an overwhelming wave of affection wash over her. In that moment, amid the brilliant colors lighting up the night sky, she turned to Kai, wanting to share her truth—the truth she had been holding close during the recent rush of emotions.

"Kai," she said as they both looked at the mesmerizing display above them, "I want you to know how much you mean to me. Being with you feels like home. Every moment, every laugh, every kiss—it's all been a part of something incredible that I'm so grateful for."

Kai turned toward her, the warmth in his eyes reflecting the sparkling fireworks above. "I feel the same way, Mei. You've brought meaning to my life that I didn't know I was missing. I want to explore every part of this journey with you."

Her heart raced as he leaned in ever so slightly, their faces close. The sounds of the festival faded, leaving only the two of them, encapsulated in a moment that felt larger than life. "I'm so glad we have this connection," she whispered, feeling both vulnerable and empowered. "With you, I feel like I can face anything—like I can be completely myself."

"I'll always be here for you," Kai responded softly, sincerity pouring out with every word. "We'll tackle whatever challenges come our way, together. And that's a promise."

As the last firework burst into the sky, casting a brilliant light over the festival, Mei felt a sense of commitment blooming within her. She leaned in, closing the distance between them, and brushed her lips softly against his—a tender kiss that spoke volumes of their shared hopes and dreams.

When they pulled away, she felt a shimmering warmth envelop her. The night felt complete, two hearts intertwined against a backdrop of light and love. "This moment is one I'll cherish forever," she said, clarity washing over her.

"Me too," Kai replied, his expression earnest. The twinkling lights of the festival surrounded them, illuminating the path they had charted together.

As they began to stroll back through the festival grounds, Mei took a moment to appreciate the beauty around her—the laughter, the joy, the warmth of the connections being forged. With Kai beside her, she felt equipped to confront whatever challenges lay ahead.

"Let's keep creating our memories," she said, a newfound strength imbued in her voice. "Now more than ever, I want to show the world what we have."

"We will." Kai nodded firmly, a playful grin touching his lips. "And maybe we'll even document our adventures along the way through photography and art, just like we talked about."

They spent the remaining hours exploring the festival, taking photos of each other amidst the colorful stalls and celebrating the vibrancy of their connection. Mei felt a rush of excitement as the evening unfolded, her heart lighter than it had been in weeks.

As the cool air wrapped around them and the stars shone brightly above, Mei's worries began to dissipate. They had created something beautiful— a bond forged through shared experiences, dreams, and loving gestures that would carry them through the trials that lay ahead.

The night embraced them, full of promise, and as they made their way home, Mei felt a sense of belonging that illuminated the path toward their future—one filled with love, acceptance, and the beauty of shared dreams.

CHAPTER 22

A MYSTICAL DAY IN KYOTO

The day had arrived for Mei and Kai's much-anticipated trip to Kyoto, a place rich in history, culture, and beauty. As they boarded the train early in the morning, the excitement bubbled over in Mei's chest, filling her with a sense of wonder. This was more than just a day trip—it was a chance to explore new places and create memories that would weave into the fabric of their relationship.

As the train sped toward its destination, Mei watched the landscape transform through the window—the dense buildings of Tokyo gradually giving way to rolling hills adorned with lush greenery and ancient temples. The scenery felt like a living painting, awakening her artistic soul.

"What do you hope to capture today?" Kai asked, glancing over at her with that familiar spark in his eye.

"I want to capture the essence of Kyoto—the hidden gems that reflect its spirit. Each temple has so much character, and the gardens tell their own stories," she replied, her heart racing with excitement about the photographic opportunities that awaited them.

"Perfect! I'll sketch while you photograph. We can create a visual story of our day together," he proposed, his enthusiasm infectious.

When the train came to a halt at Kyoto Station, they stepped off to be greeted by the smell of fresh pastries from nearby vendors. "First stop, breakfast?" Kai suggested, grinning.

"Definitely! I've heard there's a fantastic bakery around here," Mei replied, following him as they ventured towards the quaint little café. The aroma of freshly baked goods filled the air, and as they indulged in warm pastries, Mei felt a wave of happiness wash over her.

Once their bellies were full, they made their way to Kinkaku-ji, the iconic Golden Pavilion. The stunning structure, adorned with shimmering gold leaf, reflected beautifully in the surrounding pond, creating an ethereal scene that took Mei's breath away.

"Let's get some shots!" she exclaimed, pulling out her camera.

As she began capturing the picturesque temple and the tranquility around it, she felt a deep sense of contentment envelop her. Every click of the shutter allowed her to preserve the magic of the moment, and the peaceful atmosphere filled her heart with joy.

"Look at you, capturing these moments," Kai said, gazing at her with admiration. "You make everything feel more vibrant."

"Thanks, but I couldn't do it without the inspiration you provide," Mei replied, returning his gaze. "You see the world in such a unique way."

After spending time exploring the temple grounds, they ventured through the adjacent gardens, filled with cherry blossoms in full bloom. The petals danced in the breeze, and they couldn't resist the allure of taking a few more photos.

"This is like a dream!" Mei exclaimed as they walked hand in hand, the beauty of the surroundings wrapping around them. She felt giddy, her heart soaring as they explored the serene landscape.

"Do you think we're destined to experience more days like this together?" Kai asked, his tone contemplative.

"Definitely," Mei affirmed, her heart swelling. "Every moment with you reassures me that we're meant to face this journey together."

As they continued to wander, they explored the charming streets of Gion, where the traditional wooden machiya houses lined the alleyways. Their laughter echoed amidst the tranquil beauty, and with every turn, Mei felt more certain that this was where she belonged—with Kai, exploring life and everything it held.

"Let's visit a tea house and indulge in a traditional tea ceremony," Kai suggested, his excitement evident.

"That sounds amazing!" Mei replied, feeling the thrill of new experiences wash over her.

They settled into a serene tea house, the atmosphere filled with soft music and the subtle fragrance of green tea. As they participated in the ceremony—observing the rituals and savoring the delicate flavors—Mei felt a deeper connection forming. The moment felt intimate, a bonding experience that reflected the commitment they had to one another.

Later, as they made their way toward the Kiyomizu-dera temple, the sun began to dip lower in the sky, casting a golden hue over the ancient structures. Standing at the temple's famous wooden stage that jutted out over the hillside, Mei felt a surge of emotion rush through her. The view was breathtaking, the city sprawling below, an array of rooftops and shimmering lights.

"Look at this!" she exclaimed, her heart racing as she took in the panorama. "It's like we're on top of the world!"

Kai stood beside her, a knowing smile on his face as he absorbed the beauty of the moment. "This is incredible," he said softly, turning to face her. "I can't imagine sharing this with anyone else."

Feeling emboldened by the magic of the day, Mei turned to him, the warmth of the sunset lighting up their faces. "Kai, I think I might be falling in love with you," she said, her voice steady but filled with a vulnerability that made her heart race.

Kai's expression shifted, a flicker of surprise mixed with joy illuminating his features. "You think?" he said, teasing but sincere, stepping closer to her, the warmth of the moment intensifying.

"I know!" she continued, the words spilling out of her as if they were finally free. "Every moment we share, every laugh, every adventure—it's all made me realize how much you mean to me. There's something so special about what we have."

His smile widened, a heartwarming beam that made her heart flutter. "Mei, you have no idea how happy those words make me. I've been feeling the same way for a while now, but hearing you say it gives me so much confidence. You know that?"

She could hardly contain the joy spilling from her heart as she met his gaze. "Really? I thought I might have been alone in feeling this."

"Not at all," he replied, his tone earnest. "I care about you deeply, and I want to explore this connection fully. I can honestly see a future with you—one full of art, laughter, and all those beautiful moments we create together."

With the sun setting behind them, casting a warm golden light over the temple, Mei felt an overwhelming sense of rightness wrap around them. The beauty of the moment elevated their connection, and she couldn't help but smile as her heart swelled.

"Promise me we'll keep being open about our feelings," she said, the determination in her voice returning. "I want us to face everything together, no matter what comes our way."

"Always," Kai said with a nod, his eyes locked onto hers, full of sincerity. "We'll navigate all the challenges, embrace each moment, and continue building this incredible bond we have."

With the sunset turning the sky to brilliant shades of pink and orange, they turned to face the view again, soaking in the quiet yet powerful understanding that had blossomed between them. As night fell, the stars began to twinkle above, and Mei felt a sense of peace settle over her.

Tonight, beneath the vast sky, she felt truly connected to Kai. The doubts and worries that had haunted her recently faded into the backdrop of the beauty surrounding them.

"Let's take a picture to remember this moment," Kai suggested, pulling out his phone. "You look amazing in the sunset light!"

Mei grinned, positioning herself next to him as he snapped the picture—a keepsake of their journey, a memory etched in time. "We need to document all our adventures," she laughed, the joy of the evening flooding her senses.

"Definitely! This is just the beginning," he replied, his eyes bright with enthusiasm.

As they began to walk back toward the train station, hand in hand, Mei felt the tension ease more with each moment spent with Kai. The love they had discovered felt like a profound certainty, one that allowed her to step confidently into the future, ready to embrace whatever lay ahead.

That night, as they returned home, Mei reflected on the day—the beauty of Kyoto, the laughter they had shared, and the heartfelt confessions made beneath the temple. A smile touched her lips as she thought of all the moments they would continue to create together.

But as she settled into bed, peace began to wane, and the patience she had cultivated cracked slightly. Would their love withstand the test of time and outside scrutiny? Could they really navigate the pressures from their parents and the judgment of classmates?

As she drifted off to sleep, Mei resolved to focus on the strength of their bond and the beautiful moments they had yet to share. She knew that each step they took together would reaffirm their love, and they would face challenges as partners, ready to tackle whatever came their way.

CHAPTER 23

UNEXPECTED ALLIES

The following week began with the tension of rumors simmering just beneath the surface of Mei's interactions at school. Despite the beauty of her day in Kyoto with Kai and the strength of their bond, she felt the whispers escalate, gaining momentum and momentum that made her anxious. The hallways buzzed with a mix of excitement and judgment, and she had to navigate the tumultuous waters surrounding her relationship.

Yet amid the chaos, Mei found unexpected support from her friends. As lunchtime approached, she gathered with Akira and a few other close classmates in their usual spot under the large oak tree outside. The shadows offered a comforting refuge from the sun, enveloping them in camaraderie and laughter.

"Have you talked to your parents since dinner?" Akira asked, leaning forward with genuine concern as he took a sip of his drink.

"I have! They seem to be coming around a bit more," Mei replied, feeling encouraged. "But things at school have been rough. The rumors are getting worse, and I can feel the pressure weighing on me."

Her friends nodded, expressions filled with empathy. "That's tough, but you shouldn't let others control your narrative, Mei," another friend chimed in. "What you have with Kai is real—it's not just a rumor. It's something to celebrate!"

"I know, but they talk about it like it's some kind of joke," Mei confessed, frustration bubbling to the surface. "It hurts when people twist my feelings into something trivial."

"People are going to talk—especially when they don't understand. But you have to stay true to what you feel inside," Akira said, his tone steady. "Focus on what makes you happy. It's like we talked about—you have to carve your own path, regardless of what's expected."

Feeling her spirits lift, Mei nodded. "I want to be strong in the face of all this. I care about Kai, and I want to defend our relationship against the judgment."

"That's the spirit!" Akira encouraged. "And you're not alone in this. You have us. We're all here for you, cheering you on."

The warmth of their support enveloped her, soothing her doubts. "Thank you, everyone. It means so much to know you're all behind me," she said, her voice reflecting her gratitude.

As the lunch hour wore on, the conversation shifted to lighter topics, filled with laughs and reminiscing about inside jokes. Mei felt a sense of camaraderie solidify around them, a reminder that friendship, just like love, could help mend the cracks of doubt that crept into her mind.

But as they gathered their things to head back to class, a familiar voice floated toward them from across the courtyard.

"Hey, Mei!" It was Yuki, flanked by a few friends as they approached. "You've been hanging out with Kai a lot lately, huh?"

Murmurs rippled through the small group surrounding Mei, and she felt a protective instinct surge in her quickly. "We're just spending time together," she said firmly, trying to assert herself.

"Right. Must be nice to have someone like him," Yuki said, a smirk plastered on his face. "But you have to think about your future, don't you?"

Mei's friends were quick to respond, stepping in to shield her. "Leave her alone, Yuki," Akira said, a hint of anger coloring his tone. "What you're saying is just unnecessary."

"Relax! I'm just making conversation," Yuki responded, rolling his eyes.

"No, you're trying to stir up drama, and that's not cool," another friend chimed in. "Mei is happy, and that's what should matter."

Mei looked at her friends, feeling a wave of gratitude for their support. Their loyalty reminded her that she had people in her corner willing to advocate for her happiness, to stand up against those who chose to judge without understanding.

"Thanks, everyone," Mei said, her heart swelling. "Really, it means a lot to have allies like you."

As Yuki and his friends retreated, visibly frustrated, Mei felt a renewed sense of purpose and strength within herself. She turned to her friends, grateful that they understood the depths of her feelings.

"You'll always need friends who support you in love and life," one of them reminded her, their words resonating deeply.

With the rest of the day ahead of her, Mei felt hope return to her heart. The whispers at school would continue, but she now understood that she had a support system—an army of friends who believed in her and the love she had for Kai.

The evening arrived, and as she prepared to meet Kai in the park, excitement pulsed through her veins. In her heart, she knew she was ready to heighten her love, fueled by their connection and the understanding of friendship.

When she arrived at their meeting spot, she saw Kai waiting for her, leaning casually against a lamppost with that easy-going grin that always made her heart skip a beat. The soft glow of the fading sunlight framed him perfectly, creating a silhouette that felt both comforting and electric.

"Hey there, beautiful!" he called, straightening up as she approached. "You're right on time! I was just about to send out a search party."

"Honestly, I should've been worried about you getting lost!" Mei teased back, feeling her anxieties fade in the warmth of his presence.

"Trust me, I can follow a map," he replied with a faux seriousness that made her smile widen.

As they began walking, the day's earlier events looped through her mind—the whispers, the laughter, and the unwavering support of her friends. Those memories gave her strength as they strolled beneath the growing canopy of stars. "So, what's the plan for tonight?" Mei asked, glancing up at Kai, a mixture of eagerness and nervousness bubbling within her.

"I was thinking we could enjoy some ice cream and then find a quiet spot to talk about those art ideas we had!" Kai said enthusiastically.

"That sounds perfect," she replied, picturing the sweetness of ice cream contrasting with the freshness of evening air.

As they made their way to the ice cream shop, Mei couldn't shake off the lingering shadows of worry and doubt. Had she done enough to stand her ground with her parents? She wanted to be free in love, but what if their acceptance remained just out of reach?

"Everything okay?" Kai asked, glancing down at her with concern as they entered the shop, sensing her momentary distraction.

"Just thinking about my conversation with my parents earlier in the week," she confessed, shifting her gaze. "I feel like I'm still not over the hurdles we faced. The doubts lingering about us, the expectations—sometimes it feels heavy."

Kai reached for her hand, intertwining their fingers as they waited in line. "We'll face those challenges together," he insisted, squeezing her hand gently. "You have to remember that their opinions might take time to shift, but that doesn't change the reality of what we share."

"I know," she said quietly, feeling comforted by his presence. "It just worries me that society's judgments will pull us apart."

As they ordered their ice cream and stepped outside, Mei felt the coolness of the evening refreshing her spirit. Small moments like these brought them joy, a reminder that amidst the noise, there was still beauty to savor.

"Let's find a spot to sit," Kai suggested, nudging her softly with his shoulder as they walked along the pathway lined with blooming flowers.

They found a secluded bench tucked under a large cherry blossom tree, where the petals still clung to the branches, casting a gentle pink carpet on the ground below. Mei felt a wave of tranquility wash over her as they sat down, the warmth of Kai's hand still reassuring.

"Here's to new beginnings," Kai announced, raising his ice cream cone dramatically. "A sweet start to conquering whatever comes our way!"

With a soft laugh, Mei raised her cone to meet his. "To us—stronger than any rumor!"

As they savored their treats, the tension that had built up during the week began to dissolve. They talked about their art, exchanging ideas, and soon found themselves falling back into a comfortable rhythm—a blend of playful teasing and heartfelt conversations that made the world feel alive around them.

But as their laughter filled the air, Mei felt the gnawing concerns creep back in—reminders of the external pressures that still loomed over her. Just then, a familiar scene unfolded at the edge of the park, drawing her attention.

She spotted Yuki, laughing with a group of students, and a pang of anxiety coursed through her. What if they began to spread more rumors? What if Yuki decided to intervene between her and Kai again?

"Are you okay?" Kai asked, noticing her shift in demeanor.

"Yeah," she said quickly, but he could see the tension in her eyes. "It's just—might be nothing, but there's Yuki again. I can't shake the feeling he'll stir up more trouble."

"I wouldn't put it past him," Kai replied, a hint of frustration sparking in his voice. "But don't let that affect what we have. You're stronger than that!"

"Right. I shouldn't let it bother me. I want to focus on us," she said, trying to regain her inner strength. "And I really appreciate all the support from you and my friends."

"That's what we're here for," he said, gently squeezing her hand once more. "You have a team behind you and as long as we have each other, we can navigate through anything."

Taking a deep breath, Mei felt the knot in her stomach begin to loosen. The evening sun bathed the park in a golden glow, casting a warm light over their conversation—a small reminder that, despite external pressures, they were anchored by something real and genuine.

"Let's just enjoy our time together tonight," she said, shaking off the lingering worries. "I want this moment to be about us."

"Absolutely! We can let the world worry about itself while we conquer our corner of it," Kai replied with a beaming grin.

As they resumed their laughter and playful banter, Mei felt the weight of doubt begin to recede. In this moment, it was only the two of them—two artists enveloped in creativity, exploring their surroundings and each other's hearts.

After finishing their ice cream, they decided to take a leisurely stroll through the park, soaking in the beauty of nature as the last hues of sunset painted the sky. The blossoming flowers swayed gently in the breeze, and winged creatures flitted about, seemingly reveling in the same joy they felt.

"Let's get a photo!" Mei suggested suddenly, pulling out her camera. "This light is perfect for capturing the atmosphere."

"Okay, I'm in! What should I do?" Kai asked, striking a silly pose that made Mei laugh.

"Maybe try—turn your head a little to the left and flash me the biggest smile you've got!" she instructed, positioning the camera to capture the essence of the moment.

As the camera shutter clicked, she captured not just the image, but also the vibrant bond they were forging in that enchanting setting. The warmth of their laughter echoed in the stillness of the evening, and for a moment, the world outside melted away.

Once they reviewed the snap together, Mei felt a satisfying rush. The photograph encapsulated their experience—two friends navigating a blossoming relationship under a canopy of cherry blossoms, vibrant smiles reflecting an authentic connection.

They continued taking pictures, creating a scrapbook of memories that filled them with joy. But as they moved to a quieter part of the park, Mei's mind began to drift again toward the reality they would soon confront. She quietly replayed the conversations with her parents, the judgment from classmates, and the uncertainties lingering in the background.

"Kai…" she began, her voice trailing off as she found herself lost in thought, the blooms around them swaying gently.

He turned to her, concern flickering in his eyes. "What's wrong?"

Taking a deep breath, Mei poise herself to address the fears swirling within her yet again. "I want to make sure that we're both ready for whatever may come our way. I love being with you, but with all the judgment, I don't want our relationship to suffer."

"Mei, we're stronger than the negativity around us," he said firmly, a spark igniting in his voice. "We still have each other and this amazing connection. I'm not going to let any rumors change that."

"I know, but what if it gets harder? What if Yuki or someone else tries to come between us again?" Mei asked, vulnerability creeping into her voice.

"Then we will face it together." Kai took her hands and clasped them tightly. "You don't have to bear the weight alone. We can always talk through these challenges, whether they come from the outside or within."

Feeling her doubts ease slightly with his words, Mei nodded, grateful for the bond they shared. "You're right. We will navigate through whatever lies ahead."

Just then, a commotion from nearby drew their attention. A small group of students, including Yuki, had gathered nearby, laughing and pointing. Mei felt her stomach twist again at the sight of them, her insecurities surfacing as she recognized the teasing lilt in their voices.

"Look who's in love! Maybe that's the trend now," one girl called out, laughter erupting from the group like a wave crashing down on her.

Kai's expression darkened, and Mei felt a protective instinct rise within her. "Don't let them get to you," he said, noticing her tense reaction. "They're just looking for attention."

Before she could respond, Yuki approached them, his demeanor charming but with an edge that made Mei uneasy. "Hey, Mei! Still hanging out with your 'artistic boyfriend'?" he said, his tone tinged with sarcasm.

Mei took a deep breath, summoning courage as she stepped forward. "We're happy together. It's not a joke to me or Kai."

His smirk widened, but the crowd began to wane, caught off guard by her assertiveness. "Sure, but don't you think it's a little naïve? I mean, how long can this really last?"

The laughter from the group began to bubble again, and Mei felt her heart race, insecurity threatening to overwhelm her. Then she remembered Kai's words—"You don't have to bear the weight alone."

With that thought echoing in her mind, Mei felt a flicker of strength ignite within her.

"No, Yuki. What's naïve is to assume that love is something that can be dismissed or diminished by someone else's opinion," Mei said firmly, her voice steady as she met his gaze. "What I have with Kai is real and genuine, and your mocking won't change that."

Kai stood beside her, a protective nature radiating from him. "You don't get to judge what we feel. We have a connection that's important to both of us, and it's strong enough to face any noise."

Mei's friends, who had been hanging back, began to rally around her, their support infusing confidence into her words. Akira stepped forward, speaking up for her as he scoffed at Yuki's antics. "Mei knows what she wants, and it's clear that you're just trying to provoke her. Why don't you focus on your own life instead?"

"Exactly," another classmate chimed in, their tone firm. "What you're doing is unnecessary. Just let them be happy."

A surprise flickered across Yuki's face as he glanced around at the growing number of supporters in Mei's corner. The laughter that had previously surrounded them began to fade, replaced by a respectful silence.

"Whatever," Yuki replied, clearly unfazed, though the smug expression on his face had faltered. "Just don't say I didn't warn you, Mei. People will always judge. It's just how things are."

"But what if we don't give them a reason to?" Mei asked, her confidence rising further. "What if we create our own narrative? I won't let someone like you dictate my happiness."

With that declaration hanging in the air, she felt a surge of affirmation from her friends around her. They stood shoulder to shoulder, creating a protective barrier against the judgments and negativity that had haunted her.

Yuki shrugged, glancing at his friends in annoyance. "Good luck with that," he said, turning to walk away. "But just know that not everyone will be on your side."

Mei felt the invisible tension begin to dissipate as Yuki and his group retreated. She stood taller, her heart racing, fueled by the adrenaline and the support surrounding her.

"You didn't back down!" Akira said, his eyes bright with admiration.

"Honestly, I was scared, but I felt like I had a good reason to stand up for myself and for us," Mei admitted, looking at Kai, who was smiling at her with pride radiating from his expression.

"I'm proud of you," he said softly, leaning closer. "You handled that so well, and it just shows that love really can conquer the judgments of meddling voices."

Feeling their connection strengthen in that powerful moment, Mei realized that she had made a choice—to focus on love, acceptance, and creating her own narrative. With Kai beside her, she felt ready to embrace whatever challenges lay ahead.

As they walked away from the crowd, hand in hand, Mei felt buoyed by the love and support of her friends and Kai. The whispers would always exist, but they could define their relationship based on their actions, their honesty, and the resilience they had forged together.

Later that evening, when they found a quiet spot to catch their breath, Mei turned to Kai. "I know we'll face more challenges, and I'll need your support as we navigate those. But I want you to know that you've helped me grow stronger."

Kai smiled as he wrapped his arms around her, pulling her close. "And I'll always be here, ready to face whatever comes next. This is our journey, and I wouldn't want to share it with anyone else."

"Me too, Kai," Mei replied, feeling a rush of emotions. They stood together under the evening sky, the stars twinkling above them as a testament to their bond.

With renewed determination and the promise of love and support, they were ready to tackle the next phase of their journey—whatever trials awaited them felt conquerable with each other by their side.

CHAPTER 24

MOMENTS OF DOUBT UNDER RAINFALL

The early summer morning didn't bring the sunshine Mei had hoped for; instead, dark clouds loomed ominously overhead as she made her way to school. The rain began to fall lightly, the pitter-patter of drops against the pavement echoing her inner turmoil.

After the last week's triumphant moments where she stood up for her relationship with Kai, a lingering tension quietly emerged, creeping into her heart like a fog. The initial thrill of her parents' acceptance felt overshadowed by the relentless judgment of peers, and as each drop of rain fell, it seemed to mirror the anxiety washing over her.

As she arrived at school, the first feeling of doubt settled deep into her gut. The familiar buzz of students flowed around her, but murmurs of gossip echoed in her mind, pushing against the confidence she had gathered. The sky mirrored her emotions, gray and dreary with a hint of threat.

"Hey, Mei!" Akira called out, spotting her near the entrance. He rushed over, holding an umbrella above them as they hurried to cover from the drizzling rain. "Don't you think it's a perfect day for a pep talk?"

"Yeah… I guess," she muttered, her voice uncharacteristically flat.

As they dashed across the courtyard, the sound of water splashing beneath their shoes resonated with Mei's internal struggle. The thrill of having defended her relationship with Kai felt distant, and whispers still floated through the hallways, taunting her worries.

Once inside the school, sheltered from the rain, Mei felt a momentary reprieve, but anxious thoughts and lingering doubts clung to her like the dampness of her clothes.

Throughout her classes, Mei's mind drifted. She could feel the weight of expectations pressing upon her shoulders, each comment from classmates piercing her confidence. The shadows of judgment danced in her thoughts, making her question whether it was really worth facing the storm brewing among her peers.

As lunchtime approached, she made her way to the cafeteria, her heart racing with trepidation. Would Kai be there? Would their classmates continue to whisper about their relationship? Would they brush off their love as merely a passing fling?

Upon entering the cafeteria, she caught sight of Kai sitting with some friends at their usual table, and a mixture of warmth and anxiety surged within her. She yearned to run to him, to bask in the safety of their connection, but the apprehensions tugged at her heart, clouding her mind.

"Hey, you made it!" Kai greeted her, his smile radiant but tinged with concern. "You okay? You seem a little distant today."

"Just a rough morning," Mei admitted, forcing a smile as she sat beside him. "The rain is a little doom and gloom, and you know how rumors are... they linger."

Kai nodded, sensing the gravity of her words. "Let's not let them get to us. They can say what they want. We know what's real," he said, determination coloring his voice.

But even as she heard his encouraging words, Mei felt her heart weighing heavier. The soft drizzle outside continued as a backdrop, mimicking her spiraling thoughts. What if I can't overcome this? What if the judgments really do affect us?

As they shared lunch, the weight of school pressures settled deeper into her thoughts. She noticed classmates casting glances their way, whispers traveling like wildfire. It felt as if every bite of food she took was accompanied by the gnawing anxiety of outside judgment.

Soon, a familiar group approached their table. Yuki led the pack, a smug grin plastered across his face. "Well, look who's all cozy together," he remarked, his tone mocking. "Hope you're enjoying your little love story before reality hits."

A pang of irritation pierced through Mei. "What is it to you?" she said, unable to hide the fire in her voice. "We're just trying to enjoy our time together, just like everyone else."

Yuki smirked, and his friends snickered behind him. "But can you really enjoy it when everyone's watching? You know how these things go, right? People get bored. They'll move on to the next drama soon enough."

Mei felt Kai's grip on her hand tighten, and she could see frustration etched across his features. "What's the point of your comments, Yuki? Do you enjoy digging into other people's lives?" Kai challenged, standing up for her once again.

"Relax, I'm just making conversation," Yuki replied, waving his hand dismissively, but Mei felt the sharp edge of his words, their sting sharper in the confines of her mind.

As they walked away, the weight of their judgments seemed to seep into Mei's very being.

"Don't let it get to you, Mei," Kai said, concern coloring his voice. "They're just trying to provoke a reaction."

"I know, but sometimes it's hard," Mei admitted, her voice cracking slightly as frustration bubbled to the surface. "It's exhausting trying to ignore the whispers and rumors. I just want to enjoy my time with you without feeling like I'm under a spotlight."

Kai's expression softened, his concern evident as he leaned closer, their hands still intertwined. "You don't have to go through this alone, Mei. Whenever it gets overwhelming, just lean on me, okay? I'm here, and I want you to feel secure in our relationship."

Her heart fluttered at his words, but the anxiety still gnawed deep within her. "It's just that… with Yuki around and everything, I feel like I have to prove something—like I need to show everyone that what we have is real."

"You've already proved that to me," Kai replied firmly, locking eyes with her. "What we have is genuine, and it shouldn't matter what others think. We know how we feel about each other."

"I wish it were that simple," she murmured, looking down at their hands, interwoven like the paths of their lives. "What if they never accept me or us? What if I have to choose between who I love and my family?"

The thought caused a lump to form in her throat, the storm of insecurities threatening to overwhelm her once more. Kai placed a comforting hand on her back, a grounding presence against the turmoil swirling within.

"Whatever happens, we'll navigate it together," he reassured. "We have each other's backs. And we can communicate openly when doubts creep in."

As they wrapped up their lunch, Mei felt a surge of determination rising within her. With each passing moment, she realized that building their future wasn't just about confronting uncertainty; it was also about cherishing the present.

"I'm going to hold you to that," she said, finally managing a smile. "We've built something special, and I want to continue nurturing that."

"I wouldn't have it any other way," Kai replied, their hands still intertwined as they walked toward their next class, a feeling of warmth lingering in the space between them.

But as the day wore on and the rain began to fall heavier outside, Mei's thoughts drifted back to her earlier conversation—the weight of her parents' expectations and the looming judgment from classmates still tugging at her heart.

Later that evening, as she lay in bed listening to the rain patter against her window, the feelings of doubt resurfaced. The soothing sound of the rain felt comforting yet paradoxically amplifying her worries, mirroring her inner tumult.

Just when she thought she had conquered her fears, the reality of societal pressures seeped back into her mind. She recalled Yuki's initial intrusion, the unnecessary chaos that felt so out of control.

Perhaps she needed to speak with her parents again—reassure them of her feelings for Kai and how genuine their connection was. The thought filled her with a mix of determination and dread.

With the commitment they had made to one another, she knew that together they could face these obstacles. It was time to solidify her self-acceptance and the love she had for Kai, pushing back against the shadows of doubt.

As the rain drummed softly outside, Mei pulled her phone closer, contemplating reaching out to Kai, to find comfort and share her thoughts.

Finally, she began typing:

Mei: Hey Kai, can we talk? I've been thinking about some stuff.

The response came quickly.

Kai: Of course! What's on your mind?

Mei: About us and everything. I just want to make sure we're both on the same page.

Kai: Absolutely. I'm here for you anytime. Let's meet up after school tomorrow, okay?

Mei: I'd really like that. Thanks for being so supportive.

The acknowledgment of their connection brought a sense of solace, the reassurance she needed to face the upcoming challenges head-on.

Tomorrow would be a new day, a chance for them to solidify their commitment to one another and reinforce the strength that love could bring against societal pressures. Mei felt determined to embrace that love fully, no matter the tempests that lay ahead.

CHAPTER 25

REAFFIRMING LOVE WITH A BLOOMING HEART

The air in Tokyo was thick with the scent of spring as blossoms unfurled across the city, painting the landscape in soft hues of pink and white. Mei felt a sense of fresh optimism as she and Kai ventured back to Shinjuku Gyoen, a place that had become significant for their blossoming relationship.

Their last visit had brought them closer, and Mei was excited to reconnect once more beneath the cherry blossoms. As they entered the park, the vibrant beauty of flowers filled her with joyful anticipation, a perfect backdrop for the heartfelt conversation they needed to have.

"Look at all the blossoms! It's even more stunning than last time!" Kai exclaimed, his eyes sparkling as he took in the scenery.

"It really is," Mei replied, soaking in the magnificent view. The gentle rustle of leaves and the laughter of families enjoying the day created harmony in the air, and for a moment, she felt the pressures from school and the rumors fade into the background.

They found a quiet spot nestled beneath a large cherry blossom tree, where petals fluttered gracefully around them, settling softly on the grass. As they sat down, a peaceful calm enveloped them, and Mei felt the comfort of Kai's presence beside her.

"Kai," she began, taking a deep breath as she looked at him. "I've been doing a lot of thinking about everything—our relationship, the challenges we've faced, and the way we've navigated through them."

"Me too," he said, his gaze earnest. "I think it's important for us to take a moment to reaffirm what we feel for each other. It reminds us of how special our connection is amidst all the chaos."

"I've realized that our differences, whether they be cultural backgrounds or the judgments from others, don't diminish what we share. Instead, they enrich it," Mei said, her heart racing as she spoke her truth. "I appreciate that we can approach this together and celebrate our unique perspectives."

"I feel the same way," Kai replied, his expression softening. "Every challenge we face just strengthens what we have. You inspire me to embrace both who I am and what I feel—especially with you."

His words stirred something deep within her, and a rush of affection surged in her chest. "It's like you make me feel seen in ways I didn't know I needed," she continued, feeling the vulnerability in her words. "My worries about the world fade away when I'm with you."

Kai moved a little closer, his sincerity deepening as he took one of her hands in his. "Your happiness is paramount to me. No one should define how we feel or what we build together. I want to create a space where we can both feel accepted and appreciated for who we are."

Mei nodded, the connection between them solidifying in that moment. "I've never felt so free to be myself with anyone else. It's like when I'm with you, I can truly express my feelings without fear of judgment."

The cherry blossoms blossoming around them mirrored the growth of their connection—a delicate yet resilient bond that thrived amidst uncertainty. The realization settled in her heart, affirming the beauty of their journey; even when faced with challenges, they could emerge stronger together.

"Let's continue to embrace our differences and learn from one another," Kai suggested, a bright smile illuminating his face. "We can share our joys, our art, and the stories that shape us."

"I'd love that," she replied, feeling the warmth radiating from his unwavering support. "I want to make every moment count."

As they shared laughter and deeper conversations beneath the sheltering cherry blossoms, Mei felt a weight lifted from her shoulders. She embraced the joy and the love they had cultivated, a blossoming relationship that juxtaposed against the challenges from outside forces.

Yet beneath the blooming heart, shadows of doubt still lingered in her mind. As the sun began to set, she couldn't shake the feeling that the budding values of acceptance and understanding between them would continually be tested by the outside world.

"Whatever lies ahead, I'm ready to face it with you," Mei said, her determination rising. "I promise to always be honest about my feelings and to celebrate our love."

"And I promise to do the same," Kai replied softly, his gaze fixed on her. "Together, we'll turn our dreams into reality, hand in hand."

The moment felt significant, tinged with both hope and assurance. They were poised on the precipice of something beautiful, ready to nurture their bond amidst the complexities life had to offer.

As they lingered under the cherry blossoms, a graceful kiss sealed their promises and affirmed their commitment to one another. And while uncertainty loomed just beyond the horizon, they knew they would face it together with love in their hearts and a shared understanding that made their bond unique.

CHAPTER 26

DREAMING OF A FUTURE TOGETHER

The morning sun poured through Mei's window, casting a warm glow over her room as she prepared for the day ahead. Today was a special day—Kai was coming over for a creative project that Mei had been eagerly looking forward to. They had decided to create a vision board, an artistic representation of their dreams and aspirations for the future.

Mei had been inspired by their recent conversations under the cherry blossoms, where they had explored their individual hopes and dreams. The idea of visually mapping out their ambitions together felt both exciting and empowering, a way to solidify their bond further.

Once she finished her morning routine, Mei carefully laid out a large piece of poster board on her desk and gathered magazines, scissors, markers, and glue—everything they would need to create something special.

When the doorbell rang later that morning, her heart raced with excitement. "Kai!" she called as she opened the door, finding him holding a large stack of magazines and a determined expression.

"Ready to dream big?" he grinned, stepping inside and placing the magazines on her desk.

"Always! I've been thinking about this project all week!" she said, her enthusiasm bubbling over. "I can't wait to see what we come up with together."

They began flipping through the magazines, searching for images and quotes that resonated with their aspirations. Each page turned sparked lively conversations about their dreams—whether it was traveling to new countries, pursuing art, or simply living life to the fullest.

"This is so cool!" Kai said, holding up an image of a breathtaking beach scene. "I want to travel to places like this one day and capture their beauty through my sketches. We should do this together!"

Mei smiled, the idea warming her heart. "Absolutely! Imagine taking your art to beaches around the world, creating masterpieces inspired by new cultures."

As they continued to cut images and paste them to the board, their bond grew stronger as they shared insights and laughter. Mei found herself opening up about her fears—the uncertainty of following her dream of becoming a photographer. "What if I don't make it? What if I fail to capture what I envision?" she pondered aloud.

Kai paused, his expression serious as he looked at her. "You won't fail, Mei. You have talent and passion, and those qualities will take you where you want to go. Besides, I'll be right there with you every step of the way."

His words blossomed hope in her chest, and as they continued their work, she felt determination begin to solidify. "You're right! I can't let fear hold me back anymore. I want to embrace every opportunity that comes my way."

With renewed commitment, she searched through the magazines, looking for imagery that resonated with her artistic journey. She found a photo of a bustling street market, vibrant and alive, and instinctively cut it out.

"This represents the projects I want to pursue—capturing the pulse of life! I want to show how the blend of cultures and experiences can create something beautiful," she said, excitement lacing her voice as she added it to their board.

"And I found this!" Kai exclaimed, holding up an image of a cozy café filled with art displays, an inviting atmosphere that could inspire creativity. "I want to open a space one day where artists can come together, share their work, and inspire each other."

"That sounds incredible!" Mei responded, her creativity igniting at the thought. "I can picture it now—the energy, the passion. And we can host events and workshops to help others explore their creativity!"

As the hours passed, their vision board began to fill up with beautiful images and bold statements, a tapestry of dreams reflecting who they were and who they hoped to become. It was a visual declaration of commitment—not just to their relationship but to their individual journeys.

Finally, as they stood back to admire their work, Mei felt a swell of pride. The board showcased their personalities, their hopes, and the love they had nurtured. "This is more than just a board; it's a representation of our future," she said, her voice filled with wonder.

Kai nodded, his gaze soft as he looked at her. "Exactly. It's a reminder of what we're working toward, and it holds us accountable to our dreams."

With a sense of peace washing over her, Mei turned to Kai and took his hand, feeling the energy between them surge. "I can't wait to see where our paths will take us. This is just the beginning."

"Together, we'll create a life filled with art, love, and adventure," he said, squeezing her hand gently, his eyes reflecting the clarity and vision they had shared.

As they stood together, surrounded by their board filled with dreams, Mei felt the urge to capture the moment. "Let's take a picture of our vision board to commemorate this day!"

"Great idea!" Kai responded, enthusiasm radiating from him once more.

Once they captured the moment on camera, Mei felt a wave of joy as she looked at the picture, a tangible reminder of their aspirations. The vision board represented more than just artwork; it was a testament to their commitment to each other's dreams and the bond they continued to strengthen.

"Let's hang this up somewhere special in your room," Kai suggested, a playful grin on his face. "It'll serve as a constant reminder of what we're striving for."

"Yes! I definitely want to see it every day," Mei replied with enthusiasm. She quickly found a spot on her wall, clearing a space where their dreams could shine.

As she affixed the board to the wall, a feeling of excitement washed over her. This was not just a collection of images and words—it was a bold declaration of who they were and what they wanted to achieve together.

Once the board was up, they stepped back to admire their work again. "This is all so inspiring," Mei said, her eyes sparkling with enthusiasm. "It has the potential to keep pushing us toward those goals."

"Exactly! And I can't wait to see the adventures we'll experience," Kai said, a dreamy expression washing over his face. "We'll capture the beauty of the world around us."

With the sun setting outside, casting a warm glow in her room, Mei felt grateful for this moment—filled with love, hope, and the promise of a shared journey. But underneath that happiness was still a flicker of insecurity, a whisper of doubt that reminded her that their relationship would face challenges.

"Do you think we'll be able to make all of this happen?" she asked, the poignant curiosity slipping out before she could take it back.

Kai's expression shifted, turning serious, yet his intent gaze offered reassurance. "Absolutely. If we're committed to our dreams and to each other, there's no question we can make it happen. I believe in us."

"Thank you for believing in me," she said, her voice softening. "Your support has really helped me face my fears."

As they talked about their aspirations under the soft light of the evening, a sense of warmth enveloped them. Though challenges awaited, Mei felt ready to tackle them—with Kai by her side, their connection felt like an unbreakable foundation.

But as they resumed their playful banter, shadows of uncertainty still danced in the back of her mind. What if their aspirations clashed with the realities of life? Would she have the strength to navigate societal pressures while building a life with Kai?

"Whatever happens next, I'll be beside you," Kai said suddenly, as if reading her thoughts. "Let's promise to remind each other not to give in to the doubts."

"Definitely," Mei replied, her heart swelling at the thought. They would build their lives together, one dream at a time.

As the evening came to a close, and Kai promised to text her later, Mei held onto the hope ignited within her. She knew they would face challenges— external pressures, family judgments—but with their vision board as a guide and the strength of their love as a compass, they could navigate through anything.

That night, as Mei lay in bed, she gazed at the vision board she had created with Kai, feeling a tidal wave of determination wash over her. Tomorrow was a new day that held the potential for both joy and challenges, but she was ready to face it all—together.

CHAPTER 27

THE NECESSARY CONFRONTATION

The days leading up to the family meeting felt like an emotional rollercoaster for Mei. Despite the joy she shared with Kai and the supportive gestures they made toward each other, a growing sense of apprehension brewed within her. Would she be able to articulate her feelings? The fear of rejection loomed over her like a heavy cloud, threatening to overshadow the happiness they had cultivated.

On a bright Saturday afternoon, Mei stood in front of the mirror, adjusting her outfit—an elegant yet casual ensemble that radiated confidence. She had spent considerable time reflecting on her words, shaping her thoughts into a coherent narrative that she hoped would resonate with her parents.

When she finally descended the stairs, her heart was racing, anticipation mingling with anxiety. Her parents were already in the living room, seated on the couch, engaged in quiet conversation. The warmth and familiarity of home enveloped her, but the looming conversation felt surreal.

"Mei, you're just in time!" her mother said, looking up with a welcoming smile. "We were just discussing the upcoming holiday preparations."

"Thanks, Mom," Mei replied, her stomach fluttering with nervous energy as she took a seat across from them. "I actually wanted to talk to you both about something important."

Her parents exchanged glances, their expressions shifting to one of cautious curiosity. "Of course, honey. What's on your mind?" her father prompted gently.

Taking a deep breath to steady herself, Mei decided to dive in. "It's about Kai. I know that you both have concerns about our relationship, and I want to address those openly. I need you to understand just how much he means to me."

A brief silence filled the room as her parents listened closely. She had their attention, and Mei could feel the weight of their expectation resting on her shoulders. "I understand that our backgrounds are different and that it might be difficult to accept. But Kai has brought so much happiness into my life. He makes me feel seen, respected, and valued in ways I have never experienced before."

Her mother's eyes softened even more, and Mei fought the urge to sway under the scrutiny. "Mei, we just want to make sure that you are making the right choice. Relationships require consideration and understanding. It's a lot to navigate," her father began.

"I know that," Mei interjected, finding her voice in the moment. "But I also know that love can be complicated, and it doesn't always fit into neat little boxes. What I feel for Kai is real, and I want you to understand how much he supports me and encourages me to pursue my dreams."

Her parents exchanged cautious glances, and Mei took that as an opportunity to delve deeper. "It's important to me that you trust my judgment. I've seen how Kai respects me as a person, understands my values, and wants to learn more about my culture. I truly believe that with time and understanding, you will come to appreciate him as much as I do."

A flicker of concern crossed her father's face as he processed her words. "Mei, it's not that we don't see the virtues in him. It's just... it's different," he said quietly, choosing his words carefully. "You've only known him for a short while. We want you to be happy, but we need to know he's someone who can support you, not bring complexity to your life."

Mei felt a sharp pang at the thought that her parents questioned Kai's intentions. "He's not a source of complexity; he's a source of joy! The bond we have has made me a better person, more confident in expressing myself. He encourages me to explore who I am and to pursue my interests."

Her mother nodded, a flicker of acknowledgment in her eyes. "And we appreciate your honesty, but there is a reality that exists beyond your love. We just worry about the pressures society and family expectations will place on you."

"But I don't want to compromise on my happiness because of expectations," Mei insisted, her voice gaining strength. "Love should be about choosing someone who makes you feel complete, not fitting into someone else's predetermined mold of who you should be with."

"And I promise to honor your family and values," Kai said, stepping forward into the conversation even though he had remained quiet until now. "I want to understand where Mei comes from and what's important to both of you. I'll work harder to earn your trust."

Her parents looked at each other thoughtfully, their expressions beginning to soften as they processed Kai's words. She could feel the atmosphere shift, the barriers they had built slowly beginning to dissolve in the face of honesty and sincerity.

"Maybe we need to observe how everything unfolds," her father said cautiously. "We appreciate your commitment, Kai, but we want to make sure Mei's happiness is maintained. Relationships are complex, and they require care and understanding."

"Thank you for being willing to consider this," Mei said, her heart swelling with gratitude as she saw glimmers of acceptance in her parents' expressions. "I know it might take time, but I really believe that if you give Kai a chance, you'll see how great he is."

Her mother nodded slowly, an understanding softening her features. "It's not just about understanding Kai; it's also about seeing how you handle this relationship, Mei. You have to be confident in your feelings, especially if others around you don't support it."

"I am confident," Mei replied, her voice steady. "What we have is real, and I don't want to shy away from it just because of social norms or pressures. I'm ready to embrace it fully."

Her father's gaze flicked to Kai, who withstood the scrutiny like a steady pillar beside her. "Just remember—this journey isn't just about the two of you. It's also about blending two families, and that requires understanding from all sides."

"I understand," Kai said, his expression earnest. "And I'm willing to learn about Mei's culture and family values. I respect what they want for her, and I want to build that trust."

A moment of silence filled the room as Mei's parents considered his words. She could see the deliberation brewing; this was an unfamiliar territory for them, but the openness in the air spoke volumes.

"Let's take this one step at a time," her mother said finally, her tone softer than before. "We're willing to support Mei and your relationship, but we also want to see how you handle it moving forward."

"Thank you," Mei said, the gratitude pouring from her heart. It felt like a turning point—a bridge to greater understanding and acceptance within her family.

As the evening drew to a close, she thanked her parents again, still buoyed by the progress they had made together. After Kai said his goodbyes, feeling accomplished and hopeful, she felt the joy of the moment radiating from her, pushing the shadows of doubt further away.

As she settled into bed that night, her mind danced with thoughts of all that transpired. She had fought to stand up for what she believed in and, despite the lingering doubts, they were making strides toward a future built on honesty and love.

But the next day, as she stepped back into school, the familiar buzz of whispers awaited her. The rumor mill had begun to churn again, fueled by the new developments of her relationship. Glancing around at her classmates, she caught sight of Yuki leaning against a wall with his friends, smirking as he exchanged glances with a group nearby.

The confidence she had felt after dinner wavered slightly, anxiety starting to creep back in. Would they twist what she had accomplished into something hurtful again?

Each step felt heavier as she navigated through the school corridors, her heart racing with apprehension. Just when she thought the evening would provide her with enough clarity, the pressure resumed, swirling violently in her thoughts.

Navigating the day was increasingly difficult with judgment hanging over her. During lunch, she met up with Kai, desperate to share her concerns.

"Hey! How are you feeling?" Kai greeted her, concern etched on his features as he noticed her unease.

"I'm feeling good, but the rumors are still there, and I can sense they're growing louder," she said, her brow furrowing. "I overheard Yuki earlier, and I can't help but fear that he'll escalate things."

"Focus on us," Kai reassured her, leaning closer. "Their negativity doesn't define our relationship. We'll just keep being honest and open with each other, okay?"

Feeling more secure with his support, Mei nodded and tried to push the anxiety aside. "You're right. We need to stay strong."

As they finished lunch, the weight of the conversations still lingered in her mind, but Mei resolved to stand firm. She wanted to embrace her journey with Kai wholeheartedly, regardless of what others said. They had taken steps toward acceptance, and she wouldn't let the rumors shatter that resolve.

Later that evening, as she prepared to meet up with her friends to discuss their plans, the uncertainty flared again in the back of her mind. The road ahead might not be easy, but with Kai's unwavering support and the backing of her friends, she felt ready to embrace whatever challenges lay ahead.

Tonight, she would gather strength from those who believed in her—those who understood that love could conquer societal norms.

She stepped out of her room and headed downstairs, ready to navigate the whims of her school environment—in just a few short moments, she would reaffirm her commitment to her dreams while embracing the beautiful complexity of love.

CHAPTER 28

A JOURNEY OF FORGIVENESS

The sun poured through the windows of Mei's home the following week, casting a warm glow over her family's dining table, where her parents sat with contemplative expressions. Mei had revealed her heart, and now she felt the weight of anticipation as they begun to process the experiences shared during their last family gathering.

She had sensed a shift in the air, as if a veil of understanding had momentarily lifted, making room for possibilities. After her heartfelt conversation, she hoped her parents were genuinely considering their perspectives on her relationship with Kai.

Her mother sighed softly, placing her hands on the table. "I've been thinking a lot about our conversation and how I've approached everything. I've come to realize that my views have been influenced by my own upbringing and cultural values—a reality that's no longer applicable in today's world."

Mei's father furrowed his brow, contemplating. "You're right, dear. I've always held tight to traditional ideas about relationships, wanting to protect Mei from potential heartache—never considering that my perspective might limit her happiness."

Mei stood at the kitchen entrance, feeling a rush of hope. "I appreciate that you're both willing to reflect on this. It means a lot that you're trying to understand where I'm coming from."

"It's important for us as a family to grow together, especially as the world changes around us," her mother continued, lifting her gaze to Mei. "We want to connect with you and respect your choices, but we also need to confront our prejudices."

"As parents, we often project our fears onto you," her father admitted, looking down at the table. "We don't want you to struggle with the weight of societal expectations, but perhaps we've been too rigid in our thinking."

"You've always wanted what's best for me, I know that," Mei replied softly, her heart swelling with gratitude. "But love transcends cultural barriers. It should be celebrated, not judged. I want you to see that what I feel for Kai is real and meaningful."

A moment of silence filled the room as her parents mulled over her words. Mei could see them grappling with the inner conflict between their traditional values and the evolving perspective her relationship with Kai presented. She felt a surge of determination to bridge that divide, aware of how powerful love could be in shifting perceptions.

"Maybe it's time for us to embrace a broader definition of love," her mother said finally, her voice steady. "It doesn't have to fit into neat categories. It's about how someone makes you feel, how they respect you and support you."

Her father nodded, a sign of agreement as he began to soften. "And we should encourage you to pursue your happiness, wherever that may lead. If Kai truly cares for you, then perhaps we need to reevaluate our stance."

"Thank you," Mei said, her voice thick with emotion. "It means so much for you to see that love isn't about conformity; it's about connection."

After a slight pause, her mother continued, "I'd like to get to know Kai better. Perhaps we can invite him over again, maybe for dinner or another family gathering?"

"That would be great!" Mei replied, relief flooding through her. "I think spending more time together will help you see just how great he is."

"It's important for us to unlearn some of our biases, especially the ones we didn't realize we were holding," her father said thoughtfully. "As a family, we need to grow and adapt just like the world around us."

With a newfound sense of excitement, Mei felt hopeful—not only for her relationship with Kai but for her family as well. She could see her parents beginning to embrace the possibility of acceptance and understanding in ways she hadn't thought possible just weeks before.

As they continued discussing their thoughts on relationships, love, and culture, Mei felt a sense of warmth enveloping the family. Each heartfelt conversation contained a thread that bound them together—a growing understanding that love is fluid and constantly evolving.

Later, as Mei headed upstairs, she couldn't shake the surge of appreciation that filled her heart. The warmth of her family shifted something inside her, igniting a renewed sense of hope that transcended the previous doubts.

With the promise of a more accepting future buoying her spirit, Mei picked up her phone, eager to tell Kai about the heartwarming conversation she'd had with her parents.

Mei: Hey! I had a great talk with my parents, and they might be open to getting to know you better! Can we plan something soon?

The response came almost immediately.

Kai: That's amazing news! I'd love to! Let's set a date.

As Mei settled into her bed, a sense of calm washed over her. The obstacles they once faced seemed surmountable, and now the brightness of their future together sparkled brightly on the horizon.

With a smile on her face and a heart full of hope, she drifted into a peaceful sleep, dreaming of adventures and shared memories yet to come. The prospect of spending more time with Kai amid the warmth of her family's acceptance filled her with excitement.

The next day, Mei woke up to the soft light of the morning sun filtering through her curtains. She felt renewed, ready to embrace whatever unfolded in the coming days. Kai had texted her the night before, suggesting they plan something special to celebrate the growing connection between their families.

Over the following days, as they prepared for their dinner with her parents, Mei felt their excitement build. They devised plans—including a small presentation of Kai's artwork to showcase his talent, hoping it would resonate with her parents on a deeper level.

That evening, as they set up the dining room, Kai arrived bearing a selection of artwork he had completed since their last gathering—works inspired by their shared adventures over the last few weeks. Mei felt the pride swelling within her, knowing how much effort he had poured into this gesture.

"Are you ready for this?" Kai asked, his expression a blend of excitement and nervousness as he unloaded his sketches onto the dining table.

"More than ready! I think this will really impress them," Mei replied, her confidence unwavering in that moment of shared vulnerability.

As she helped him arrange the pieces, she glanced at each artwork, marveling at how he captured their experiences. One piece depicted a lively scene from the art festival, while another showcased their time at the beach—a beautiful reminder of the happiness they had found together.

"Let's hang these up, so they catch the first glimpse," Mei suggested, her heart racing with anticipation.

"Absolutely! This will show them how much I appreciate the effort they've made to understand us," Kai grinned, hanging the artwork with care.

Once everything was set up, it felt as though the moment was heavy with potential. The table was adorned with a lovely dinner spread, and the artwork added a personal touch, weaving their stories into the fabric of the evening.

When her parents arrived, they greeted Kai with warm smiles, appreciation apparent in their expressions as they stepped inside. "Welcome back, Kai! It's lovely to see you," Mei's mother said genuinely, her demeanor welcoming.

"Thank you for having me again, Mrs. Suki," Kai said respectfully, bowing slightly.

As everyone settled around the table, the rapport between them felt light, and Mei could see the small shifts in her parents' attitudes. Their engagement with Kai during dinner carried an air of openness, and they began to share more about their lives as the evening unfolded.

After enjoying the delicious meal, the time came for Mei and Kai to share the artwork. "We've both been working together to capture the essence of our experiences—especially our adventures and how they relate to our journey," Mei announced, her heart racing with pride.

Kai began explaining each piece, sharing the inspirations and emotions that drove him to create them. Mei watched as her parents leaned in, genuinely interested in his thoughts. The conversation flowed naturally, and for a moment, it felt like the barriers had crumbled completely.

"This is beautiful!" her father said, examining one piece closely. "You have an exceptional talent for capturing emotion, Kai. I can see the joy that radiates from these moments."

Her mother nodded in agreement, a soft smile gracing her face. "It's wonderful to see how you express your experiences through art. I truly appreciate the effort you put into this."

The warmth of their acceptance washed over Mei, invigorating her spirit. The conversation felt like a breakthrough—a testament to the love they had carefully cultivated.

Later, as the dinner came to an end, they all expressed how they hoped for future gatherings filled with more conversation and creativity. When her parents spoke of a family outing to an arts festival, Mei's heart soared; she could see their willingness to embrace not only Kai but her happiness as well.

As Kai and Mei stood by the door, preparing to say their goodbyes, venturing back into the evening air, Mei felt a sense of fulfillment. "Thank you for tonight," she said, glancing at Kai. "You were incredible, and I think my parents truly began to see you for who you are."

Kai smiled warmly at her, the sparkle in his eyes mirroring her own happiness. "I'm grateful for this opportunity. Your parents are wonderful, and I knew we could find a way to connect."

With their hearts buoyed by the evening's successes, they headed back into the night, ready to continue their journey together.

As they walked hand in hand through the softly lit streets, Mei felt a swell of hope for the future. Perhaps the challenges they faced did not need to overshadow the beauty of their connection; together, they could bridge the gaps between love and acceptance, weaving the story of their journey with both courage and creativity.

CHAPTER 29

A LOVE RECOGNIZED WITH NEW UNDERSTANDING

The day of the family outing arrived, and Mei felt a mix of excitement and lingering apprehension as she prepared for the day's events. It was a sunny Saturday, perfect for their planned trip to a nearby art festival. Mei glanced in the mirror, smoothing down her outfit—a comfortable dress that felt infused with confidence.

After the previous dinner when she and Kai showcased his artwork, Mei had sensed a shift within her parents. The willingness to get to know him had opened the door to deeper understanding, but she was still anxious about the day ahead. Would they see the bond that had blossomed between them? Would they truly accept Kai into their family?

As she and her parents drove to the festival, the atmosphere in the car was charged with anticipation. Mei stole glances at her mother and father, who exchanged apprehensive yet hopeful looks. She could sense that they had been preparing for this moment as well, both curious and concerned about what their experience would hold.

When they arrived at the festival, the sun glinted off vibrant art displays and the cheerful sounds of laughter filled the air. Mei's heart raced with excitement at the colorful surroundings, but she could also feel a slight tension creeping back in as they approached the entrance.

"Are you ready?" her mother asked gently, glancing back at Mei, whose stomach churned with a mix of eagerness and anxiety.

"Yeah, let's go!" Mei replied, forcing a smile as they walked in together.

Once inside, Kai spotted them immediately, waving excitedly with his characteristic enthusiasm. "Hey! You made it!" he exclaimed, his eyes bright with joy.

"Hi, Kai!" Mei called back, her spirits lifting at the sight of him. There was something about sharing this experience that felt significant, as if it could either solidify their bond or present new challenges.

As they approached, Mei stepped in front of her parents. "Kai, I want to introduce you again to my family. These are my mom and dad," she said, her heart racing as she made the introductions.

Kai bowed slightly in respect, confidence radiating in his demeanor. "It's great to see you again! Thank you for having me join your family today."

Her parents returned the greeting, their expressions warm but still tinged with caution. "Thank you for coming, Kai. We hope this outing will help us get to know you better," her father said, his voice steady yet careful.

"Absolutely! I'm looking forward to sharing this experience," Kai responded cheerfully, his infectious enthusiasm cutting through the tension in the air.

As they walked through the festival together, the initial nervousness began to fade. They wandered from booth to booth, checking out a variety of art pieces, participating in workshops, and enjoying the festivities along the way. Laughter bubbled around them, and slowly but surely, Mei could feel her parents soften as they witnessed the bond between her and Kai.

At one booth, they watched an artist skillfully constructing traditional crafts, and Kai stepped in to engage with the process. "This is so fascinating!" he said, dipping his hands into the vibrant colors. "I've always admired this art form."

"Mei has a great appreciation for art too," her mother chimed in, watching as Kai interacted with the artisans.

"I do!" Mei said, excitement bubbling in her voice. "Kai inspires me to explore more of my artistic side. I think sharing this with my family is important, especially since we've been talking about blending cultures together."

Her father nodded, clearly warming up to the idea. "It's nice to see that you both have such a strong interest in art that extends beyond your individual styles."

As the day wore on, Mei noticed her parents engaging more naturally with Kai, laughing at his jokes and sharing stories about their own experiences with art and creativity. The barriers that had seemed to stretch between them began to dissolve, little pieces at a time.

Eventually, they stopped at a booth featuring handcrafted items influenced by various cultural traditions—paintings, textiles, ceramics. The vibrant colors and intricate designs reflected Mei and Kai's love as well as the fusion of their backgrounds.

"This booth is beautiful," Mei said, glancing between her parents and Kai. "It really shows how art can merge different styles and cultures into something extraordinary."

"It's a perfect representation of love and understanding," Kai added, addressing Mei's parents. "Just like how love can weave its way through differences, creating something unique and beautiful."

For the first time, Mei's mother seemed to contemplate his words thoughtfully, a hint of understanding sparking in her eyes. "Yes, I see that now. Art, like love, can transcend boundaries."

As they continued to admire the artwork, her father turned to Kai. "We apologize for any preconceived notions we might have had," he said, the sincerity in his voice palpable. "It's evident that you care deeply for Mei. We appreciate the respect you show toward our family and values."

Mei's heart soared at her father's acknowledgment, feeling the weight of tension within her begin to lift. She glanced at Kai, who appeared just as surprised. "Thank you, sir. It means a lot to me to be welcomed," he replied, his tone respectful yet genuinely grateful.

"We know that love can take many forms," her mother added, her earlier hesitation softening as she observed the rapport blossoming before her eyes. "And if Mei is happy, that is what truly matters."

Having witnessed Kai's integrity and Mei's unwavering affection for him, their acceptance felt like a breakthrough. Her parents were beginning to dismantle those barriers they had built, allowing space for embracing love's complexities.

"I want to be a positive influence in Mei's life," Kai said earnestly as he turned to Mei's parents. "I'm committed to understanding both her culture and your family values. Together, we can create a harmonious bond."

"Creating a harmonious bond is key," Mei's father responded, nodding thoughtfully. "Finding common ground while respecting each other's differences is essential in any relationship."

As they stood surrounded by the vibrant displays of art and culture, Mei felt the connection between her family and Kai deepen. The earlier apprehension that had filled the air gradually transformed into warmth and understanding, like the gentle breeze rustling through the trees.

"Let's pledge to keep this level of communication open between us," she suggested, looking at her parents and then at Kai, who nodded in agreement. "Love grows when everyone is on the same page."

"Absolutely," Kai said, a smile of encouragement on his face. "I hope we can build not just our relationship but also the relationships with your family."

The ambience of camaraderie enveloped them as they continued exploring the festival, indulging in several tasty treats and giggling at the various live performances they encountered. Mei's parents engaged with Kai like they were friends, sharing anecdotes about their own experiences and exchanging playful teasing.

As they approached a culminating spot—a beautiful art installation decorated with twinkling fairy lights that illuminated the night—Mei felt a sense of gratitude and happiness sweep through her.

"This is beautiful," her mother said, her eyes sparkling as she took in the intricate designs. "It reminds me of the connections we've all formed tonight."

"Yes, it does," Mei agreed, her heart swelling with joy. "It symbolizes our journey and growth as a family, embracing each other's differences while showing love."

Kai looked at Mei, appreciation shining in his eyes. "You have a way with words. It's inspirational."

Before she could respond, her father looked at Kai, a newfound warmth in his gaze. "We thank you for your patience with us, Kai. It takes time to shift perspectives, and we appreciate your willingness to engage with our family."

"Thank you, sir. I'm honored to be a part of this," Kai said, his sincerity cutting through the air.

As they took a moment to enjoy the festivities and the installation before them, Mei felt a wave of hope fill her heart. Tonight had been a journey toward acceptance, and she sensed that they had taken steps closer to a future where love could flourish, unrestricted by preconceived notions.

Eventually, they were drawn back to the bustling atmosphere of the festival, filled with laughter and joy. As noise and color swirled around them, Mei's parents looked at Kai with curiosity rather than skepticism, a shift she had longed to see.

As the night wore on and they departed from the festival, Mei felt a renewed sense of commitment to both her relationship with Kai and her family.

Days later, as she sat with her friends at lunch, the sunlight streaming through the windows, she felt empowered and uplifted. She wanted to maintain the momentum they had built, reminding herself to stay resilient against the judgments that had initially rattled her.

"Did dinner go well?" Akira asked, noticing the subtle glow of happiness about her.

"Better than I could have hoped," she replied, her heart bursting with pride. "I think my parents are beginning to understand Kai and the love we share."

"That's fantastic! You deserve to enjoy your happiness without the noise interfering," Akira said, lifting his drink to toast her.

"Here's to growth and love!" Mei exclaimed, laughter spilling over as they clinked their cups together.

As she relished the joy surrounding her, she felt fortified—a reminder that love, when nurtured and supported, could break through barriers, leading to acceptance and understanding.

But outside the bubble of joy her friends provided lay the challenges of navigating class dynamics, where rumors and judgment still loomed like a tempest. The whispers from classmates had yet to dissipate, and every glance from students in the hallways reminded Mei of the scrutiny they faced.

As the days continued to pass, she found herself increasingly aware of Yuki's smirking presence. He had become more vocal about her relationship with Kai, making snide comments that rippled through the crowd, causing Mei's confidence to waver. With every quip he made, the earlier warmth and acceptance she had felt from her parents felt distant again.

"Don't let Yuki get to you," Akira said one day as they walked to class, observing her worried fidgeting. "His comments are just attempts to stir the pot and create drama."

"I know," Mei replied, trying her best to stay focused on the positive experiences. "But it's hard when I feel like everyone is watching, waiting for us to fail. I want to prove them wrong."

"Then do that. Focus on you and Kai, and the bond you share. That's what matters," he said, his voice steady and encouraging. "You two are forging something special, incredible even. Don't let anyone else diminish that."

Mei appreciated Akira's support, but the external pressures loomed larger every day. As the rumors intensified, whispers started to circulate around school that distorted her relationship with Kai, painting it in unflattering colors. She felt as if she were losing control of her narrative, and her heart ached at the thought of her love being trivialized.

One afternoon, as she waited for Kai to meet her by their usual spot, the clouds rolled in ominously, and raindrops began to fall, echoing the heaviness in her heart. The weather felt like a reflection of her mood, and as the rain became heavier, she felt her mounting panic.

"Hey, Mei!" Kai called, rushing over with an umbrella, his hair damp from the rain. "Sorry I'm late! Didn't want to get you soaked!"

She looked up at him, a rush of warmth sparking inside her despite the gloom. "It's okay! I'm just glad to see you!" The momentary distraction eased her worries, and she couldn't help but feel the love and support radiating from him as he held the umbrella overhead.

As they took cover, huddling closely beneath the umbrella, Kai turned serious. "What's on your mind? You look a bit worried."

"I don't know… It's just been hard trying to ignore the rumors," Mei confessed, a tightness forming in her throat. "The more I try to focus on us, the louder they seem to get. Yuki and his friends haven't stopped making comments."

Kai nodded, understanding her feelings. "Let's not allow them to take away from what we've built. You know that what we have is real, and we don't owe anyone an explanation."

"I know, but it hurts hearing them laugh about us," Mei said, frustration bubbling to the surface. "I want everyone to see that being with you makes me happy instead of reducing our connection to something trivial."

"I care about you, Mei. You mean the world to me, and I'll always stand by you. If confronting those rumors will help clear the air, we can tackle it together," Kai said, his tone filled with determination.

Feeling invigorated by his words, Mei nodded as conviction surged within her. "You're right. I just need to remember that our love is valid, no matter what anyone thinks. But how do we handle Yuki without it becoming a big spectacle?"

"I think standing together openly can help, showing them that we're not afraid to express what we feel," he advised. "We can show our strength through honesty."

As they lingered in the rain, huddled together under the umbrella, Mei felt the worries of the day begin to lift. "Thank you for being here, for believing in us," she said softly. "Your support means everything."

"I wouldn't have it any other way," Kai said, pulling her closer as the raindrops continued to fall around them, creating a gentle melody.

Emboldened by their conversation, Mei made a decision. "Let's face them together. This is our relationship, and I want to be proud of it."

"That's the spirit, Mei," he said, his eyes shining with encouragement.

As the rain began to ease, they stepped out from under the umbrella and walked together, hand in hand, feeling a renewed sense of strength. The challenge ahead still loomed large, but now they felt like a team ready to forge ahead, ready to confront whatever awaited them.

That night, as Mei returned home, she felt empowered for the first time in a while; the love she had for Kai overshadowing the noise of judgment and the weight of rumors. The conversations they had shared under the rain had ignited a fire within her, propelling her forward into a space where she could embrace her truth more openly.

As she settled into her room, removing her wet shoes and shrugging off her damp jacket, she glanced around the space that had always been her sanctuary. A sense of warmth emanated from the vibrant photos and art pieces that adorned her walls, each one telling a story of her journey thus far.

She gingerly picked up her phone, her heart racing at the thought of reaching out to Kai. After the day they had shared and the bonds they reinforced, she felt a burst of joy knowing they were in this together. Quickly, she typed out a message.

Mei: Hey! I just wanted to say thank you for today. I feel like I'm ready to face whatever comes our way.

The reply came almost instantly.

Kai: Always! I'm proud of you for owning your feelings. Together, we've got this!

With a contented sigh, Mei leaned back against her pillows, letting the warmth of his words wash over her like a gentle wave. As her heart continued to flutter, she began to think of what their future might hold. How could they handle the challenges of society together?

The next morning, a sense of purpose guided her through her routine. The anticipation of facing school again filled her with both excitement and apprehension. But she vowed not to let fear prevent her from enjoying the connection she and Kai shared.

Once she arrived at school, her steps felt lighter, strengthened by the promise of love and partnership. But just as she began to relax, she spotted a group of classmates huddled together near her locker. Their conspiratorial whispers heightened her anxiety once again and as she approached, the laughter cut through the air.

"Look who is back—Mei and her 'boyfriend,'" one girl exclaimed, her voice dripping with sarcasm. "What a cute little love story!"

Mei felt the heat rise in her cheeks, but as she approached her locker, she reminded herself of the strength she had fostered in the past days. "What's it to you?" she challenged, trying to keep her voice steady.

"Oh, nothing. Just concerned about how this whole thing is going to blow up in your face," another girl chimed in, laughter following her words. "You really think a relationship like this is going to last?"

Before she could respond, Kai came up beside her, sensing her tension. "Hey, let's just ignore the chatter. We are happy together, and that's what matters," he said firmly, standing protectively beside Mei.

The group paused, taken aback by his confidence. "You don't have to be defensive, it was just a question," one of them replied, trying to mask the tension with a casual tone.

"It's not just a question. It's a reflection of your judgment. And it's unnecessary," Kai replied, his voice steady and sincere, unwavering against the negativity around them.

Mei felt courage welling within her at how Kai stood up for her, how passionately he defended their love in the face of criticism. With a newfound determination, she turned toward her classmates, her voice firm. "I know you might not understand our relationship, but I won't allow your opinions to dictate how I feel or who I choose to love. This is my choice."

There was a moment of shock that hung in the air, and for the first time, Mei noticed nodding heads from a few supportive classmates standing nearby—beneath all the chatter, there were allies beginning to surface.

"Yeah, Mei!" one of her friends exclaimed. "You're happy, and that's what matters. You don't need to apologize for who you love."

"Exactly. We're all friends here. Let's celebrate that!" another friend joined in, backing her up.

Feeling bolstered by their support, Mei held her head high. "Thank you! I won't let this negativity diminish what I have with Kai. We're in this together!"

As the tension began to break, Mei felt a surge of triumph wash over her. She had stood up for her love and herself, daring to be brave, fiercely holding onto what they had built.

"Let's all move on. It's time we stop spreading negativity and start supporting one another," Kai said, purposefully stepping between Mei and the group, directing the conversation away from any confrontation.

As the hallways bustled around them, Mei could feel the momentum shift. The whispers that had stung so badly began to fade, replaced by a sense of empowerment and unity forged through friendship.

When she and Kai stepped away from the gathering, a wave of relief washed over Mei, mingling with the adrenaline still coursing through her veins. "I can't believe I actually said that," she admitted, laughter spilling from her lips as she felt the tension begin to fade. "It was exhilarating!"

Kai chuckled, squeezing her hand reassuringly. "You were amazing! That took so much courage, and I'm proud of you for standing up for what you believe in."

"Thank you for having my back," Mei said, glancing over at him. His unwavering support gave her the strength she needed to face the noise swirling around their relationship.

As they made their way toward their next class, Mei felt a weight lift—her earlier insecurities had been challenged and pushed aside. The warmth of Kai's presence continued to bolster her confidence, reminding her of the love they had built together amidst the doubts.

Yet, as the day wore on, the shadows of uncertainty still lurked in the back of her mind. The rumors surrounding Yuki and his group would likely resurface; she knew they would seize any opportunity to sow discord in her life. With each passing moment, she could feel the simmering tension returning, threatening to overshadow the triumph she had just felt.

"Do you want to hang out after school?" Kai asked as they approached their classroom, his expression bright and inviting. "We could work more on our photography ideas and plan for our next outing!"

"Definitely! I would love that," Mei replied, trying to push the worries aside. "I think spending more time together will help strengthen things, especially with everything happening at school."

After a long day of classes, the bell finally rang, and they made their way outside, the fresh air filling their lungs like a welcome embrace. The conversations and laughter of their classmates surrounded them, but Mei felt a sense of calm wrapping around her like a comforting cloak.

As they walked through the bustling school grounds, Kai suddenly looked thoughtful. "You know, I really admire how you handled today. Not everyone has the courage to confront rumors head-on like you did. It shows your strength."

Mei felt the warmth of his approval radiate through her heart. "It really wasn't easy, and I still feel anxious about what might come next. I guess part of me always fears what others might think."

Kai paused mid-step, turning to face her fully. "Listen, Mei. We can't let others dictate our happiness or define who we are. You can't control their opinions, but you can control your reaction to them. Let's focus on the love we share and how much we support each other, no matter what."

"What if they try to drive a wedge between us?" she asked, her voice trembling slightly as the weight of her fears crept back in. "What if they succeed?"

"I promise you, Mei, they won't," he said confidently, cupping her face with his hand. "What we have is too strong, too real. And if we encounter any rough patches, we'll face them together."

"What if that becomes harder?" she pressed gently, feeling a mix of hope and doubt intertwining in her heart. "With families and societal pressures at play, can we really stand our ground?"

Kai's eyes met hers with a fierce intensity. "We can and we will. Love isn't easy, but it's worth fighting for. And we're already stronger for having faced challenges together. This is just another layer of our story."

Feeling buoyed by his conviction, Mei nodded, the reassuring warmth of his words infusing her with newfound determination. "You're right. We have to keep expressing our love, regardless of what anyone else thinks. I won't let fear dictate our journey anymore."

With that resolve solidified, they made their way home, their hands clasped tightly together—a symbol of unity and of the promises they had made to each other.

As they reached Mei's home, she felt a sense of contentment wash over her, prepared to face whatever came next. A brief glance back at Kai solidified her confidence; they were a team, and she was ready to navigate their journey with him.

Later that evening, as she settled down to review her day, the upcoming challenges hovered just at the edges of her mind. But as she pulled out her camera and flipped through the pictures they had taken during their recent outings, she felt the warmth of their connection, the beauty of their shared experiences reminding her that love could be a source of strength.

Tomorrow would reveal what challenges awaited, but tonight she would hold onto the joy and optimism Kai inspired in her heart. Together, they could conquer anything.

CHAPTER 30

A NEW BEGINNING

The sun shone brightly on the vibrant streets of Tokyo, illuminating the bustling scene as the annual summer festival kicked off in full swing. The air was alive with the sounds of laughter, music, and the delicious scent of festival treats wafting through the crowd. Mei and Kai stood hand in hand, excitement bubbling between them as they prepared to celebrate a new chapter in their relationship.

As they approached the festival grounds, Mei couldn't help but feel a rush of joy. This event was more than just a celebration; it represented resilience, acceptance, and the culmination of all the challenges they had faced together. After successfully bringing her parents and Kai's worlds together, she felt lighter, free from the weight of previous doubts.

"Look at all the decorations!" Kai exclaimed, pointing toward booths laden with colorful lanterns and streamers, fluttering in the warm summer breeze. "It's even more festive than I imagined!"

"Isn't it beautiful?" Mei replied, her eyes sparkling as they explored the festivities. "I'm so glad we could come together for this."

As they strolled through the lively scene, joyous music filled the air, and they were greeted by friends and family who shared in the excitement. Akira waved enthusiastically from a nearby stall, his expression glowing with happiness when he caught sight of them.

"Hey, you two lovebirds! Over here!" he called out, beckoning them to join him.

Mei and Kai exchanged delighted looks and headed over to their friend. The camaraderie felt celebratory—an energy that reaffirmed their connection to one another and the unwavering support of their friends.

"Thanks for inviting us to the festival!" Kai said, bumping fists with Akira.

"Of course! We've made plans to enjoy the evening together," Akira replied. "I want to see you both having fun without a care in the world!"

Mei felt a swell of gratitude for the allies she had found along the way, friends who had stood by her during her challenging moments. The atmosphere felt warm and accepting, and as they entered the festival, she felt as though every shadow of self-doubt drifted away.

They tried various festival foods—takoyaki, yakitori, and sweet mochi—each bite bursting with flavor and accompanied by laughter as they shared stories over the delicious treats. The joy surrounding them felt tangible, infusing their hearts with hope and love.

At one booth, they attempted to toss rings onto bottles, the friendly competition heightening the excitement. Kai's competitive spirit shone brightly as he cheered Mei on with unwavering support.

"You've got this! Just aim and let it flow!" he encouraged, and as Mei focused intently on the target, she felt the warmth of his belief lifting her confidence.

With a determined flick of her wrist, she tossed the ring, scoring a perfect hit. Cheers erupted, and she danced with excitement, Kai's laughter filling the air like music. "We make a great team!" she exclaimed, pulling him in for a joyful hug.

"Yes! Master ring-tossers!" he replied, a gleam of triumph in his eyes.

As the sun set, a beautiful twilight glow enveloped the festival, illuminating the faces of the crowd and the collective joy they felt. Mei found herself pulled toward a stage where performers showcased traditional dances, the vibrant colors of their clothing blending beautifully into the surroundings.

"This is magical," she said softly as they stood together, hand in hand, feeling the rhythmic beat of the drums resonate in their chests.

"It really is," Kai said, turning to her. "But what's even more magical is being here with you. It feels like we've come full circle."

With a gentle smile, Mei leaned against him, feeling a blend of contentment and excitement for the future. "You're right. Everything we've faced has led us to this moment. I'm so grateful for the journey."

As they stood together, wrapped in each other's warmth, they shared a tender kiss, the connection between them reaffirmed against the backdrop of the festival's lights. It was a sweet moment that encapsulated their love—a promise that expanded beyond the boundaries of judgment and doubt.

With each passing moment at the festival, Mei felt her heart swell with hope as they celebrated the beauty of acceptance, the unity of their families, and the bond they had nurtured. Those who had once questioned their relationship were now silently gathering, reassessing their perceptions of love as they witnessed the authenticity radiating from Mei and Kai.

As the night progressed, fireworks soared into the sky with bursts of color, illuminating the faces of everyone gathered below. Mei and Kai stood together, awe-struck by the display, feeling the beauty of their love reflected in the brilliance of the fireworks.

"Let's make a wish!" Mei exclaimed as the finale began, the vibrant lights flickering in sync with her racing heart.

Together, they whispered their wishes into the night, filled with hope for their future. The last of the fireworks painted the sky above them in brilliant colors, the light illuminating their faces and reflecting the joy bursting in their hearts.

As they stood hand in hand, the romance of the moment enveloped them, the magic of the festival becoming a part of their story. Mei looked at Kai, her heart swelling with gratitude for every challenge they had faced together, reminding her of how far they had come.

"I wish for us to always have moments like this," she said softly, her voice barely above a whisper.

Kai smiled, brushing a stray hair behind her ear. "And I wish for our love to be as adventurous as tonight. To steal the moments that matter most."

"Steal?" Mei chuckled, a playful glint in her eyes. "You mean like a love heist?"

"Exactly!" he exclaimed, his enthusiasm contagious. "We've already conquered so much together. Why not take on life's adventures with the same daring spirit?"

Their laughter mingled with the crackles of the fireworks, but in that moment, they shared a deeper understanding. It wasn't just about the thrill of the festival. It was about the promise of the future, the memories they would create together, and the unwavering bond they had forged.

"Then let's make a pact," Mei said, her face alight with excitement. "To always seek out those moments worth stealing—those lifetimes of memories that no one can take from us."

Kai's gaze softened, and he pulled her closer, his forehead resting against hers. "A love heist, indeed. We'll capture joy, chase adventures, and cherish every second. No heist is too great when we're in it together."

With renewed determination, they turned back towards the festival, exhilarated by the shared anticipation of life ahead. As they joined their friends, the energy of joy surrounded them once more. They danced, laughed, and celebrated the beauty of acceptance, buoyed by the love that had blossomed between them.

As midnight approached, Mei took a moment to glance around at the glowing faces of their friends and family. She felt a profound sense of belonging and saw the echoes of their shared journey reflected in everyone's smiles. The love that had once been doubted was now celebrated.

But just as they began to lose themselves in the festive atmosphere, she felt Kai's hand brush against hers, a silent cue. Stepping away from the crowd once more, he led her to a secluded spot overlooking the city, where the lights twinkled like stars.

"This is where the real magic happens," he said, wrapping his arm around her shoulders. "Just us."

As they gazed into the breathtaking view below, Mei felt a wave of emotion wash over her. "This journey has been one incredible heist," she declared, a sense of fulfillment blossoming within her. "We've stolen happiness, carved out acceptance, and blossomed into something beautiful."

"Let's keep it going," Kai said with promise in his eyes. "There are many more treasures to capture together."

With a shared glance filled with unspoken dreams, they sealed their words with a kiss, embodying the essence of their love—an undeniable adventure worth every risk.

As they stood together, the vibrant celebration of the festival faded into a faint memory, replaced by the magnificence of their moment—the greatest heist of all: stealing each other's hearts and forging a love that would stand the test of time.

In that embrace, they understood that their story was just beginning. There were places to explore, dreams to chase, and many more adventures waiting to be seized. Love, they discovered, was the ultimate heist—one that would continue to surprise and delight them every step of the way. And with that, they whispered their final wish into the night, silently promising to cherish every moment, for they had already stolen the best treasure of all: each other.

THE END

ABOUT THE AUTHOR

Jamar Berry is a British writer of Caribbean and Portuguese descent, navigating the complexities of identity and belonging. As a light-skinned male, Jamar has faced unique challenges in dating within the Asian community, often confronting stereotypes and biases that stem from the color of his skin. Despite achieving success as a young professional, the experiences of feeling marginalized deeply influence his perspective on relationships and love.

These challenges inspired him to write this novel, which explores the intertwining of diverse cultures and the journey toward acceptance in a world often divided by difference. Through the characters of Mei and Kai, Jamar seeks to illuminate the beauty of love that transcends societal barriers while also addressing the emotional struggles that come with navigating such complexities.

www.ingramcontent.com/pod-product-compliance
Lightning Source LLC
Chambersburg PA
CBHW061921130726
47908CB00016B/542